ON THE HUNT

ON THE HUNT

IRIS
JOHANSEN

GRAND
CENTRAL

New York   Boston

Copyright © 2024 by IJ Development

Cover design by Flag. Cover images by Getty Images and Maggie McCall/Trevillion Images. Cover copyright © 2024 by Hachette Book Group, Inc.

Grand Central Publishing

Hachette Book Group

1290 Avenue of the Americas, New York, NY 10104

grandcentralpublishing.com

@grandcentralpub

First Edition: September 2024

Grand Central Publishing is a division of Hachette Book Group, Inc.
The Grand Central Publishing name and logo is a registered trademark of Hachette Book Group, Inc.

The publisher is not responsible for websites (or their content) that are not owned by the publisher.

The Hachette Speakers Bureau provides a wide range of authors for speaking events. To find out more, go to hachettespeakersbureau.com or email HachetteSpeakers@hbgusa.com.

Grand Central Publishing books may be purchased in bulk for business, educational, or promotional use. For information, please contact your local bookseller or the Hachette Book Group Special Markets Department at special.markets@hbgusa.com.

Library of Congress Control Number: 2024937058

ISBNs: 978-1-5387-2641-9 (hardcover), 978-1-5387-5869-4 (large type), 978-1-5387-2643-3 (Canadian trade), 978-1-5387-2644-0 (ebook)

Printed in the United States of America

LSC-C

Printing 1, 2024

ON THE HUNT

CHAPTER

1

QUAI BRANLY MUSEUM COMPLEX
PARIS, FRANCE

Damn, it was still burning.

Kira Drake and her dog, Mack, moved through the fiery rubble of what was once one of the most beautiful museums in Paris. There was almost nothing left of the glass buildings and picturesque grounds. It had been more than thirty-six hours since a string of explosions had decimated the museum, and a dark haze still lingered, almost completely obscuring the Eiffel Tower, which loomed over the scene from just blocks away. The tower and the businesses within a radius of almost a mile were closed, and the surrounding neighborhoods were cordoned off to everyone except investigators and rescue workers.

Kira leaned over and rubbed the back of Mack's neck. He was a four-year-old golden retriever, and they had worked together in disaster scenes all over the world. Mack sniffed the air, which was thick with an acrid odor they'd smelled practically from the moment they'd landed at Charles de Gaulle Airport an hour before. Kira glanced around the depressing scene. Hot spots had erupted in flame pockets all over the grounds, and more appeared as quickly as firefighters could extinguish them.

"What are you getting, boy?" she whispered to Mack.

Her dog was on high alert, sniffing in every direction as he led her through the narrow pathways that crews had swept free of the twisted metal and shards of glass.

This wasn't a body hunt; 230 corpses had already been removed from the scene and identified, and she'd been assured there were no more to be found. She and Mack were there for a different reason.

"Kira!" a voice called out behind her.

She turned to see that it was Matt Graves, who had practically begged her to come to Paris and visit the site with Mack. Graves was a special investigator with the United Nations Office of Counter-Terrorism. She'd never seen him in anything but a business suit, but today he was wearing a long yellow firefighter's jacket and tall boots. He stepped closer and spoke with his usual French accent. "Thank you for coming. Good flight?"

"Fine." She looked around the still-smoldering scene. "This is sickening. Any theories about who's responsible?"

"Lots of theories, but little concrete evidence yet. This museum features artwork by indigenous peoples of Europe, Africa, Asia, and the Americas. There have been protests calling for the return of some of the artifacts to their homelands, so it could be related to that. Half the law enforcement agencies in Europe are here trying to make sense of this. You'll see some familiar faces."

"I've already seen a few. French police, Interpol, Scotland Yard...Are there any other dogs working the case?"

"Henry Jaffer flew in from Holland yesterday."

"With his white shepherd, Dancer?"

"Yes. They found the last two surviving victims in what was left of the parking structure. Vince McCall and his little terrier were among the first to arrive. They found several corpses that the rescue workers had missed."

She nodded. "I'm not surprised. Harper is one of the best body dogs in the business." She looked ahead. "Can you get us close to one of the main blast points?"

He pointed to the right. "The explosions started in the new modern art building. Jack Harlan was here for the dedication just last week. Detonations continued across the main building and finally to the administrative offices. Our best bet is to start at the offices. They're the most intact."

Kira looked at the heap of concrete and melted glass. "'Intact' is a relative term."

"Absolutely. This way."

He led her and Mack around a mound of blackened concrete to what was once a five-story administrative building. She had spent much of her flight from the U.S. familiarizing herself with the layout of the buildings and surrounding grounds, but there was little still standing that related to the online maps she'd studied. At least here, part of the superstructure remained.

Mack pulled on his harness and guided her around a hot spot she and Graves hadn't seen.

"Good boy." Kira turned back to Graves. "Were the explosions at the lower level?"

"Yes, all the way across. They were carefully placed to cause maximum damage. The bomber may have had some professional demolition experience."

She unclipped the leash from Mack's harness, and the golden retriever bolted through the smoldering piles of steel and roofing material, stopping to sniff every few feet before moving on.

Graves watched for a moment, his face wrinkled with concern. "There's a lot of broken shards of glass out there, and they're still trying to tamp down the hot spots. Will he be okay?"

"He's wearing protective booties, and Mack knows his way around disaster areas. Remember the stadium collapse in Barcelona?"

He grimaced. "I remember."

"Trust me, he'll be safer than we will. We just need to keep up."

Kira and Graves followed Mack through the rubble. Graves finally raised an N95 mask over his nose and mouth. "When the wind changes, the smell is overpowering. Will he be able to pick up the scents?"

"I think he already has." She pointed toward her dog, whose tail was furiously wagging as he darted past globs of melted glass. "He's zeroing in on something now." They broke into a run as Mack finally stopped short in front of a gaping hole and started barking.

Kira caught up and knelt beside him. "Got something, boy?"

Mack barked again and looked at her with his big brown eyes.

"Good, Mack." Kira extended her arms in front of her.

Mack faced her and placed his right paw on her left hand, then rested his chin on her right arm. Kira put down her arms, then raised them again. Mack repeated his motions. Kira rubbed his neck and gave him a treat. "You're the best boy ever, Mack."

She stood and turned back toward Graves. "It was RDX."

He looked down in surprise. "He just told you that?"

"Mack can detect over two hundred explosive compounds. That's why you brought us here, isn't it?"

"Yes, but . . . the Paris police thinks it was C-4. We're still waiting on lab results."

Kira shook her head. "Mack doesn't need a lab. It was probably transported here shortly before the blast. Otherwise, the museum security's own bomb-sniffing dogs would have picked it up before detonation. More than likely, it was transported here in a well-ventilated vehicle. Which means . . ."

Mack took off, running for a nearby street. Kira ran after him and called over her shoulder, "Get some of your men. Now!"

Kira followed Mack down Avenue Rapp, and she'd gone barely half a block before she turned and saw that Graves had enlisted two plainclothes agents and a pair of Paris patrolmen to join them. She had no idea where this would lead, but she was glad to have backup if the situation demanded it.

"Slow down, Mack. We'll get there soon enough."

She hoped. The bombs could have come from anywhere, but she

assumed the bomber wouldn't want to transport unstable explosive devices over a long and potentially bumpy journey.

Graves and the others caught up to her just as she and Mack turned left on Avenue de la Bourdonnais. "How certain are you of this?" Graves asked Kira.

She shrugged. "For now, extremely certain. But he could lose the scent at any time. We'll have to see."

The group followed Mack until they finally found themselves at an empty storefront on Rue Duroc, situated next to a dry cleaner. Kira and Graves peered into the plate-glass window and saw only a few dirty tarps on a concrete floor.

"There's nothing here," Graves said.

Mack barked and ran down a narrow alley next to the building. He stood in a driveway behind the empty store and barked at the rear entrance. The dog then spun around several times.

Kira pointed to the back door. "We need to go in there."

Graves nodded to the patrolmen, and the taller of the two kicked the door repeatedly until it finally splintered open. They rushed through an empty storeroom and glanced around the front area they'd seen through the windows.

The place was empty.

Graves sighed. "Wild goose chase?"

Kira grabbed one of the patrolmen's flashlights and trained the beam on the storeroom floor. "No. Look!"

They gathered around her and leaned over to see short lengths of wire, metal shavings, and pieces of insulation.

Kira backed away. "The bombs were assembled here."

Graves nodded and motioned for everyone to exit out of the back door. "Yes. Everyone out. I'm calling Interpol."

———————— • ————————

RUE DUROC

FOUR HOURS LATER

Night had fallen over the city, and the empty storefront was now the center of activity for dozens of forensics specialists and representatives from scores of law enforcement agencies. Across the street, Kira could see all the television news crews that had set up shop; their reporters were doing stand-ups in the glare of bright camera lights.

She had just taken Mack for a walk around the block when Graves approached her at the corner. "Interpol thinks they have a lead. A security camera caught someone going in and out of this place a few days ago, and their facial recognition system matched an American who was in the country for a few days."

"That was fast."

"Yes. They're not fooling around. They've had a lot of pressure on them this time."

"Who is it?"

"They haven't released that information yet. It's probably no one you've heard of."

She shrugged. "It doesn't matter. Mack did his job." She scratched the dog's back, and he looked up at her with sublime appreciation.

Graves smiled. "Yes, he did. You both did. Thank you. If you'd like to spend another couple of days here, the hotel is already paid for. There are worse places than Paris for a little R and R."

Kira thought of the wreckage of the once beautiful museum area and slowly shook her head. Lord, she was weary of the acrid smell of smoke and the sight of death that clung to that place.

"Thanks, Graves. Maybe another time. There's someplace else we need to be right now." She tried not to show how eager she was to leave as she turned away. "Good luck with your investigation."

———————— • ————————

"Did you see this morning's headlines, Harlan?" Belson came into the study and threw the newspapers on Jack Harlan's desk. "They've identified the Paris bomber. It was our old friend Joseph Taylor. You called it."

Harlan brushed the newspapers aside. "Old news, my friend. My contacts at Interpol tipped me off last night. If you hadn't taken the day off, you would have known that." He grimaced. "I've been doing my best not to feel responsible."

"Why? Because you donated that new museum building? No one could possibly think that makes this your fault."

"You and I both know that's exactly why Taylor targeted this museum. Interpol knows it, the Paris police know it, and the reporters for these newspapers know it. He knew he couldn't get past the security here at my home. Taylor's been looking for a way to strike back at me. Up to now, he failed every time he tried, but he finally found a way to do it. Even if it meant killing two hundred and thirty innocent people."

Belson paced across the study to stand before the bank of television monitors. They were in a magnificent chalet on the outskirts of Paris, which became Harlan's home base when he oversaw the Western European operations of Harlan Enterprises, a multinational tech company that had burst onto the scene and come to dominate several consumer product categories in the space of just a few years. Floor-to-ceiling windows offered a magnificent view of the Paris skyline; the Eiffel Tower was slowly becoming visible again as the post-blast haze finally dissipated. Belson pointed to the bank of six screens, all still displaying international news broadcasts covering the bombing. "You've seen, of course, how they found out it was Taylor."

"I could hardly miss it." Harlan stared at the TVs. Three of the six broadcasts were showing footage of a golden retriever being guided by an attractive young woman near the blast site. "It's Kira Drake. She's the one you've been pestering me to put on my payroll."

" 'Pestering' is too strong a word," Belson said. "I'd never be that crass. 'Strongly suggesting' is more like it. If you're looking for someone, she's the one you want in your corner."

"Is she really that good?"

"She *got* the bastard. The entire city of Paris was crawling with police and military, and she's the one who managed to zero in on Joseph Taylor."

"But he still got away."

"That isn't her fault. He'd left the country before she even arrived. He's back in the U.S. somewhere. It's only the latest in a long line of successes for her."

"Like what?"

"Did you even read the magazine I gave you last week?" Belson picked up a journal from the coffee table and tossed it on top of the newspapers. "Why do you pay me an exorbitant salary if you're not going to pay attention to me?"

Harlan glanced at the cover of the magazine. "Maybe because most of your ideas aren't as weird as the one you threw at me this time. Besides, I was busy with that conference in India. But I remember that when you mentioned her, I did tell you to try to engage her services. You had nothing to do with bringing her here?"

"No, she was flown in by a UN investigative team. I'd reached out to her less than a week before, but I didn't detect a lot of interest."

"Why not?"

"She's always in demand. But it seemed like a good idea to me, and it still does. Every time Taylor comes up on our radar, he manages to slip away. It wouldn't hurt to have Kira Drake on call to track him the next time we get a report on his location."

"There are other trackers and other dogs."

"Not like her. That's why I wanted you to read that article. She's extraordinary. She's a veterinarian, but her emphasis is on research. She's helped develop drugs to double and perhaps even triple the normal life spans of dogs."

This piqued Harlan's interest. "My friend's wife is doing much the same thing."

Belson nodded. "Sarah Logan. She actually mentored Kira Drake at her Summer Island facility. They've worked together for years."

"Interesting."

"But Drake is probably better known for her work as a tracker. Most dogs are trained for one specialty, be it bomb sniffing, cadaver seeking, or straight-out tracking based on a scent. She's trained her dog, Mack, for all these things, and he's accompanied her all over the world for a variety of missions. She's even used him for a few archaeological projects. The dog can identify areas where foreign objects have been placed in the earth hundreds or even thousands of years ago. Like I said, extraordinary."

Harlan looked down at the photo of Kira Drake on the magazine cover. Long gold-brown hair pulled back from a face that was dominated by huge dark brown eyes and a smile that held a hint of mischief. "Lovely," he said absently. "And character in every line of her features. I suppose it couldn't hurt to take a chance interviewing her."

"If she'd permit it," Belson said. "Like I said, she turned me down flat when I approached her last week." He grinned. "I don't know if she even knew who you were. Amazing. Rich as Croesus, two Nobel Prizes, and a Presidential Medal of Freedom. Do you want me to keep on trying? It might be worth it." His eyes were twinkling. "If your ego can take it."

"You're enjoying this, aren't you?" Harlan asked with a small smile. "It might be worthwhile to make another try at persuading her to take my money. I'm sure you'll enjoy a second opportunity to watch me fail to impress her with all that hype you're so eager to spread. It's one of your favorite sports, and you relish the chance to tell me about it later."

"Perhaps," Belson said. "Everyone needs to face an occasional put-down. Even me. But I don't think that this will be one. I believe I have a way to get to her this time. I know someone who might persuade her that she wouldn't be doing you a favor but saving the world. That way, she won't think she's wasting her time in the service of a rich, selfish playboy. My plan might work, but you'll need to do something."

"Heaven forbid. Marching orders, Belson?"

"Just a phone call. You'll need to reach out to your friend John Logan and his wife and see if they'd be willing to put a good word in. As I said, Sarah Logan mentored her, and John has poured hundreds of millions of dollars into the Summer Island research facility. Kira Drake might be more willing to listen to them than to either of us."

Harlan nodded. "You want me to use my friendship with them to recruit her?"

"For the very best cause. To catch someone who just murdered two hundred and thirty people. I know John Logan casually, and he might be willing to do it if I talked to him…"

"I don't doubt it," Harlan said dryly. "John Logan gave you a fantastic reference when you were applying for this job with me. You certainly managed to do a terrific con, talking him into doing it."

"Con? I'm hurt. You know I'm a man who can reach out and make anyone come to terms with the world around them. It's one of my gifts. This is relatively simple. One phone call from you, and then I'll follow up myself. Yes or no: Should I tap the person who might lure Drake into your camp?"

"John Logan?"

"John's wife, Sarah. He gave her Summer Island when they were newlyweds, and she allows Kira to use the island for training whenever she's not on a mission. It's fortunate Sarah has wonderful taste and finds me appealing and fairly brilliant."

Harlan thought about it. "Why not? I've been after Taylor for a number of years and haven't been able to catch him. I'm willing to try any avenue at the moment." He dropped down in his office chair and opened the magazine. "I'll research Kira Drake in depth and see what she has to offer."

"That's all I wanted," Belson said. "You and Taylor have been playing cat and mouse ever since Taylor killed your brother, Colin. It's become an obsession. You need to try something different. I like this job and don't want to have to look for another one anytime soon. I told you that I investigated this woman, and she has the reputation of being a bloody wonder. There might be a way to use her to help you get to Taylor. He almost cut your throat in Rome last year."

"And I was within a breath of getting him in Athens two months later." Harlan's lips twisted bitterly. "It's only a matter of time." He held up his hand as Belson started to interrupt. "But I admit I've reached a point where I'm desperate enough to listen to you. I'll even read about this woman and her blasted dog and try to see what you see in her. Heaven forbid you end up on the unemployment line."

"I won't," Belson said. "You wouldn't let me. I'm too valuable. You'll find you can't exist without me. You just have to listen to me. It's time you tried something new. So let's go hunting. We can start near Mount Blue Sky in Colorado, where Taylor is rumored to have a hideout. You're almost as good a tracker as that woman you're so scornful about. You might even be able to get your hands on Taylor before she does. It's what you wanted anyway. She's unique enough that both the local cops and the Colorado governor might go for the idea of bringing her in just for the media exposure. They wouldn't touch you given that you're practically a national treasure."

Belson chuckled as Harlan made a rude sound. "It's true. No one wants to antagonize NATO or Congress. And this woman is something of an outlier, but she just might be able to help in some way. Give her a chance." He got to his feet. "It's time for me to get out of here. By the time you talk to John Logan, I'll be on my way to

Summer Island to try to persuade Sarah Logan to talk Kira Drake into giving you a chance to get what you want." He tapped the magazine. "Be sure you read about how our dog lady managed to find that pirate treasure trove in the Bahamas. That should amuse you."

"I doubt it. The only thing that will amuse me is getting Taylor in my sights."

"Which might be the same thing," Belson said. "Kira and her dog spent almost a year on that Caribbean island searching for those Spanish doubloons. When she found them, she insisted it was her dog's keen nose that located the site where they had been buried. A bit hard to believe."

"Don't worry," Harlan said grimly. "I'll research everything about her before I interview her."

"*If* you interview her," Belson said as he left the office. "It depends on whether your connections and my charm are still as potent as ever. But you've got a great chance…"

———— • ————

SUMMER ISLAND
TWO DAYS LATER

Kira pressed her forehead against the private jet's side window and looked down. "Feels good to be here, doesn't it, Mack?"

The dog licked her hand appreciatively.

"It's good to have you back," the pilot said as he guided the plane over the island. "Both of you."

"Thanks, Edward. I never feel better than I do when I'm on Summer Island. It's a magical place."

As they flew over the island, Kira smiled as she saw some of the site's oldest residents, a group of dogs in their late twenties and early thirties who ran and played on an obstacle course as if they were puppies. A moment later, the jet swooped over a tall suspension bridge spanning a wide river that nearly cleaved the island in two. For all its majesty, the bridge melded with its surroundings, fitting in with the simple architecture and lush vegetation that characterized Summer Island.

Soon they touched down on the airstrip near the main research lab. Edward tapped his headset. "I've just been told Sarah is greeting us today. She's finishing up an evaluation in the lab and will be out in a minute or two."

"No problem. I'll play with Mack for a while. He always gets excited when he comes here."

They jumped out of the jet and started running in the large field next to the airstrip.

Mack dashed one way, then another, as Kira tried to grab him in a spirited game of tag. She finally cornered him against the communications shack.

"Got you, Mack. It's about time," she grumbled. "You could have remembered that I don't have four legs like you. You ran me ragged." She ran the rest of the way to where the dog was crouching and tagged him on the neck, which was the official victory signal in this particular game. "I win! My game. But you were particularly determined today." She put her arms around him and gave him a hug. "I was actually very proud of you. You were exceptionally clever."

He nodded solemnly.

She laughed. "Don't be arrogant. You almost missed that last turn at the bottom of the hill."

But Mack was no longer listening to her. His head rose, and suddenly he was howling with joy and running down the hill toward the lake.

"Mack!" She jumped to her feet. Then she saw who was coming out of the research lab and sighed in resignation. Of course Mack wasn't paying any attention to her. She waved and started down the hill herself. "Hi, Sarah. There's no way Mack is going to be able to concentrate with you and Monty here. He'll think it's playtime." She watched Mack jumping around Sarah's dog Monty like a young puppy. She hadn't seen him so happy since the last time Sarah had brought him to the island. Monty was Mack's sire, and they had been together for the first two years of Mack's life as well as during his early training. "But it's not time for Monty's shots. I told you we should stagger them."

"I'm not jumping the gun." Sarah was climbing the hill toward her, but she was forced to leap around the two dogs. "I wasn't going to miss bringing them together, though, since I was coming here anyway." She was looking at the two romping dogs with affection.

"I love to see them together. Admit it, so do you." She held up a picnic basket. "So I brought lunch for all of us." Her eyes were twinkling. "I'll have to see if Monty can keep his son in line at the chow line. It's the ultimate test of obedience."

Kira's eyes narrowed. "But that's not the reason you showed up today," she said. "Are you worried about Monty?"

"No," Sarah said quickly. "I have faith in your latest versions of our serum. I couldn't be more grateful to you. He has the health and energy of a five-year-old pup. It's a miracle."

"It's only the first stages. I'm working on an advanced blend if this one shows signs of weakening."

"No sign yet." Sarah opened the basket. "Wine? You may need it." She made a face. "I brought more than Monty tucked away in my bag of tricks."

Kira stiffened. She went over possibilities with lightning speed and came up with the most recent. "The Paris bomber. Taylor. Is that what you're talking about?"

Sarah nodded. "How did you know?"

"I heard from Carl Belson last week. He said he worked for Jack Harlan and wanted to know if I'd be interested in working on a retainer with the idea that I'd help them track down someone who's been on international most-wanted lists for a few years. I had the impression that it was a personal grudge of Harlan's, and I passed." She made a face. "This was before Taylor became Public Enemy Number One after the Paris bombing. I knew Harlan must have really wanted him after that. The great man must have been furious that Taylor destroyed the Paris museum whose shiny new building had his own name on it. And everyone knows that Harlan was already obsessed with finding his younger brother's killer."

"One can hardly blame him," Sarah said quietly. "It was a brutal murder, and the word was that Harlan always took care of Colin. But I think you should consider that Jack Harlan has also donated millions to the survivors of those killed in Paris. There's more than one side to him. Still, the murder of his brother probably had a defining effect on his character."

"You're being very defensive." Kira's gaze narrowed on Sarah's face. "Why?"

"Because I might detect a hint of resentment toward Jack Harlan and his employees. True?"

"Maybe. I think I'm just tired of being pressured by all the rich and powerful who want to get their way and sometimes seem to leave the peasants behind. Belson was polite enough, but he really annoyed me when all I wanted was to get back to work." She scowled. "Actually, I don't know that much about Jack Harlan. Other than he's rumored to be some kind of genius." Kira wrinkled her nose. "Okay, maybe I'm not being fair. Why are you laughing?"

"Because John and I have worked hard and managed to acquire a good amount of money over the years. I don't believe you'd say we were completely ungenerous. And there's nary a suffering peasant in sight."

"Of course not. You're the most generous people I know. You're absolutely exceptional." Kira was laughing, too. "Okay, your point is that Harlan could also be exceptional? I'm listening. Convince me. How did the killing of Colin Harlan happen?"

"Colin worked at Harvard University and ran across Taylor when they had a computer lab together. Taylor was an assistant professor and usually managed to be charming if he made the effort. He must have made the effort with Colin, who said that Taylor was impressed when he learned what a celebrity his big brother, Jack Harlan, was, so he invited him home to the castle at the end of the quarter. He even persuaded Harlan to give Taylor some minor work to do on one of his latest projects. The two of them were supposed to be working on it together." Her lips twisted. "But Taylor abused that generosity and stole Harlan's algorithm for a new encryption program he had developed for online purchases. It was potentially worth billions. Taylor murdered Colin to cover up his crime and blew up the lab in an attempt to make Colin's death look like an accident. We know Taylor stole the technology because he licensed it to companies in scores of other countries and pocketed almost a hundred million dollars before Harlan uncovered the crime himself and exposed him for the thief and murderer he was. That was the start of Taylor's criminal activities, but far from the end. The museum bombing may be the most horrific thing Taylor has done, but it's only the latest in a long line of horrible attacks against Harlan and his interests."

Kira nodded. "I can see why Jack Harlan would want to put the bastard away. But tell him to talk to the FBI or the CIA. I gave in when Interpol asked me to look over that bombed museum, and it horrified me. So all I want to do now is go back to working with Mack and refining that serum. I don't have the time to deal with Harlan's personal problems. I'm busy doing something worthwhile that has to do with life, not death."

"And I applaud it," Sarah said. "I wouldn't have asked if John didn't want you to consider the possibilities. Harlan has done him a lot of favors, and he says he's a great guy. They're on several charity boards together."

"I don't have time," Kira repeated. "I don't want to do this, Sarah."

"Then don't do it," Sarah said. "But explore it and have a good reason to refuse. This Joseph Taylor is obviously a terrible man. Not only is he a master thief and murderer, but he has his own private criminal organization in a number of countries that rivals the mafia in effectiveness. Which makes it difficult for the Harlans to use the law to bring him to justice and keeps even the governor of Colorado from having him arrested for killing his daughter."

"Charming," Kira said. "He sounds like a total beast. However, I'm sure Harlan wasn't entirely innocent from all the stories and reports I've heard about their encounters."

"Harlan is a good man, Kira. Do you know what his two Nobel Prizes are for? One was for an incredibly effective water purification system that he developed and gives away to impoverished coastal and river communities all over the world. In some of these places, childhood morbidity rates have fallen sixty percent or more because of him. The second Nobel was for the atmosphere purification plants that he constructed in New Zealand. They're helping repair the ozone hole over that part of the world. In a few years, that same technology may help reverse global warming on the rest of the planet. He's making a difference."

Kira thought for a moment. "Where do they think Taylor is now?"

"Near Blue Sky, Colorado, although he may have already left there. Taylor has a way of staying one step ahead of the people after him."

Kira paused for another long moment. "I guess I can spare a few days in Colorado to see if Mack and I can find anything that might help. Okay?"

Sarah nodded. "Thank you, Kira."

"You're welcome," Kira said. "Now can we talk about something else, hopefully more pleasant?"

"Anything is more pleasant." Sarah frowned. "And I hated having to bring it up. So eat your sandwich and drink your wine, and we'll watch the dogs, and I'll tell you how impressed the International Veterinarian Council is with Monty's progress. It's my dream, but you've made it your reality."

Kira was silent for an instant but was still not happy. She knew that Sarah would not ask her again about Taylor, but it didn't change the fact that she also knew Sarah had listened to her ideas, brought her to this island, and taught her all she knew about veterinary science and rescue. She'd been orphaned as a ten-year-old child on one of Sarah's search-and-rescue operations, and Sarah had not only paid for her education but actually given her a career in this field of her choice. After college, Kira had come knocking on Sarah's door, and she had never regretted it. Sarah had become a teacher and a friend and had opened doors that Kira valued enormously. She'd never asked anything that Kira wasn't willing to give. She was having difficulty refusing her now.

She slowly nodded. "I'll explore the possibility of finding and bringing Joseph Taylor to justice, but I won't deal with Harlan. I'm sick about all that horror I saw in Paris, but I won't be caught between him and Taylor with their ugly revenge games. That's not what I do."

"Harlan wouldn't ask it of you," Sarah said.

"I won't deal with Harlan," Kira repeated. "But you can bet I won't go in blind. And if he tries to use me, I'll walk away."

"I doubt it." Sarah shook her head. "John gave me a few sickening autopsy reports, which I'll leave with you. They're probably copies of the same documents Belson gave you that you've been ignoring. I found I couldn't ignore them." She handed Kira a glass of wine. "Just be careful and don't be afraid of asking Harlan for help if you need it."

Kira shook her head. "I won't need it. All I need is Mack."

"I believe it." Sarah touched her own glass to Kira's. "And may you be happy together. But if that changes, call me. I had Monty but somewhere along the way I found that search and rescue wasn't enough for me. I gave you Mack, Monty's son, and you gave life to many other dogs over the years with that serum we invented. But I don't want you to entirely block out the possibility of some actual human intimacy. I want there to be a John in your life."

"I assure you I haven't been a nun," Kira said, laughing. "I'm just selective. You don't believe there are any men as good as your John anyway."

"True. So you can continue to do your work here for a little while longer while I look the field over for you. Now tell me how Mack is doing at the games." She handed her a sandwich. "I'd like to have the two dogs play a game together in a couple hours. I want to see if Mack has learned any tricks from you that he could teach Monty. But after that, I've got to get back to the mainland to meet John and drive back to our town house. He's been in London at a meeting for the last week."

"It's just as well." Kira made a face. "I've got to plan my trip to Colorado and then send a message to the governor to tell him that Mack and I will be paying a professional visit to his state in the next couple of days. I'm not looking forward to it."

"You can back out," Sarah said.

"Not likely," Kira said. "On the other hand, I could strike out. In that mountain area where this particular monster lives, it's almost impossible to track down criminals. The governor sent his people out to get Taylor and never located a sign of him. Besides, you wouldn't have asked me if you didn't really want it." She got to her feet. "Mack and I will go after this Taylor, but I gave you the rules." She suddenly grinned. "Now that I've discouraged you, let me show you how good Mack has gotten over the last year. Prepare to have your Monty put in the shade..."

Sarah was laughing as she ran after her. "Be a little respectful. Monty will show that young whippersnapper what maturity is all about..."

CHAPTER

2

MESA VERDE NATIONAL PARK, COLORADO
EIGHT DAYS LATER

"You're still watching her?" Belson asked curiously as Harlan trained his infrared binoculars on Kira Drake. She was moving swiftly around the first level of the museum cliff dwelling community followed closely by her golden retriever. "It's the fourth time this week that I've seen you go to the trouble of staking her out yourself since she arrived in Colorado. Which means you've been practically stalking her since she showed up. Why? Didn't you believe me when I told you that she was good?"

"You might say that," Harlan said. "Or maybe I wanted to make certain she wasn't getting ahead of me, given that she's refused to even meet with me since she arrived. It's enough to annoy me, isn't it?"

"But somehow I don't think it is. You look like you're enjoying yourself too much," Belson said speculatively. "So which one is it?"

Harlan lowered his glasses. "Yes, she's as good as you told me she was. Yes, I'm annoyed that she could screw up the entire capture if I'm not careful. But she's also very interesting, quite unique. For instance, why did she come here? Would anyone else show up at an archaeological site built centuries ago when they were searching for a bloodthirsty killer?" He leaned back against the pueblo wall. "But she not only came today, she's been searching the entire area for any clues that he's been here in the past."

"And has he?" Belson asked.

"He must have been. The dog must have picked up his scent at some point near this location. It would have been an excellent hideout for him until he could arrange transport to whisk him away from Colorado. Some of those ancient Pueblo communities have almost a hundred and fifty rooms. He could get lost in that much space. At any rate, either way it would have been clever of her to lead me here, don't you think?"

"If she cared one way or the other," Belson said. "She's made an art of ignoring you since she's been here. You have to appreciate that fact."

"Oh, I do. Let me count the many ways," Harlan said caustically. "And if Taylor's scent still lingers, she may not even know whether or not he's in that cliff dwelling or somewhere else entirely. It's a crapshoot."

"What's your guess?"

Harlan shrugged. "That we'll have to wait until she leaves and then go search the place ourselves. In the meantime, we'll just send one of our team to follow her and keep an eagle eye out in case she already has an idea where else she can locate Taylor and is only trying to find him before we do." He added thoughtfully, "She's very sharp. That could be the way she'll play it. We'll have to see, won't we?" He lifted his binoculars to his eyes again before settling back against the pueblo wall. "She's started working at the dwelling called the Cliff Palace right now. She should find it interesting. It dates back over seven hundred years and is built of sandstone, wooden beams, and mortar. At one time, it was painted entirely in brilliant colors."

"Fascinating. I'm sure you find those esoteric facts intriguing, but I don't regard them as particularly appealing."

Harlan grinned. "No, but evidently Drake does. Otherwise she wouldn't have come here or looked for Taylor at an ancestral Pueblo national park. Not exactly the usual action for an expert tracker to take."

"So we just sit here in the sun and watch and wait to see if Kira and her favorite pooch will furnish us with the direction where Taylor can be found?"

"That's it exactly. But while we're waiting, we'll let her entertain us and admire the way she's handled herself so far in tracking the bastard. Aren't you proud that you managed to talk me into hiring such a pearl above price?"

"Sarcasm, Harlan?"

"Perhaps a little. It all depends on what happens in the next few hours and what Kira Drake is really up to . . ."

"Yes, he's watching us again, Mack." Kira bent and stroked Mack's neck. "But he's not making any moves yet. We'll still have time to finish up and get out of here." She chuckled with amusement as she finished up checking out the last room at Mesa Verde's Cliff Palace. "No sign of Taylor here. Well, it could have gone either way. Do you think Harlan is enjoying himself? We do hope so, don't we? But we'll be out of here soon, and then we can go back and make sure that we actually locate Taylor before he does. I've found an opening on the lower level near the juniper trees where we can slip out and get back to that place where you first picked up his scent here." She deliberately turned and stared directly at where Harlan was probably sitting, watching her. She smiled and insolently flipped her hand at him. "Have a great day, Jack Harlan. See you later..."

———— • ————

JONES CREEK, COLORADO

Shortly after nightfall, Kira called Harlan. He sounded shocked to hear from her. "To what do I owe the pleasure?"

"I thought it was time I checked in."

"Well, you've been treating me like a pariah, and you won't even discuss working with me when we're actually after the same thing. If I'm the problem, I'll be glad to send Belson instead."

"Don't you dare. I don't trust Belson, and I certainly don't trust you. Do you think I didn't know that you've been on the hunt for me ever since I arrived here in Colorado?" She didn't wait for an answer. "You must've known. I could *feel* you tracking me."

"Of course I did. It was quite entertaining. You're exceptionally talented."

"I'm happy you enjoyed yourself. But suppose I give you a counteroffer. As soon as I capture Taylor, I'll turn him over to the governor with the stipulation that he's to let you and your lawyers know he's in custody and allow you access. That would be fair and wouldn't allow you total power over a prisoner that I've already apprehended."

"I guarantee the governor won't mind if I have jurisdiction over the bastard," Harlan said curtly.

"But he also has a reason for revenge," Kira said. "I don't mind being connected to the administration of justice, if necessary. It's revenge I don't like." She rushed on to stop the protest she knew was coming. "Yes, I saw the photos of the governor's daughter. It made me sad, but I can't be judge and jury."

"You'd rather be the cop on the beat?" Harlan paused. "Yes, I can see you in that role."

"I can't. I'd rather not be involved at all. But my offer will remain in place until further notice. I've told you my terms. They're better than you deserve, but Sarah Logan appears to think you're worth it. Goodbye, Harlan." She hung up.

She drew a deep breath and turned back to face the porch of the ranch house. She didn't know what she expected, but nothing had changed since she'd zeroed in on Joseph Taylor a few moments before. She had located Taylor's hideout earlier this week, and she was almost sure that the man she had caught sight of in the rocking chair on the ranch house porch today was her target. He had been sitting in that same position just now, leaning back, casually holding a rifle across his lap, except he was talking to someone on his phone. From the way he looked up and occasionally nodded, she guessed he was talking to someone in the helicopter that was almost overhead now; she could see the blue lights streaming down from the cockpit. She couldn't make out what they were saying, but she had to be absolutely certain that the man in the rocking chair was Taylor. Which meant she had to go back to that porch and get a closer look at him. It might also mean that she and Mack would go after Taylor if the opportunity presented itself. She began crawling down the cliff, her gaze still glued to the figure on the porch. She gave a short whistle for Mack to follow her more closely.

She knew he would make no sound as he came toward her. One of his lessons involved making sure he would never betray her while they were on the trail. The people in that helicopter were almost definitely some of the men who had been summoned to help Taylor escape, and the craft was slowly descending toward a clearing she remembered seeing behind the cabin. They weren't close enough to be a danger yet, but the lights would make it more dangerous by the minute. Better to move fast and grab the target when the opportunity presented itself.

However, those lights might be an opportunity in themselves, she thought suddenly. There was more than one way to bring a monster like Taylor down. She just had to bide her time. But she could see now that the man with the rifle had the general build and features of Taylor; he seemed to match the photos that had been forwarded to her. She would get a little closer to the porch and see if an opportunity presented itself to go after Taylor that didn't involve Mack in the capture. She would have to be very careful...

The man on the porch was now shouting angrily into the phone. She heard an expletive and the name Donovan. Instinct told her that this person was subservient to him. If she brought Harlan into the picture, he might be able to get a trace on Donovan, which might be a way to pin down the identities of Taylor's gang. But she didn't want to involve Harlan if she could avoid it. Better to go with her own tried-and-true tracking methods...

———————— • ————————

"Where the hell have you been, Donovan?" Taylor shouted into the phone. "You were supposed to be here forty minutes ago."

"I had to pick up the helicopter. Then you said you wanted me to do a little scouting around for that mutt that belongs to Drake. It took me a while, but I managed to spot him on the cliffs near the pueblo a little bit ago. I think he's on the hunt for you just like you thought he'd be. Do you want me to go after him and take him out?"

"No, the timing is wrong," Taylor said impatiently. "It has to be me, and the Drake woman has to see it."

"I don't understand," Donovan said blankly.

"I know you don't," Taylor said. "You don't understand any of the subtleties of the relationship that exists between Harlan and me. It's all about punishment and pain and making sure Harlan knows that he can't bring in outsiders and expect me not to punish them. But he'll know all that after tonight. How close are you to picking me up, Donovan?"

"Five minutes. We'll do one more sweep, then land at the clearing."

"That's good enough. I might have to perform a demonstration to illustrate how our tracker is to be treated. But all you'll have to worry about is lining up her faithful pooch exactly where I want him."

"Whatever you say," Donovan said. "You're the boss."

"Exactly. Now get down here and let's start moving. I admit I'm getting a little impatient..."

———— • ————

Although Kira had been on the far side of the porch and too far away to hear much of the conversation, she'd been able to get the gist of the emotion from Taylor's body language. No fear. Arrogance. Now he was stroking the stock of his rifle almost caressingly and leaning back in the rocker, his thoughtful gaze staring into the darkness. The aircraft appeared to be preparing to set down. She felt a sudden chill. She was sure he didn't know she was anywhere near this hideout. She'd been careful whenever she'd hiked this area recently. But she'd had the eerie feeling that he not only knew she was there but had been smiling mockingly at her from the porch.

Imagination?

The feeling was so intense that she carefully backed away from the porch and then, just as cautiously, made her way around the side of the ranch house until she was halfway back to the cliff where she'd left Mack. She would take her time and approach the house from a different direction. She believed in trusting her instincts, and she'd never had a stronger sense of warning than tonight. Once she had positive confirmation of his identity, she'd get Mack off the cliff, go after Taylor, take away that rifle, put the son of a bitch down, and then get the hell out. She gave Mack another short whistle as she increased her pace to bring him closer to her. "It's okay, boy," she whispered as he looked up at her, cocking his head inquiringly. "We just have to wait a little longer. I have to be sure about what we're doing. We'll go slowly and steadily. Okay?" She gave him a hand signal and Mack started at a trot, looking over his shoulder to make sure she was following. It was the way they usually worked, and Mack was eager to resume the status quo.

Her head rose as she suddenly heard something! A familiar low hum in the distance. Was it the helicopter again? She tensed. She'd done a preliminary search of the area earlier in the day for possible co-conspirators and found nothing. This could be members of his team in another vehicle. A late arrival? But she had been sure Taylor had been communicating with someone in the helicopter while he'd been sitting on that porch. It could be either.

Mack could hear the sound, too. She could feel it in the tension of his body. Was Taylor on the move? She put out a hand to soothe

35

him. "Soon," she murmured. "I'll let you go when I'm sure we can close in on the damn bastard. Yes, I know that helicopter is getting closer." She reached in her pocket for her infrared binoculars. "Just give me a few more minutes..." She trained the glasses on the porch as she spoke, quickly scanning the entire ranch property.

Shadows. Only shadows. "Come on, Taylor. Let me see you..."

Light from the helicopter played across the back porch, illuminating the figure in the rocking chair for a moment. It was definitely Taylor. Unmistakable.

Yes!

"We've got him, Mack," she whispered. "Go!"

But Mack was already on his way, climbing toward the bottom of the cliff. Not a sound emerged from his throat. Even the pads of his feet were quiet on the stone and rocks of the cliff.

And Kira knew she had to be just as quiet as she and Mack set a trap for that bastard...

CHAPTER

3

"I'm heading out," Harlan told Belson curtly as he headed for the cliffs. "Kira Drake is getting close to Taylor and could cause big trouble. And I need to clean up the mess before it becomes terminal. I can't get her to listen to me."

"What a surprise," Belson said. "Do you want company?"

"I think I'd rather deal with her myself. I'll call if I need you."

"Which is what I told you was probably going to happen anyway."

"Because you're so psychic?" Harlan asked sarcastically. Still, he had to admit that Belson had been right: Here Harlan was on this blasted mountain, running after that woman and her dog while she tracked that damn murderer. It was damn fortunate Harlan had made his own maps and plans to go after Taylor from the beginning.

There had always been the possibility that he'd end up on his own, as he always had been where the hunt for Taylor was concerned. Kira Drake had always been just a way to get the police, FBI, and governor to let him participate in the search. At least now he wasn't worried that the media wouldn't be on his side at every turn of the mountain.

But Kira and her dog had done their job, finding Taylor in an area of hundreds of square miles. Although Taylor had become the most wanted man on the globe, the world's investigative agencies still came up short compared with this one woman and her canine companion.

"He's there," Harlan said grimly. "I tracked the woman to within two miles of the property, and she was still heading north. There's nothing else around there. The bastard is the most arrogant son of a bitch on the planet. He's waiting for me. I wouldn't want to disappoint him."

"Don't be conceited. It may not be you he's after right now. Maybe he's actually waiting for Kira Drake, what with all that media coverage. Several news outlets have revealed that it was you who hired her. She's new blood. Taylor would like that. To strike at her would be like striking at you."

Harlan shook his head. "I shot him in the stomach after he killed Colin and blew up the lab. I guarantee he won't forget that. I'll bet he still has some lousy nights from that wound. And he knows I'll never stop now. A mere dog and his tracker buddy wouldn't stand up to that kind of competition." Harlan added mockingly, "Though they might be good enough to give him a reason to prove what a good shot he is." He glanced over his shoulder. "I revealed his crimes to the world, and I've been getting in his way ever since.

She doesn't have nearly the appeal I do for him." His teeth were suddenly bared in a tigerish smile. "So follow if you like, but don't expect me to wait around for you. I'm going to go get him." He increased his pace, feeling the adrenaline begin to pump through him. He was impatient. He wanted Taylor with a hunger that had dominated his life since that moment at the lab when he had realized the son of a bitch had blown Colin to kingdom come. The waiting was almost over now, though Taylor's recent ascension to the world's Most Wanted Man had made things more complicated. Harlan didn't want to risk someone else getting their hands on Taylor first. "You can bet I've no desire to see either that tracker dog or Kira Drake get in my way and prevent me from finding Taylor tonight."

***

ONE HOUR LATER

Where the hell was Donovan? Taylor moved from the back of the ranch house toward the cliff. He'd sighted Kira Drake's slim, athletic figure at least fifteen minutes ago, and he wanted to put the plans he'd made into motion. He'd been anticipating them ever since he'd heard about Harlan's hiring her to track him. At first it had made him angry, but then he'd realized it was only going to make his victory more complete. It would be perfect...

But his phone was ringing now. Donovan. It was about time, Taylor thought in disgust. "Where the hell are you?" he growled.

"You were supposed to be here more than an hour ago. Why are you running late?"

"Only a little," Donovan said. "There are too many cops and state troopers bustling around here. I had to find another landing spot. Meet me near the lake. I'll give you time to get there and move in for the pickup. Fifteen minutes should do it." He paused. "Unless you want me to zero in on the woman myself instead of just giving you an assist to get out of there? I could do that for you."

"Do you think I don't know that? Obey my orders," Taylor said. "You're an idiot, Donovan. If I'd wanted anything else, I'd have told you. I want her punished. I have to find the way I can hurt her the most. She's got to realize she can't take orders from Harlan where it concerns me. I won't let him humiliate me like that. She'll learn she can't take his money and think it will buy me. Our relationship is all about pain. Now obey those orders."

"It's still a risk," Donovan said.

"Not if you do exactly what I said. I'll take care of the rest. Move!"

"Okay, okay." Donovan turned the helicopter and veered in the direction of the lake.

Taylor sat back down in the rocking chair and stared out into the darkness. He knew she was out there somewhere. Harlan, as always, was probably so impressed with himself for hiring the famous Kira Drake to hunt him down. But she wouldn't succeed. He had his own plans in place now. Though he had gone through hell avoiding her since she had arrived in Colorado. She knew what she was doing, but now all he had to do was show himself one more time and bring Kira Drake running toward him again...

Come on along, pretty woman. Step into my parlor...

———•———

Mack was just ahead. Kira could feel his tension, and she knew the golden retriever could sense her presence. It was true they could almost anticipate each other's movements when they were on the trail, and tonight was no different. Perhaps it was even more intense now that Mack was able to feel her own desire to bring Taylor down. Good heavens, she found she was actually trembling. And all because she had encountered Joseph Taylor on the edge of that porch a few minutes ago. This hunt had obviously become too important to her and thrown her a trifle off base. Not only had she recognized Taylor, he had actually been close to her, sitting in his damn rocking chair, so why hadn't she confronted him? It was only now that she had stopped and paused, her gaze flicking over toward the back of the property. No sign of him. She didn't hear him moving on the porch, either. She listened a little longer anyway. No sound. But he was there. She could *feel* him, moving quietly. She closed her eyes.

You're out there. Her heart leaped when she realized Taylor was now heading for the ranch house.

Time to go after Mack.

She started to crawl down the hillside toward the lake, where

41

IRIS JOHANSEN

she was sure the circling helicopter would soon touch down. She
scoped out the terrain using every skill and instinct she'd learned
through the years. She knew these mountains and had spent
more than the usual time bringing Mack to razor-sharpness after
she'd agreed to go after Taylor. She could feel Mack tense out
there in the darkness as he sensed that she was close to making
the final move. She closed out everything else around her and
concentrated on the final rendezvous with Mack. She'd never
admitted to all that bullshit in the tabloids about the so-called
magical bond that existed between Mack and her. It would have
pleased them too much. They would have gotten all sentimental,
and she wouldn't allow the affection that existed between them
to be used in that way. It would have cheapened the bond that she
cherished, and no one would have understood it anyway. How
could they when she really didn't understand it herself? It had
always just been...there.

Her pace increased. "Come on, Mack. We've both got a job to
do. It's showtime. He's a very bad man. I'm more sure than ever
now. Let's take the asshole down."

She frowned as she glanced over her shoulder again, and her
lips tightened with determination. "It's just you and me again, and
that's the way it should be. Harlan doesn't deserve consideration
since we're the ones who actually found Taylor..." Yet despite her
words, Kira was experiencing that same uneasiness she'd known
at the porch. "Hey, I'm not the only one who's involved in this hunt
when Taylor could be a hundred yards away. What's your call,
Mack?"

But Mack whimpered with eagerness and was already running toward the lake!

Evidently Mack wasn't having any doubts, Kira thought, ruefully. He was as eager as he always was at the thought of the game ahead. Not the death of Taylor but the game itself. They both wanted to get back to Summer Island where they had spent their lives doing what they should be doing. She should stop questioning herself and Harlan and just rely on the usual tried-and-true methods. She increased her speed.

Are you waiting for me, Taylor? The lake was just ahead of her now. When she'd located what she was almost sure was Taylor's hideout several days ago, it had been deserted, and she'd hidden out in the mountains and waited until she'd actually caught sight of Taylor earlier this evening. She'd scoped the acreage out a few days ago but she never took anything for granted. She'd have to look the property over again before she confronted him tonight if she didn't want any surprises.

There was only one more thing to do. She quickly phoned Jack Harlan. "I just wanted to let you know that Mack and I have located Taylor's cabin and ranch house, and I have no need of your help. I'll let you know when I'm ready to bring him in and hand him over to the local police. You can try to pull strings with them, if you like."

"That's very generous of you to include me," Harlan said sarcastically. "Since I've already deposited a very handsome fee in your bank account."

"I thought I made it clear I don't accept blood money. I'll return it to you."

"I prefer you don't." His voice was suddenly rough. "Don't be a fool. Let me help you. Money is cheap compared with you being able to hold me hostage for a favor owed. I've always found that's more expensive for me in the long run."

"I can see how it could turn out that way for a man of your means. It won't with me," she said flatly. "Back off, Harlan. I hate looking over my shoulder. You've already gotten in my way. You decided to trust me to find Taylor, and I did it. It wasn't easy but I'll be damned if I let you step in to take credit at the last minute. I told you that when you sent your errand boy Belson to nag Sarah. But she seems to think you're worthwhile, so I thought I'd give you fair warning." She hung up with a definite click. "It's okay," she whispered to Mack as she reached out and rubbed his neck. "Though our genius isn't going to like me treating him like that. Tough. We don't care, do we? It's better than having him get in our way." She realized how impatient Mack was becoming. He never wanted strangers interfering between them. It had always been just the two of them from the moment she had begun training him on Summer Island. They were a team. Working together to bring in either the bad guys or the grand prize. No wonder Mack was so impatient. Well, Harlan couldn't have it the way he wanted this time. He had come to her, and Taylor would be handled in such a way that she could keep Mack as well as herself safe. Mack was looking impatiently over his shoulder again, and she waved to him to go ahead. But a moment later, she heard it.

A motor! It was a low throb, and at first, she thought it might be a boat on the dark lake. But soon she realized it had to be the helicopter again. It was much closer now. It seemed Taylor had definitely decided to call in some help to get himself out of this particular fix. It didn't surprise her, though she'd thought he might be too arrogant. But it meant she'd have to move even faster. From the sound of those engines, the pilot was still circling, but he had cut his lights to avoid being seen. A risky move, but she guessed he might be using night-vision goggles. She heard the helicopter rotors getting louder.

Mack gave a low whimper and looked back toward her again. "Soon," she murmured. She gave a hand signal to let him know that he had to wait. He clearly longed to bolt ahead but didn't want to leave her.

The helicopter grew louder.

Kira pointed forward with both hands. "Go! Slow and steady."

Mack knew that signal. Even from several yards ahead, he'd been matching her pace and rhythm. But now he ran toward the lake as she made her way down.

Then Mack stopped. He'd picked something up.

Course correction.

The dog turned back in the direction of the ranch house.

She turned just in time to catch a glimpse of Taylor near the edge of the porch. He'd circled back! "Go, Mack!"

Mack took off at a dead run toward the bottom of the cliff, heading for the ranch house! Kira followed him, letting Mack set the pace. She caught another swift glimpse of Taylor on the porch.

But the next moment Taylor was gone!

Nowhere to be seen.

An instant later, she realized why.

"Stop and freeze where you are, Kira Drake," Taylor said with deadly softness from directly behind her. "Don't make a move except to put your hands up. Particularly don't reach for the .38 revolver you usually keep in your side pocket or anything else lethal that you might decide to use to take me down."

Kira raised her hands.

Taylor smiled. "Did you really think I didn't know you'd tracked me down? I've been looking forward to this. How clumsy of you not to know how good I am. Harlan clearly hired the wrong gun for his hunt this time."

Kira's heart was beating hard. Taylor was clever; she had to give him that. He'd managed to circle back. She'd figure out how later. Now she needed to get out of this trap he'd sprung. "You knew I was there? I thought perhaps you did. You were too cocky. But Harlan had nothing to do with how I intended to capture you or who I was going to turn you over to when I took charge of the operation. We don't agree on many things."

Taylor laughed. "That must have annoyed him."

She took a cautious sidewise glance over her shoulder and caught a glimpse of the metal barrel of the rifle gleaming in the moonlight. How could she get hold of the damn thing? "Not really. He didn't seem worried about you."

Taylor muttered a curse. "You're lying. He should have been very worried. Just as you should be worried right now, bitch!"

Kira gazed cautiously over her shoulder again and then froze as she'd been commanded, but now it was in sheer *horror*. Because Taylor's rifle was not aimed at her but straight at Mack on the hill above her! The retriever was dangling from a rope tied around his chest. Muzzled, unable to make a sound, he was caught in the blue floodlights now beaming down from the helicopter. He was obviously helplessly blinded by the lights.

No! Dear God, this was Kira's worst nightmare. She had to stop Taylor from firing. She instinctively whirled and launched herself at him, striking him in the chest. Too late! Mack yelped as the bullet hit somewhere in his upper body. Kira watched in horror as he pitched off the hillside to lie at Taylor's feet.

"Bitch!" Taylor swung his rifle and knocked Kira to the ground. Then he kicked her in the ribs.

Kira barely felt the pain. She was too absorbed with gazing at Mack lying on the ground a short distance away. Blood! Was he dead? *Please don't let him be dead*, Kira prayed.

And that bastard Taylor was laughing at her. "Look at you. I told Donovan that you'd be in agony if I killed that mutt. He couldn't understand why I wanted to rely only on the pain factor as a punishment. He didn't like the idea of just knocking the dog out with a hypodermic gun and then bringing him to me to kill in front of you. He thought it was inefficient." Taylor's expression was filled with malice. "But now he's probably seen the light. You screamed louder than the dog did!"

"You monster," Kira said through set teeth as she got to her knees. "He's a helpless animal. If you haven't killed him, I'll hunt you down and let Mack tear you apart. Or maybe I'll do it myself."

Taylor stopped laughing. "So much venom. Then perhaps I'd better make certain. I told you to put up your hands. Do it now." He pointed his rifle at Mack. "You might have spoiled my shot by lunging at me. I thought I saw him moving just now. Perhaps Donovan needs another demonstration. I've decided to take both of you with us when he lands. I've been hearing rumors about you and how clever you are at finding hidden treasure. I think I'll have you tell me about it. It shouldn't take me too long to persuade you to do that."

"Rumors?" she asked scornfully. "You mean lies. What a fool you are."

"Perhaps. But don't you think this would show how superior I am to him? Perhaps a little expertly applied torture would also be what you both need. Using a dog and a weak woman was poor strategy anyway—it was not worthy of either me or him. But when they see the condition I leave you in after spending a few hours with you tonight, Harlan will definitely learn a few lessons. And the entire world will know that I'm much more intelligent than some bookish scientist who thought he could outsmart me because of all those medals they gave him."

Kira was already desperately planning her next move as he shaded his eyes from the glaring blue lights of the descending helicopter. Maybe she could gain a small advantage if she could use that weakness to get to the gun in her pocket or knock the rifle down and away from Mack. Her only hope was that he might not expect another attack from her: She was still kneeling at his feet, and he probably thought she was helpless and defeated now. "I don't anticipate any problem," she said. "I was told Harlan almost killed you several times in the past. He just hired me as a backup measure. I don't need either him or my dog when I have my own plan in mind. I've been doing this for years, Taylor. I've trained law enforcement agencies all over the world. In return, many of those agencies have also trained me." She added one additional goad: "This poor, weak woman has had to learn how to handle blowhards like you."

He scowled. She was walking a tightrope here, hoping to antagonize him enough to throw him off balance but not enrage him to the point that he would immediately put a bullet in her brain. "You don't think this mountain is crawling with FBI, police, and state troopers right now? You've made yourself a famous man, Taylor. You're the slimeball responsible for the Paris massacre. These mountains are like one hellish fun house." She paused. "But maybe we can make a deal..."

The helicopter was descending rapidly now.

She had to continue distracting him. She wouldn't be able to reach her weapon, but the helicopter lights would soon be upon them, and she could wait for a moment when the glare was shining in his eyes. Maybe then she'd be able to lunge for that rifle and keep him from doing more harm to Mack.

His lips twisted. "That has to be a bluff. You have to be lying. If not, then you're doubly ignorant. You can't play games or get between Harlan and me. You're a dead woman right after I kill this hound. Don't you realize when you've met your—" He flinched as the blue beam of light hit him squarely in the eyes, blinding him!

"Yes!" It was what Kira had been waiting for. She spun around to put the blinding light behind her and then tackled Taylor and knocked the rifle from his grasp. The next instant, she had her .38 revolver in her hand and was struggling with him.

Pain!

Hot agony as a bullet tore into the flesh of her shoulder. Where in the hell had that come from? The helicopter?

Ignore it. Get to his rifle lying on the ground.

She was fighting him desperately now but getting weaker every minute.

"Dammit, stop struggling. I'm trying to stop the bleeding."

Not Taylor. It was Harlan's voice! She recognized it though she'd only heard it on the phone.

"Mack..." Kira gasped. "Help...Mack." If anyone could find a way to save Mack, it would be Harlan with his military background. "You've got to save...my dog. You can't let Mack die..."

"Shut up. I'll give you anything you want if you'll just be quiet and let me stop this blasted bleeding. I'm trying to keep you alive. I'll tend to everyone else later."

"Be careful...Taylor!"

"He's gone. I squeezed off a few shots, and he ran into the woods. I don't think I got him, but both he and the helicopter are gone now."

"Mack...Promise me..."

"I promise, dammit. Be quiet and let me work."

She heard a low whimper and tried to turn her head. "Mack?"

Harlan glared impatiently down at Kira. "Satisfied? Your dog is still alive. I patched him up as best I could. But he's been trying to crawl over to you since I got here and got rid of Taylor and his pilot buddy."

"No." It was painful for her to speak. "Let Mack come...he doesn't understand." And Harlan didn't understand, either. But she had to make him know what to do. "You're going to have to make him better...Make him...right."

"Okay, I promise that, too. I'll give him everything he wants. Now relax and let me try to keep you alive and Taylor from getting his way this time."

"He won't...do it. I won't let him. He hurt...Mack."

"Keep that thought in mind. Now will you calm down and let me help you?"

"Help...Mack." But she could let go now. She'd heard that Harlan never broke his promises, and Mack would be safe...

She slid down into the darkness...

CHAPTER

4

"You're awake again? Thank heavens. That dog of yours has been driving me crazy. Want some water?" The red-haired teenage girl wearing jodhpurs and a suede vest was sitting in the chair beside Kira's bed and was holding a crystal glass to Kira's lips for her to sip. Then she snapped her fingers. "Come on, Mack. She's back with us again."

"Mack..." The golden retriever jumped on Kira's bed and cuddled closer to her, making whimpering noises.

She gave him a relieved hug as she realized how well and blessedly *alive* he was looking. "How is he?" Kira was frantically examining Mack's bandages more closely as she spoke. "He was hurt, but he looks...okay now?"

"Better than you." The girl made a face. "You had a bad fever that kept flaring up even after the wound in your shoulder was almost healed. Harlan raised hell with your physician because he was worried about it. But you're both on the way back now. Harlan wouldn't have it any other way. He said he made you a promise. By the way, I'm Fiona, Harlan's niece." She grinned. "Mack has kind of adopted me in the days since Harlan assigned me to take care of you. Harlan's been busy searching for that scumbag Joseph Taylor after he escaped from Colorado. At first your snooty dog wouldn't have anything to do with me, but then he decided to give me a break and we came to an understanding. Of course, he was positively crazy about Harlan. But I guess Mack decided that you needed someone to keep watch on you if Harlan wasn't there to keep you company any longer."

"Keep me company?" Kira lifted her hand to her temple. "Where the hell am I?" She was looking around the chamber, taking in all the luxurious furnishings and antiques surrounding her and trying to put the pieces together. The room was all comfort and luxury. In the alcove within the far wall, she saw a group of several sketches of magnificent horses that appeared so real, she felt as if she could reach out and stroke them. There was also a sketch of a man whom she recognized all too well. Those glittering green eyes, that hard yet expressive face. "I...suppose this has to be one of Jack Harlan's houses if he was giving orders about Mack."

"Of course it is." Fiona's gaze followed Kira's to the sketch. "Do you like my sketches? People are much harder than my horses. But I thought I drew Harlan well."

"It's very good. Completely recognizable."

"He wouldn't let me touch Mack for the first couple of days you were under a doctor's care. After you left the hospital, you were brought here to the manor and he imported one of the vets who generally takes care of my horses to live here and watch over Mack." She shrugged. "Otherwise Harlan himself was in here and took care of both of you."

"Wait a minute," Kira said. "You're going too fast. Where is this manor?"

"It's a castle in northern France. Not too far from Paris. It's where we live when Harlan is overseeing his factories in Europe."

"Factories for what?"

"He's invented a lot of things. Phones, satellites, cars...all kinds of stuff."

"Okay, another question," Kira said. "Harlan took care of me? Why would he do that?"

Fiona frowned. "You don't remember?"

"I don't think..." But she did remember...or at least some of it was coming back. She recalled desperately fighting with Taylor and that bastard shooting Mack. Not...much more. Everything else was blurred. Maybe Harlan bringing Mack to lie on the ground beside her as he tried to stop her bleeding and him yelling at her to be quiet and let him work. "I guess all I really remember is that I told him he had to take care of Mack. You're sure Mack is going to be all right?"

Fiona nodded. "So the vet told Harlan. Final checkup tomorrow." She added caustically, "It would have been nice if you could have brought yourself to have worried a little about Harlan. I approve of treating animals well, but from what Belson told me, you caused Harlan a good deal of trouble in those mountains. He could have died before he got you and Mack out of there."

"We both could have died," Kira said dully. "Taylor had a rifle, and someone may have even shot at me from the helicopter." She rubbed her temple again. "I don't remember much about it, but I probably owe Harlan a debt. I'll have to repay him. He did do what I asked..."

"Isn't that great?" Fiona's voice was dripping with sarcasm. "He practically saved your life *and* Mack's. What about all the time and effort he spent getting both of you well here at the manor?" The young girl's voice was laden with bitterness. "Doesn't that count for anything?"

"Of course it does," Kira said quickly. "But he shouldn't have done it. He should have just shipped me home to Summer Island and not bothered with me. I only asked him to take care of Mack."

"He did take care of him, and he took fantastic care of you. Because that's what he does. Harlan always takes care of his responsibilities." She smiled ruefully. "Who should know better than me? He's been taking care of me since my father died. Maybe someday I'll tell you about it." Fiona shook her head. "But this might not be the time. And I might not be the person. I tend to get annoyed if anyone fails to appreciate Harlan when he does something for them. And since Belson said that Harlan could have died before he got you away from that creep in Colorado, I believe I should have Belson tell you about it." She shrugged. "Never mind. What do you care? You don't know him at all."

56

Kira tried to be polite. "I didn't mean to be rude. I'm just bewildered and a little confused. I'm sure I also owe a debt to you for taking care of Mack, and I'll try to repay you."

Fiona whirled to face her. "I don't want your thanks. It's Harlan who did everything for you. Why can't you get that through your head? See that you make it right with *him*! Harlan's the one who makes our world go around here." Fiona's voice took on an edge. "He saved your life, dammit." She put Mack's collar on him as she spoke and was heading for the bedroom door. "It's time I took Mack for his afternoon walk. You should probably rest right now. I'll call Harlan and tell him that you're awake. He'll want to know. He was truly concerned about you."

Kira flinched as the door slammed behind Fiona.

Well, that had not gone well, she thought wryly. She'd been a trifle woozy and had not been able to remember much about what had happened, plus the girl's resentment had been crystal-clear. The best thing Kira could think to do was to get out of this fancy manor house and find a way back to Summer Island where she belonged. To accomplish that probably meant making contact with Harlan or one of his employees. Definitely not Harlan's niece, whom she would try to avoid until she could get out of the Harlan domain.

So get dressed, get out, and get transportation home.

But first she had to go find Mack, make certain she'd been told the truth about his condition, and get him ready to leave with her. Neither of them belonged here. If she had to, she could put him in her own vet's quarters when she got back to the island. But Mack had willingly, even eagerly, gone with Fiona when she'd leashed him for his walk, Kira remembered. He must have liked her—Mack was very picky about companions of any sort. So apparently he had truly been happy with Harlan's niece while he was here. That was good to know.

And perhaps Harlan had been a little more than a glorified dog-sitter, too, she thought wryly. But that was another mystery that would have to be solved later.

Take it easy. You're going to be fine. I'll make sure to keep you safe. No one is going to hurt you again. Trust me… That voice was clearly repeating in her head.

She did have a vague memory of someone holding her hand in the night, even rocking her when she was burning with fever or the pain was bad. She couldn't seem to forget it.

Still, Kira was definitely not welcome here and it was time for her to make her exit. She waited for only one more minute to pass before she tossed the quilt covering her aside and started to go through the drawers of the oak bureau for something to wear. In a few minutes, she'd found a loose shirt and slacks and a pair of tennis shoes. This would be all right for now. She would bathe and go find Belson; maybe later she'd find Harlan, after she was at least semi-presentable.

But things didn't turn out to be quite that simple. She was half-way down the grand staircase leading to the foyer when she had to stop a moment and grab hold of the banister to keep from falling.

"Shit!"

She recognized that voice instantly.

Jack Harlan!

He was behind her on the stairs and swearing softly as he turned her around and half lifted, half carried her down the rest of the stairs toward a huge open study adjoining the living room. He sat her down on a couch. "Fiona said she thought you were upset," he muttered. "But being Fiona, she sometimes interprets her own feelings as belonging to others. Evidently, she was right this time."

"I wasn't upset." Kira was trying to push herself away from him. "I was just confused and wanted to make sure I knew everything that had happened after I passed out on those cliffs that night." She moistened her lips. "And particularly what had happened to Joseph Taylor. Your Fiona didn't seem to want to give me details."

"So you decided to find out for yourself?" Harlan asked. "Did you come looking for me? If so, did it occur to you that it wouldn't have helped if you'd ended up in a heap at the foot of these stairs? I would have told you everything you needed to know if you'd given me the chance. The doctor said you might not be in good enough shape to face whatever trauma you might have to go through after you regained consciousness. He said to give you another week or two to rest."

"Bullshit," Kira said bluntly as she finally managed to pull away from him. "I've always been very strong. I don't need to be coddled. Fiona told me the doctor said both Mack and I were on the mend, and all I really needed to know was that Mack was well and strong. The rest I can find out for myself after I get back to Summer Island. Since I'm obviously a bother to you and your family under the circumstances, it's best that I leave here as soon as possible."

"Perhaps that's not exactly all you need to know," he said. "There are a few more items that might be important for me to bring to your attention. You mentioned Taylor specifically as a concern." He added grimly, "As well you might. I was so busy trying to keep you and Mack alive that night on the cliffs, I let Taylor and his pet thug Donovan slip away from me. I almost had him and then the son of a bitch was gone."

"No wonder you're so angry with me," Kira whispered. "I not only got in your way but kept you from getting Taylor, too, after all your years of hunting him down. But I'll make it up to you. I have every intention of going after Taylor as soon as I get the clearance from the doctor. I'll make certain that I capture him and turn him over to the authorities. He won't get away again."

"No second thoughts?" Harlan asked.

"He tried to kill my dog," she said coldly. "He would have butchered Mack if he'd had his way. Mack wouldn't have stood a chance. I'll let the authorities deal with him. If I have my way, they'll lock Taylor in a bulletproof prison and throw away the key."

"How very ruthless of you," Harlan said mockingly. "No more tough cop on the beat?"

"Mack saves lives. That's tough enough. He deserves having me to protect him and guard his interests." She grimaced. "Which I didn't do this time. I made mistakes. That will never happen again."

Harlan was silent for a moment, staring at her. "Really? You may not have a choice," he said. "It appears that you may be a prime target. Taylor is a bit irate with you, I understand."

She stiffened as she slowly got to her feet. "What are you saying?"

"Exactly what you think. It seems that as soon as Taylor escaped Colorado, he started to track you down. It didn't take him long to find out I'd brought you here. He began to write you cozy little notes in care of the manor telling you all the things he's going to do to you when he gets the chance. Very ugly notes."

Kira could imagine how ugly. "It doesn't surprise me. He gave me a verbal preview of what he'd like to do to me before I jumped him to get the rifle." She stared him in the eye. "I want to see those notes."

"You will. I'm not hiding anything from you from now on. It will be your choice. But you should sit down and have a little nourishment before you make that decision. You're just out of bed and it won't hurt to take it easy for a while. Will you go into the study and relax while I call the cook and order your dinner? You're not going anywhere until we've had a discussion. There are things you need to know, and I don't want a repeat of Colorado in any shape or form. I don't believe you do, either."

"There won't be a repeat." She was nibbling at her lower lip. "I made a mistake, and I don't usually do that. I had no idea he'd zero in on Mack instead of me. No one has ever done that. You made no mistakes, and I regret that I wasn't able to bring Taylor to the authorities as I promised. But it happened and I won't let it happen again. Just let me go back to Summer Island and I'll bring Taylor in as I promised."

"No way on earth," Harlan said as he shook his head. "Not until after dinner and we've come to an agreement. I wasn't pleased about having to bring you here and having to explain not only to the governor but also to my old friend John Logan why you were almost a dead woman before I could yank you out of there. John happens to trust me, and Belson told him I'd take care of you."

"You shouldn't have done that," she said curtly. "I always take care of myself. I even told Sarah that you were to have nothing to do with my tracking Taylor."

"Too bad. You also told Belson and left that message for me, but once I'd made the decision to use you, I had to go through with it. Even you must have heard that Taylor killed my brother. He has to belong to me. There's no question about it." His lips twisted savagely for an instant before he regained total composure. "So there's no way I'll let you go after him without me."

"Use me?" Kira repeated through set teeth. "No one uses me, Harlan. I thought I'd made that clear."

"Really?" Harlan echoed. "What about Taylor? I believe he has every intention of using you. And I might be the only one who can stop him. Because I'm the only one who wants him bad enough to make sure I'll do anything to get my hands on him." He gestured toward the library door. "I'm going to order your dinner, and it should be here in the next thirty minutes. I'll leave your notes from Taylor here in the office for you to read if you choose. But I wouldn't advise it. It won't be pleasant and might even upset your stomach and ruin your dinner. Just know that whatever he threatens, I won't let it happen. If you stand by me and help me take him down, I promise he won't touch you or yours."

"What are you saying?" Kira's hands clenched into fists at her sides. "I told you I take care of myself."

"Taylor has access to some formidable resources."

"So do I, when the occasion demands it. But Mack and I are usually all it takes."

"And I told you that I find that unacceptable." He gave a slightly mocking sigh. "It seems I've became accustomed to taking care of you during the last few days. After reading the very poisonous notes he sent, it appears he regards you almost as an adopted member of my family now. That means you're an automatic target in his eyes." He paused. "And I take care of my own, Kira."

She shook her head incredulously. "Ridiculous."

He shrugged. "Perhaps. However, I won't have Taylor getting in my way in any shape or form. That includes any future plans he has for you." Harlan opened the library door for her and gestured for her to enter. "Just rest, have dinner, and later you can read all Taylor's notes in my desk. Then we'll discuss any plans we might have for any future action."

"You're not listening. I have no plans that involve you."

"I believe you will after you read those notes. You might be stubborn, but you're also very clever, as I found out following you through those mountains. You'll do what's best for you and the people you care about."

The library door shut behind him.

Kira hesitated and then slowly entered the library and headed for the desk across the room. She needed at least a few minutes to recover her strength while she could be alone and brace herself for whatever she had to do next. That encounter with Harlan hadn't been easy despite her assertions. She was feeling infinitely weary after dealing with Harlan and his niece today, but she knew she should probably sit and read the notes in the desk. Harlan's attitude had been a little forceful as well as intimidating, and she had to realize she wasn't quite sure what he had meant by it. He had never tried to intimidate her before, when they were at odds hunting for Taylor. They had only been foes going after a common enemy. He'd annoyed her, but he hadn't tried to frighten her. This might be different. What was the reason he'd changed tactics? Did he think Taylor's letters would frighten her?

Oh, what the hell. She knew what monsters could be like. Face Taylor and get it over with. She sat down at the desk, opened the middle drawer, and pulled out the collection of notes.

She picked up the first one and slowly opened it.

The first sentence caught her eye and caused her to stiffen.

Dear God! Sarah?

She felt her stomach wrench as she started reading. By the time she finished the third letter, she felt the nausea beginning again and she had to stop for a few moments. Damn Taylor. Damn him. Damn him. She was shaking by the time she finished the fourth letter, but she still had three to go.

"You're reading those hideous letters?" Kira looked up to see Fiona standing at the study door holding Mack's leash. She was gazing in horror at the tears running down Kira's cheeks. "Stop it! Do you hear me?" She ran across the room and deliberately threw her jacket over the letters on the desk. "I was afraid that you might get hold of them. That's why I ran back down here when I found out you'd left your room. I knew I shouldn't have lost my temper. Harlan always says I don't know when to keep my mouth shut. But I never meant to let you see those letters. Harlan didn't even want me to see them." Tears suddenly poured down Fiona's own cheeks. "But when Belson told me how Harlan had saved you, I wanted to find out what kind of monster Taylor really was. He killed my father, you know. People whispered about him around me, but Harlan wouldn't talk about him to me." Her trembling hand shoved the letters roughly aside. "And I found out, didn't I? But I never meant for you to see them when I read all those ugly threats to you."

"Not only to me." Kira was trying to keep her voice from shaking. "I could have stood that, but what he said he was going to do to the people I cared about to punish me...that was horrible. I wanted to run and stop him." She drew a deep breath. "And I will. It will just take time. It only hurt so much at first because of the shock. I don't have that many friends, but those I do have, I try to keep and cherish. Taylor seems to have found out the names or addresses of most of them."

Fiona nodded. "And it was my fault you found out. I had no

business interfering in anything he says or does when he's always so good to me."

Kira shook her head. "It's not all your fault. You were just trying to protect him, weren't you? He shouldn't have kept those letters where you could find them. He should have realized you'd be curious."

"You're being very generous," Fiona said. "I don't deserve it. But he would have trusted me not to go through his desk and intercept this garbage. I'd never done it before."

"There's always a first time, Fiona," Harlan said coldly from the doorway. "And evidently you picked a hideous time to choose to do it." His gaze was fastened on the notes scattered on the top of the desk and then to Kira's tear-wet face. "I was going to leave the choice to her whether or not she wanted to read his poison pen letters."

"I'm sorry," Fiona whispered as she ran across the study and into his arms. "I shouldn't have done it, Harlan. I was mad at her because Belson had told me how she'd treated you on the mountain. He said Taylor might have even managed to kill you while you were trying to save her. But then it was too late when I ran after her because I remembered she might stumble across those blasted letters. She'd already started to read them by then."

"Did you actually believe I couldn't take care of myself?" Harlan asked wearily. "Haven't I taken care of you during all these years? I don't think you've had any complaints. Right?"

"You know I haven't." Fiona buried her face in his shoulder.

"I promise it won't happen again." She lifted her head and gazed across the room at Kira. "I apologize. And if there's any way I can make things right, tell me."

"There isn't. You've already made things right," Kira said. "You took care of my dog when he was ill. Both Mack and I are very grateful."

"No, that was really Harlan," Fiona said. "I just filled in now and then. However, now I have to pay my dues." She gave Harlan a hug and headed for the door. "But he'll give me my marching orders, won't you, Harlan?"

"It depends on whether Kira decides you're worth the bother."

"I will be. Let me know when and where I can help."

As the door closed behind her, Harlan started across the study toward the desk. "Sorry about that." He gestured toward the notes scattered on the desktop. "I really did want to give you a choice whether you read Taylor's nasty little missiles."

"And they were nasty," Kira said. "I wasn't sure when you left me." She shuddered. "But I had to find out. Then when I read what Taylor had written, I went into a form of shock. It was even uglier than I dreamed."

"It was exactly what he wanted you to feel," Harlan said grimly. "Every word. Every act he intended to commit. Don't think he wasn't sincere."

"I won't. I can't afford to let anything happen to my friends, and most of those letters were aimed at them. The first thing I have to do is make certain that I can keep Sarah and John safe from him."

"I can help make sure they will be taken care of. I have quite a few people on the payroll who will keep them from being victims of Taylor and company."

"I'd rather do it myself," Kira said bitterly. "But it's not only friends and other people I care about whom he could be targeting. There have been wild rumors floating around lately that I located another sunken treasure several months ago off Egypt's north coast. He mentioned that he was going to force me to tell him where it was located when I was fighting with him on the cliffs. He said that again in one of these letters." Then her lips tightened. "There's no way I'd ever let him get his hands on that or any other treasure. It would make him far too powerful. No one would be able to tolerate what he'd do to everyone around him." She glanced at him again. "But you knew about the treasure, didn't you?"

He nodded. "I couldn't help but be aware of it from those letters. Plus, the media did a hell of a lot of coverage on that Spanish medallion treasure you located in the Caribbean last year. It was in all the magazines Belson threw at me to lure me to hire you. There was one article that particularly intrigued him. I imagine the treasure hunters who have been chasing after you over the years have been giving you a rough time?"

She shrugged. "Treasure hunting is more a hobby to me than anything else at the moment. Exciting, but my prime interest is my work with the dogs plus my work on age extension. That's my prime job and vocation." Her lips tightened. "But there's no way I'll let Taylor get near anything he wants ever again."

"I'll start working on that right away," Harlan said lightly. "I can hardly wait."

"I haven't promised you anything," Kira said. "Not yet."

"But I have high hopes." Harlan held her chair for her. "And now sit down. We'll have dinner and then talk. Okay?"

"Maybe."

"All you have to know is that I'll keep your friends and mine safe and then we'll find a way to bring Taylor down. Deal?"

"We'll talk about it."

"I regard that as an affirmative."

"Regard it how you like. It will be what it will be." She spread her napkin on her lap. "And what I choose it to be." She looked at him across the table. "But I do wish to tell you that I appreciate how you saved Mack. I'll never forget it."

He smiled ruefully. "Even though my niece has been a bit... troublesome?"

She shrugged. "She must care a great deal for you if she was ready to attack me when she thought that I might have caused you to be injured. And she let me know how sorry she was when she realized how much those letters hurt me."

"She's a good girl...most of the time." He added affectionately, "She's had only me around for most of her life. Her mother died in a car accident when she was just a baby. And she's gone through a good deal since her father, Colin, was murdered by Taylor. I'm probably not the best substitute she could have, but I do my best. And if she said she'll make it up to you, it will happen."

"If you tell her that's what you want?"

69

"Maybe. But she'd do it anyway. She's only fifteen, but you'll find she can be amazingly mature if her emotions aren't actively involved. She's a great equestrian, and I've supplied her with a number of horses she adores. She won two medals at the Olympics last year, and I was very proud. Either way, I always know where she's coming from." He put sliced turkey roulade on Kira's plate before adding some Parmesan-roasted vegetables and handing it to her. "Understanding can move mountains. That's what we need to get us through this, Kira."

She didn't answer, just began to eat her dinner.

"Kira?" He was staring curiously at her. "What the devil are you thinking? Sometimes I can't make you out."

She looked back at him. What was she thinking? That he was complicated, and she didn't know quite what to do or where to go with him. That now that he was smiling, he was everything intelligent and powerful that spoke of intensity and appeal. But she couldn't let him see the effect he was having on her. She lifted her chin defiantly. "I was thinking that you're used to getting what you want from almost everyone."

He nodded. "Frequently. But it's principally because I work very hard to go after it. And I'm always willing to make certain that my partners aren't cheated and get what they want as well." His voice lowered. "You'll find that out, Kira."

"Will I? You might be right. We'll have to see." She changed the subject. "This is a very good meal, by the way."

"I'll tell the cook. She'll be pleased."

"But you should realize that I'm not accustomed to meals like this. I usually eat very simply." She added, "I'm used to getting what I want, too, and I don't cheat. But that doesn't matter. Because I also work hard, and I've found good things usually just come to me if I do."

"I don't doubt it." He was grinning. "I watched you go after what you wanted in the mountains. You're quite incredible. One of the best trackers I've ever seen. Now finish your meal and we'll go have a glass of wine and talk. Okay?"

She shook her head. "I've had enough. And I'm still not certain I don't want to just walk out of here."

"Let's see...how could I make you want to stay? Tell me and I'll give it to you. I believe there's one thing I've got on my side." He got to his feet, took her hand, and led her to the chair beside the fireplace. "You want to keep yourself and your friends safe. I've already promised that. Do you think I'd betray you?"

She stared at him a moment and then shook her head. "You promised to help Mack, and you did it. Fiona said you saved me, too." Kira made a face. "She was angry with me for not worshipping humbly at your feet."

"Humbly?" He threw back his head and laughed. "She would have been amused if she'd heard some of our conversations. Nothing humble about you, Kira."

"Nor you." She sipped her wine and reached over to pet Mack, who had just come into the room. "And I admit I don't like feeling as if I owe you some kind of debt. It pisses me off."

71

"How ungenerous of you." He tilted his head. "Though I'd be glad to let you repay me any way you'd like."

"Ugh." She wrinkled her nose. "It would be even worse with it hanging over me."

His lips were twitching. "I thought so. Then name your terms. I'm sure you'll be able to tell me how I can best please you. Since you appear to be averse to letting me murder that son of a bitch." He snapped his fingers. "Though you sounded more promising when you were talking about throwing him into prison without a key. I admit that encouraged me."

"I don't like murder."

"Nor do I," Harlan said. "That's why I've been hunting Taylor down all these years." He waved his hand. "But I believe that the problem is going to solve itself. Not as satisfying, and not to my liking, but I suppose I can't have everything."

She was frowning. "What are you saying?"

"That Taylor is going to take it out of our hands," he said simply. "I don't believe anyone is going to take the option away from him no matter what we do. I've never seen more violent and poisonous thoughts than in his letters. If I felt that way, what must you have gone through reading them?"

"Sick to my stomach."

He nodded. "That was obvious. Anyone who helps me becomes an immediate enemy of his, and for that I'm sorry. That makes your safety my responsibility. But his threats come with a definite advantage for us."

"Advantage?"

"I guarantee he'll try to make every one of those promises he made come true. All we have to do is sit and wait for him."

"And if I don't choose to do that?"

"Then you'll run the risk of getting people you care about killed. He'll go after them. The best place for them is right here where I can keep them safe."

"You can try," she said bitterly. "But your best may not be good enough."

"Check with the local police or military officials. They know I've made certain to keep this property and the people on it safe for years. I'm telling you the truth. As for Summer Island, I'll send out teams to watch over all your friends." He paused. "Until you have some faith in me."

She shook her head. "That might take a long time. I'm not a very trusting soul."

"Will you give me a week in which to get to know me? You should allow yourself that amount of time anyway to rest and get a final okay from your physician. After all, you didn't object when I suggested we do it for Mack. Then can we talk again?"

She was silent. "I'll think about it."

He gave a low whistle. "Okay, three days. You're one tough lady."

She smiled faintly. "It's how I make my living."

He nodded. "I promise I'll bring my vet back first thing tomorrow morning to give Mack his final walking papers. I suppose you'll want to take care of him yourself from now on?"

"Of course."

"He's a good boy. Fiona and I both enjoy him."

"Naturally. He's a wonder. Ask anyone." She watched him put the collar on Mack's neck. "He likes you." She smiled faintly. "He has good taste. You might not be so bad after all."

"He'd better approve of me after what he put me through," Harlan said lightly. "And I have a favor to ask while you're still here at the property."

She stiffened. "A favor?"

"If you decide to go away, all I ask is that you let me know when you're going to leave her."

"Her?"

"Fiona. I know she may not be your favorite person, but she'll probably be hanging around you and trying to make up for being a pain in the ass. I'd appreciate it if you'd keep an eye on her and let me know if there's anything wonky going on."

"Wonky?"

"Heartbreak, kidnapping, murder, et cetera, and so forth."

Her eyes narrowed on his face. "I take it that Fiona is also a target?"

"Her father was killed when she was only seven," Harlan said. "Naturally, I have her watched like a hawk, particularly when she's out of the country competing in the Olympics. But she can be both reckless and emotional, as you saw today."

"Seven years old?" She shuddered. "Did Taylor ever manage to get hold of her?"

Harlan shook his head. "But he's been trying ever since he

realized that it would be a great way to cause me pain and suffering. He scared her a couple of times, but I didn't let him get near her." He added grimly, "Though I had to kill one of his men the second time they went after her."

"Was she scared?"

"Terrified. But I had a long talk with her and then I bought her a new horse and told her how she had to protect the animals who were her friends. She has a very protective soul, and she forgot about being afraid for herself after that."

"But you didn't forget."

"Never," he said bluntly. "And I never will. She's a top priority."

"A child..." She shook her head. "How could anyone..."

"Easily. Taylor doesn't care. Remember that. But we care, and we have to make certain that we make him know it. She still has guards on duty, but as I told you, she can be reckless. Will you keep an eye on her for me?"

"Of course I will," she said. "Dogs and children." She was still shivering. "What a beast he must be."

"Yes," Harlan said as he prepared to leave the study. "But you knew that. You had all the figures and reports. Try to sleep tonight, Kira. We'll talk tomorrow. I promise there won't be anything to disturb you. I've already made the arrangements to protect your Summer Island." He looked back at her. "By the way, your friend Sarah Logan has been checking on you practically every day this week. You might give her a call so that she won't think I'm keeping you prisoner here."

"Not tonight. Maybe tomorrow. I haven't made up my mind

what I'm going to do yet. Evidently John and Sarah both trust you. And I want to be able to tell Sarah something definite, if you don't mind. I'll go back to that bedroom where you've been keeping Mack and me and I'll do some thinking about ways and means."

Harlan nodded. "I'd be the last to discourage you. The more you consider what your options are, the better. It will all point in my direction as your best bet." He opened the door for her. "Should I warn Fiona to leave you alone tonight?"

"That's up to you." She led Mack out of the study and started up the ornate winding staircase. "I can handle her, and at the moment, I'm feeling a little sorry for her."

"That was never my intention. And it's not what she'd want," Harlan said. "She can be extremely tough when it's necessary."

"Good. With you as head of the household, I can see that might be a very good trait to cultivate..."

---·---

Five minutes later, Kira was upstairs and hesitating outside the bedroom door. Then she knocked and let herself into the bedchamber.

Fiona sat up straight in bed and smiled at her. "I was hoping that you'd come back and talk to me. You let me off the hook with Harlan, and I owe you."

"I believe Harlan makes up his own mind," Kira said. "At least that's my impression. However, you know him much better than I do. He told me that he's been taking care of you since you were seven."

"That's true," Fiona said. "I was just a kid, and sometimes I didn't realize what was going on. But he's always been there for me since I lost my dad. Even when he was so busy because of all the people trying to get his attention. But then everyone practically worships him, you know. He has all kinds of officers and diplomats and other important people coming to see him and giving him medals and awards. He invents all kinds of important stuff, and people pay him zillions to do it."

"Really?" Kira's lips twitched. "Zillions?"

"Maybe I'm exaggerating a little. But not very much. He's like you in that."

"Me? I don't have zillions, and I guarantee that I don't compare monetarily with your uncle Harlan in any way," Kira said. "Why would you think I was anything but a working girl making a decent living?"

"Because Harlan told me that you're famous and have all kinds of veterinary and dog training degrees and you travel all over the world and hunt down criminals and even invent medicines to help dogs live longer. That's why we have to get you well—so you can keep doing that." She made a face. "But then I blew it. Because I couldn't stand the thought that you wouldn't help Harlan if he needed you. That pissed me off royally."

"Obviously."

"And then of course there were the horses," Fiona said. "I couldn't see why you were discriminating."

"I beg your pardon?"

Fiona's gaze went to the sketches of horses on the wall in the alcove. "You've been working with dogs and extending their lives. I have fourteen wonderful horses, and they're not getting any younger. Why not give them a break?"

Kira shook her head. "I'd be delighted. I love horses. But I work with dogs because I'm familiar with them. I have to accept and work with each species individually, exploring their differences. Understand?"

"Not really. You've not let yourself become familiar with *my* horses. They're absolutely terrific and deserve to live long, healthy lives. Now do you understand?"

"So I've been told," Kira grinned. "Many times. I hear it from everyone with a wonderful animal they can't bear to lose."

"But mine are especially fantastic," Fiona said wistfully, "and I love them so much. I believe I might have to work with you to help you stop that dratted discrimination."

Kira smiled. "There are always ways to bring miracles about if you try hard enough."

Fiona patted the bed next to her. "Then come and sit beside me and tell me what kind of miracles you've managed to perform on Summer Island and other places you've been. Will you do that?"

"I'll try," Kira said. "But I hear you've managed to perform a few miracles at the Olympics you attended last year. And evidently, you're quite an artist as well. It will have to be a joint revelation."

"Fair enough." Fiona settled herself more comfortably and then punched her pillow a couple of times to soften it. "You first..."

CHAPTER

5

"I heard you were up and about, Kira," Belson said as he strolled across the stable yard toward Fiona and Kira the next morning. He stopped a moment to stroke the mane of Domino, the black stallion Kira was riding. Belson looked up at Fiona. "I heard you got me in big trouble with Harlan, young lady. I don't remember telling you that Kira might have caused him serious bodily harm when he went after her on the cliffs. As I recall, Harlan made the decision himself, as usual."

"I might have exaggerated a little," Fiona said quickly. "But I could see how upset you were, Belson, and so was Harlan. And you know I hate it when Harlan goes after Taylor or one of his men." She shook her head. "Anything could have happened."

"But it didn't," Kira interceded. She stared down at Belson. "And I'm glad you didn't interfere with my dealings with Harlan. I told you from the beginning that's not what I wanted."

"Yes, you did. Though I have to admit that I was right behind Harlan when he became concerned and went after you that night." He shrugged. "There'd be an international incident if anything happened to him. And when you're around him, you have to be prepared for that frequently."

"But I probably won't be around him all that often." Kira was stroking Domino's neck. "I'm just here for the next few days so that I can get a good look at Fiona's beautiful horses. Particularly this lovely boy. They're truly magnificent, aren't they?" She gazed at the sleekness of the chestnut Harlan was mounting beside the fountain in the courtyard. He was handling the spirited horse with effortless skill and appeared every bit as competent as Fiona. Absolutely faultless technique, Kira thought as she watched him ride around the stables and trot over a nearby hill with Mack in tow. She had noticed that Fiona was an amazing horsewoman, but she had expected that when she heard about the Olympic medals. She had not anticipated the care and love Fiona had shown the horses this morning. It had even reminded Kira of a few horse whisperers she had run across during her career. She'd displayed so much affection and persuasiveness, it had been almost mesmerizing. Not only for her horse, Golden Boy, but for all the other horses in the stable. Kira was beginning to look at this teenager in an entirely different way. "But then it appears the entire stable is filled with gorgeous horses," Kira said. "Is it a family affair?"

Belson shook his head. "Not as much as Harlan would like. He tries to get out here if he gets the chance when he's on the property.

But he almost always has a lab project he's working on or a conference he has to conduct."

"Or a bloodthirsty Joseph Taylor to go after?" Kira murmured.

"I'd say you were very fortunate he decided to do that, Kira," Belson said. "Just my opinion, of course. By the way, should you really be up and riding today? Harlan noticed that he'd inherited Mack and a message from Fiona saying that he should take care of him for the day while she conducted important business with Kira. I'm supposed to report back to Harlan if you've been cleared by the doctor yet. He wants to be very sure he got the message right."

"Early this morning," she said curtly. "Fiona took care of dragging me to see Dr. Sazar in his quarters before she brought me here to the stables. You can tell Harlan it wasn't my choice. She didn't want me to be distracted by Mack, and she was very determined."

"She usually is. And Harlan didn't mind taking over Mack's care, but he wanted it to be for a valid reason. Now I can assure him that it is, and I do like to spread good tidings." Belson smiled at Fiona. "And I agree that your horses are splendid and well worth our Kira's attention."

"I told her they were." Fiona's eyes were glittering with excitement. "Now go away, Belson, so that we can get in a run on the marsh before breakfast. I'm trying to convince Kira that the black stallion she's riding would make a wonderful first equine subject for Summer Island. I'd let her use my palomino here, but I just can't give Golden Boy up right now. I have plans to take him to the next Olympics."

"I should have known." Belson chuckled. "Good luck to you, Kira." He tipped his hat to her. "I think I'd better go tell Harlan what Fiona is up to now."

"But Harlan would approve," Fiona called impatiently after him. "He gave me these horses. We picked most of them out together!"

"It's still going to be no," Kira told Fiona. "I'm not quite ready for those experiments yet. Look, it's not that I don't like working with horses. I've dealt extensively with them in the past. I just want to make sure I'm ready before I make any mistakes with your property." She was still stroking Domino's neck. The black stallion was absolutely beautiful, with a single white blaze on his forehead. "But he's superb, isn't he?"

Fiona nodded eagerly. "And terribly smart and fast. He can leap over practically any barrier you set before him. Why don't you just stick around and try him for a little while longer? Then I'll let you try a few more of my horses before you go back home to Summer Island."

"That's not practical. I have other work to do with Mack. I can't just start to concentrate on a new species without in-depth research."

"Then work harder. I'll help you."

"Not now, okay? I don't have to tell you how much is going on right now."

"I won't give up," Fiona said. "It's important. You said that Mack saves lives. Maybe these horses can save lives, too. We should at least try to give them their chance. Right?"

"It would seem that we should," Kira admitted. "I'll think about it. But your Harlan might not approve." She held up her hand to halt the protests she could see were coming. "Give me some time to consider the options."

The young girl obviously wasn't happy. But she sighed and shrugged. "Okay, I suppose. I guess that means we go for a run in the marsh after all?"

Kira nodded. "That plan has a much better chance for approval than the one you've been trying to sell me all morning. Unless you can come up with a more compelling way to present it. Show me the way!"

She was laughing as she watched Fiona bolting out of the courtyard on her palomino. Kira raced out over the marsh after her, realizing how intensely exciting it was to let this particular horse have its head. It was almost magical, and she could feel the tempo and the speed with the wind tearing at her hair and face as she followed Fiona.

It was like being with Mack and yet... different. All the joy was still very much there. She bent over Domino's neck as they ran over the green earth. She could feel the soft-hardness of the moist ground and then the rocks scarring the trail all around them as they moved in and out of the trees...

"I told you," Fiona shouted, now behind her. "Isn't it wonderful? Don't you want it to go on forever?"

"Yes, blast it! Your Domino is fantastic." She glanced at her over her shoulder. "But that can't change what I have to do with my own career."

"No, but I bet my horse can change your mind. Did I tell you there are rumors Domino was born in the Egyptian desert? And there were stories that his forebearers were almost always sold to the sons of pharaohs?"

"You know you didn't. What difference does it make? He's just a great horse. You're lucky to have him. Now be quiet and let me enjoy the ride!"

Fiona was chuckling. "Just giving you all the details so that you can appreciate him more."

"Duly noted," Kira said as she nudged Domino to greater speed. "But I'll appreciate him even more if I can make him race a bit faster. I want to see if I can get him to run as fast as Mack does. Then I'll know he's a true champion."

"And you'll consider taking him to Summer Island for training?"

"I didn't say that."

"You'll do it. I know it!"

"Then you know more than I do," Kira said. "And I won't promise to—"

Splat! The tree next to Kira was pierced by a bullet as she turned to look at Fiona!

Another shot! This time it hit the tree next to Fiona.

That was too close. Kira dove sideways and knocked Fiona off her horse to the ground. Then she was dragging her into the brush behind the trees. "Be still!" she whispered. "Don't move!"

More shots spattered the earth in front of the path. Then there came an entire barrage of bullets striking the trees all around them. Kira rolled Fiona into a ditch on the other side of the road and covered her with her body.

"Are either of you hurt?" Harlan was suddenly beside them and jumping off his horse and lifting Kira to her feet. "Fiona?"

"I'm fine." Kira brushed the tousled hair out of her eyes. "And I think Fiona is okay, too. But I knocked her off her horse when I heard the shot." She made a face. "I thought you were bragging how safe it is here at your fine manor house."

"It usually is," Belson said dryly as he pulled up beside them. "Today we had a few intruders. But the military patrol took care of them when they spotted you two out here. They should be under arrest by now."

"And I have a number of questions for them to answer once we have a chance to find out how they got onto the property," Harlan added grimly. "You're sure neither of you is injured?"

"I'm fine," Fiona said as she got to her knees. Then Belson was helping her to her feet. "A little scared maybe, but Kira knocked me off my horse and then into the ditch and that was enough to clear my head." Her smile was a little shaky. "I didn't mean to get her that angry just because I was nagging her."

"Be quiet. That's not funny," Kira said as she checked out Domino's condition. Lucky? One of those bullets might have struck either one of these horses, she realized. "That bullet was close enough to ricochet off the tree right next to you." She turned to Harlan. "You're right to keep someone close to her."

"I'm glad you approve," he said deadpan. "But I wanted her to have your company, not your protection. I believed she was safe here and at the stables. Your presence here on the grounds must have inspired Taylor. I guarantee that it won't happen again." He was getting back on his horse. "Take them back to the manor, Belson. I need to go back and talk to the captain of the guard and do a little investigation about why they *weren't* safe here today." He whistled for Mack to follow him. Then he was gone.

Kira stood looking after him. "What's he going to do?"

"Nothing very violent." Belson shrugged. "Stop looking so troubled. It might be different if either of you had been hurt. But Harlan won't be going after those bastards with anything too lethal if he doesn't find a reason to do it. He's not a killer like Taylor, who's an entirely different kettle of fish. All bets are off when it comes to him." He frowned thoughtfully. "Though probably some of the men who were firing at you during this raid just now were paid by him. I think I recognized a couple whom the military brought down. Harlan will be checking that out as soon as they're brought to the manor dungeon."

"Dungeon? This place actually has a dungeon?" Kira said; then she dismissed the thought as unimportant. "But I want to see what's going on now. Fiona could have been badly hurt. Those asses certainly tried to do it. I promised I'd look out for her."

"That's up to Harlan now," Belson said. "Look, Kira. There were at least four men in that group shooting at the two of you. Those are dangerous odds. Harlan has plenty of men who can go after them and keep you safe. They're probably only being kept in the castle dungeon until Harlan decides what he wants to do with them."

"Let her go on, Belson," Fiona said impatiently as one of the grooms helped her to mount her palomino. "You know that Harlan will watch out for her. Besides, I want him to see her on Domino.

If anyone can persuade her that my horses are worthy of her attention, it will be him. He usually manages to sway anyone the way he wants them to go."

"Don't you ever give up?" Kira asked in exasperation. "For heaven's sake, you've just been shot at. Then I tackled you and rolled you into a ditch. I'd think you'd be a little discouraged."

Fiona shook her head. "That's nothing. I had worse lumps when I first started to ride. I bet you didn't give up when you were first teaching Mack. Domino is just as worthwhile, and I have to make you see it."

Kira shook her head. "Keep a watch on her, Belson. I'll see you both back at the manor." She prodded Domino, and he leaped forward at a run.

The first thing Kira noticed was that Belson had been right about the forest being full of men. Some obviously wore livery or military uniforms and belonged to the manor as employees, but there were others whose rough garb seemed to indicate they were probably Taylor's men, now prisoners as Belson had indicated. All of their expressions appeared to be both grim and very cautious.

And then Kira stiffened as she saw a body lying by the side of the road near a massive round stone building where Harlan was talking to a guard. Blood...

The body was crumpled and there was blood on the man's shirt.

Harlan saw her reaction, and his lips tightened as he strolled toward her. "Good morning again. I told Belson to keep an eye on the two of you. Where the hell is he?"

"With your niece. Fiona is quite safe. She had several other people watching over her, too."

"Exactly my intention. So then why are you here?"

"I wanted to see what was going on. I believe I was shot at today, and so was Fiona. You told me that your manor was safe, and Belson told me the same thing. And yet I'm looking at a body and blood…" She had to swallow. "Quite a bit of blood on that body. Is he dead?"

"Very."

"Did you do it?"

"No. As a matter of fact, it was done by one of Taylor's own men. Though I suppose it could possibly be laid at my door."

She frowned, puzzled. "When you didn't do it?"

Harlan showed her his cell phone screen, which had an image of the dead man's face. "I got a facial recognition hit on him. His name was Mark Latham, and he flew a helicopter in Afghanistan before he went to work for Taylor. There's a good chance he was flying that copter in Colorado. It was an unsuccessful mission, and Taylor doesn't tolerate failure. It's possible he gave another of his men the task of eliminating the pilot who displeased him by sending him on a suicide mission straight to me, here at the castle."

Kira looked back at the dead man. "Your people didn't kill him?"

"Not according to my men." He shrugged. "Either way, I'll accept it. Particularly since the assassin left a note in this asshole's jacket pocket addressed to you."

"Me?"

"Yes, Captain Darue, the head of the guards, has it now. He'll give it to you after they process it." He paused. "Though I'd prefer he didn't."

Her gaze flew to his face. "That bad?"

"Not good. Nothing for you to worry about. You're among friends."

"Am I?" She glanced back at the bloody corpse. "I still need to see that note. Unless..."

He shook his head as he met her eyes. "No, and it's not because I'm afraid that you'll think that I'm guilty as charged. Trust me, I would've been happy to shoot him myself. Isn't that always what you think first?"

"Blood. Death. You? There does seems to be a connection, doesn't there?"

"But there wasn't one on the cliffs that night?"

"No, not that night. You saved Mack." She hesitated. "And me, Harlan."

"Does that mean I'm making progress?" he asked quietly.

"Perhaps." She glanced at the stone wall that formed part of the manor's subterranean level. "That really is a dungeon, isn't it?"

"It really is," Harlan said. "It came with the castle when I bought it. It does become useful on occasion. Many properties are equipped with dungeons here in France. You find the concept a bit medieval?"

"All I know is I didn't like the idea that a fifteen-year-old girl was a victim and you had to stop it. I *like* her, Harlan. She's a little crazy, but she loves those horses. And it scared me when I had to tackle her to get her off that palomino."

"It scares me whenever I remember that bastard who wants to bring her down," he said. "I can't let it happen. By the way, did I tell you that she's right about how good you and Domino are going to be together? You look fantastic on him."

"Not you, too?" Kira groaned and shook her head. "I've been having enough trouble with her."

"Then I'll back off." Harlan was pushing her toward the dungeon. "Come and sit down in the office and I'll let the police tell you how much they like my staff and appreciate how I include them when I have to organize a particularly difficult search. They really do think I do an okay job, Kira."

"So does everyone in your hemisphere," Kira said with a small smile.

"But not you," Harlan said. "First you look for the blood, and then you make me work very hard so that I can prove my worthiness in your eyes. You're a very difficult woman, Kira."

"Then find someone easier."

"But then there would be no challenge." He opened the door of the dungeon. "Just listen and learn, and then we'll discuss everything of importance."

"I need to talk to Sarah. She's the most important person in my life right now."

"It's already in the works. We'll be seeing Summer Island very soon."

"You don't know that. I haven't made any firm decisions yet."

"I think you have. You've already told me that you're going to go after Taylor. That's all that's necessary."

"Because you believe that he'll be coming after me, too?"

"It's the way he operates," Harlan said. "There are signs that he's already beginning. Can't you tell by what happened today? I'm not going to let you go it alone no matter how stubborn you are."

"My choice," she said. "I can do what has to be done myself. And I want to see that note that was delivered in the helicopter pilot's pocket today. Will you go tell the policeman you keep on hand to give it to me?"

Harlan muttered a curse. "You're a glutton for punishment. Stay here. Sit down. He'll come to you." He turned and strode out of the dungeon.

But the man who came through the door five minutes later was in his late thirties and good looking, with a strong jawline and cheekbones that she could imagine seeing as the subject of a classical French painting. Though frowning, he was obviously trying to be as charming as possible. He bowed gracefully to her. "I'm Captain Charles Darue, and I have something to give you. Though I really disapprove of Harlan's decision to let you see this horror. You're not being very wise to ignore his advice."

She held out her hand, then he reached into a brown manila folder and held out the envelope. "Harlan clearly is only trying to save you from yourself. He's much admired in my department. He's also a personal friend."

"I'm sure he is, and everywhere else in the civilized world. I'd just rather he kept all his zillions of admirers away from me." She was scanning the letter and trying to keep from flinching.

Darue's brows rose. "Zillions?"

"One of his niece's favorite terms."

"Oh, yes." He smiled. "The lovely young girl we're all so fond of. What a great horsewoman. My men and I take good care of her."

"Do you?" She had come to the end of the letter and felt almost numb. "Then by all means continue." She handed the letter back to him. "But I'd be even more careful if I were you."

"Of course. But since the threat was clearly aimed at you, our efforts must also reflect that fact. Don't worry. We'll make certain Taylor won't touch either of you."

"I can't thank you enough." Her hand clenched. She had to get out of here. She felt suffocated. "I'll let Harlan know all the good advice you've given me. I'm sure he'll appreciate it." Then she turned and ran from the dungeon.

———— · ————

She met Harlan as soon as she tore out of the dungeon. "There you are." She grabbed him by the arm and dragged him around to where she'd left Domino tied in the castle's side yard. "Why did you do that? Do you know how it would have made me feel if I'd really thought I was responsible for hurting Fiona?"

Harlan grabbed her wrists and held them tightly. "Why are you so angry? You're the one who insisted on reading the damn letter. I tried to stop you."

She knew that was true, and it only made her feel more guilty. "I thought it was just going to be more of Taylor's same bullshit. I didn't believe he'd aim that poison directly at *me*. I didn't think about the possibility that if I didn't do something to stop it, I would be considered responsible for any of the crimes Taylor might commit."

"You won't be responsible for anything. It's all Taylor," Harlan said roughly. "You're not thinking straight."

"The hell I'm not." Her voice was shaking. "You might be partially right, but you know what was in that letter."

"I do."

"So do I." She turned away. She'd already memorized what it said.

Kira:

Did you think that I'd allow you to ignore me? You managed to escape with Harlan to his hideout in France but that's only temporary. I'm sending my men to make certain you don't feel too comfortable there with his family and all his many employees. You should be almost well now, and so should that hound you love so much. It won't be long before I'll feel ready to come and get both of you. I can hardly wait. I promised you that I'd show Harlan how I'd make you suffer. If you're reading this letter, he managed to cheat me of that pleasure today. But that time has almost come. If you want to talk terms to me and are ready to share the treasure you've tucked away somewhere off the coast of Egypt, I might be willing to let you live, as long as you turn over Harlan to me. I doubt you would do that, since he rescued both you and that mutt, but do think about it. Either way he dies, and you might as well live as long as you're reasonable. Though I'd be disappointed, because I have very special plans for you. No one close to you is safe . . . not Harlan, not his charming niece, not your friends at Summer Island. I fully intend to lay that death at your door. It will be my gift specially dedicated to you, bitch. And it will also be my infinite pleasure, Kira.

"I *hate* him. He's not going to win. I won't let him."

She whirled on Harlan. "And no one is going to kill Fiona. I like her, and Taylor isn't going to dedicate any of his damn kills to me. I won't have it. Do you hear me?"

"You couldn't be more clear. Will you stop shouting at me now? I'm on your side."

"You'd better be. Because Taylor evidently wants me to kill you, too."

"Undoubtedly. It would be a great advantage for him to use you to do that. Anything else?"

She looked away for a moment. "He mentions Summer Island in this note. I'm sorry. He's hitting me where it hurts."

"Taylor excels at that."

She quickly mounted Domino. "I'm going back to the manor and check on Fiona."

"She's quite safe with Belson, Kira. I guarantee it."

"I'd feel better if I was there myself. I shouldn't have let anything else interfere."

"And you're nervous and you want to be sure."

She nodded curtly. "That about covers it. I have some thinking to do. I'm angry and frustrated, and I want to be certain that she's okay and nowhere near Taylor."

He waved his hand and gestured for her to leave. "Then I'll see you in a few hours. Though I assure you that Taylor isn't anywhere nearby. But I agree that you should definitely do some thinking. I don't want you to attack me again without good reason..."

She lightly snapped the reins to push Domino into a fast trot and headed toward the manor.

But she went past the manor and took the first trail toward the forest again.

She had to stay here in the woods and think about what she needed to do and how she might be able to save Sarah from any other attack engineered by Taylor, if that was possible...

What was she thinking? Of course that was possible. She just had to figure it out. Yet the threats had also been specifically aimed at Fiona and Harlan in that latest note. She would just stay here in the dimness and make certain there were no mistakes in her plans. Start with what she had to do and then move forward to keep Taylor at bay...

CHAPTER

6

Darkness had already started to fall when she saw Harlan driving up the trail in his jeep with Mack sitting beside him on the front seat. He put on the brakes and stayed in the vehicle while he waited for Mack to see her and then dash out of the jeep and run toward Kira in a delirium of joy.

He watched while she got her usual greeting and then got out and strode toward her. "I thought you might be ready to take charge of Mack and let me escort Domino back to the stable. It was clear Mack was missing you."

"I doubt it. He's far too well trained." But she was kneeling down to give the retriever a hug anyway. "And Domino and I are getting along just fine at the moment."

"Then maybe I was the one who was missing you," Harlan said solemnly. "Of course it could be mere curiosity that brought me running after you. You'll have to decide that for yourself. But you have to admit, your exit line back at the jailhouse was intriguing."

"Intriguing enough to cause you to send a couple of your men running around to check on where I'd gone? Don't you think I realize when I'm being followed? I knew that the first day in Colorado, when you started to follow me in the mountains."

"And I was aware that you knew. I thought you'd feel more secure if you believed that you had at least a modicum of power." He grinned. "I realized you had far more than that by the end of the first day. But by then I was too interested to stop. You were too good at what you did. It was fun just to watch you. It had become a game. I thought you might have had the same idea."

She was silent a moment. "I was just doing my job."

"Truly? I don't think so. We were both annoyed and both determined, but there were too many elements of chance in the chase not to intrigue us both. Yes?"

She shrugged. "Perhaps." But she wasn't going to give up entirely. "That isn't why you sent your men to hunt me down here in the woods today, though."

He shook his head. "Guilty as charged. But I told them not to disturb you. And you have to admit that I had a right to be concerned about your safety at this particular moment." He paused. "And what decision you might make while you were brooding out here by yourself."

"I don't brood," she said curtly. "And I can take care of myself... if that's what I want to do."

"Ah, but you've left me an opening there." His eyes narrowed. "Haven't you, Kira?"

"Yes, I've left you an opening," she said. "I told you that I had to think about what I wanted to do. I only agreed to spend three days with you. Do you want to know what I've decided?"

"I can hardly wait." He started to gently stroke Domino's jaw. "But wouldn't you rather go back to the manor where we'll be more comfortable?"

"No, I like the woods. And I'm not sure I want you to be too comfortable. Because I've decided that I might need you. If you turn me down, I might have to work out some other way to accomplish the same end."

He shrugged. "I try my best to be irreplaceable, so let's hear if you succeeded." He dropped down and leaned back beside her against the pine tree, crossing his arms over his chest. "By all means proceed."

"That's my intention." She reached into her pocket and pulled out her notebook. "You know what was in that letter. Well, I won't let Taylor use me to do his dirty work. But there could be a problem. I might need a partner who wants to get rid of Taylor as much as I do, but also has influence and unlimited funds since I have neither."

"And you've chosen me? I must admit you're not the first to so honor me. But it does come as a surprise. One, I'm not looking for a partner; two, you've indicated in no uncertain terms that I wouldn't be your choice in the next thousand years or so; and three, if I did choose a partner, it would be one who brought something into the game that appealed to me."

She nodded. "I thought about all that while I was sitting here, but I think I've found solutions for both of us."

"Really? Fascinating."

"Naturally, you're mostly interested in what you're going to have to give me."

"Not necessarily. The entire process is riveting."

"Stop joking. I'm trying to be serious. I can't tell you how much it would cost you to link up with me, but I'm sure it would be considerable. Though Fiona says that you have a good deal of capital. I believe she called it zillions."

"That sounds like her," Harlan said, shrugging. "And how many of those zillions are you going to have to take from me?"

"I'm not sure, but it's not as if you won't get it back. I'll see to it."

"From your nonexistent bank account?"

"It won't be nonexistent by then. I'm going to be making a deal that will allow me to reimburse you."

"May I ask with whom?"

"Of course. You have a right to know." She drew a deep breath before she continued in a rush, "There are only two things that Taylor mentioned he wanted in the letter he sent me." She made a face. "One of them was your head on a platter. The other was a similar fate for Fiona, with a suitable dedication to me. I decided the bastard can't have either one."

"For which we're both very grateful," Harlan said. "So we'd better go back to ways and means."

She firmly shook her head. "No, that's where my share of the booty comes in. After we safeguard Summer Island, we go to a place I've become very familiar with in the past few years while I've been doing some in-depth treasure hunting. It's in the Mediterranean and totally owned by an Egyptian national. Which means that any deal I make with him regarding the treasure will stand up in an international court."

"And you've already made such a deal?" Harlan asked. "I thought the 'wild' rumors about your finding another even more profitable treasure were probably true. So much for totally devoting yourself to taking care of Mack and company."

"Everything I said was true," she said. "I just left a few details to be filled in later. The treasure is real. I can't document how big it is yet. I've seen emeralds, gold, and sapphires. But as I've said, I don't have all the details."

"Details about a treasure that will probably net a fairly fabulous sum? And will cost an equally fabulous amount to retrieve?"

"I could hardly expect you to donate your money or time to anything less. I'll split my share fifty–fifty with you." She stared him straight in the eye. "Well, is it a deal, Harlan? You should be glad I offered it to you. You'll probably make another fortune on it."

"It's definitely a possibility," he said slowly.

"Then say yes. What's holding you up? I'm being more than fair."

"And, as usual, very impatient. I prefer to go at a business arrangement like this slowly and make sure I know what I'm doing."

She stiffened. "Don't you trust me? The treasure is there. I've seen it."

"That's not the question." He got to his feet. "You have excellent credentials. And why shouldn't I believe you'd want to go after Taylor any way you could? You're angry and you want to put him away." He smiled crookedly. "What I should be worried about is exactly what method you'd use to do it. We might be very far apart on that score."

"You're right. I don't approve of taking a life for any reason." She paused. "Though I can see how you might have cause. Taylor is a beast."

"Granted." He added, "But the farthest I could go along with you would be to promise not to go after Taylor without your express approval. If you could accept that, a partnership might be possible—providing that you agree it's a full partnership in every way." He smiled as he saw her frown. "You don't like that? But it's a perfectly reasonable requirement. It protects what both of us want. Since I'm almost certain that Taylor will be the one who goes after me at his earliest convenience, I'll be able to keep my word. While you will remain ethically pure as you try to trap Taylor any way you can, I'd be a mere victim struggling to survive. Consider it. In my place, wouldn't you ask for the same terms?"

"Yes, I would," she said reluctantly. "And I'll think about it."

"But that last item isn't negotiable with me," he added. "No way. Forget it."

"You seem very determined. Why?"

"Why do you think? Because I don't want to ever feel the way I did when I had to tear you away from Taylor that night on the cliffs," he said grimly. "It never would have happened if I'd had more control over the situation. Hell, I shouldn't have let Belson pull you into that Colorado search. But I was too damn eager to go after the bastard, and he knew it. You can bet I won't permit it to interfere again."

She gazed at him incredulously. "What are you talking about? I'm the one who made the final choice to go after Taylor. You had nothing to do with it. I make my own decisions."

He shook his head. "You're wrong. I had everything to do with it. But have it your way. We'll be heading for Summer Island at dawn tomorrow. My private jet will take us there. If you still want to continue our arrangement." He was striding back toward the jeep. "Mack can come with us tomorrow, and I can have Domino brought by air transport the next day." He looked back over his shoulder. "If you've decided that you want Domino on your island?"

She nodded. "I might as well have him examined by my vet and set him up with a few preliminary evaluations. It will make Fiona happy even if it doesn't lead anywhere."

"Why did I know that was going to be your answer?" Harlan asked wryly. "My niece is nothing if not persuasive." He got into the jeep. "Go ahead and take Domino back to the stables. I'll follow you."

"That's not necessary."

"It is for me." He paused. "Look, Kira, I agree to your terms. But I'm going to insist you let me know what you're planning very soon so that I can make my own arrangements. Other than that and a few other minor disagreements, you'll find me to be an excellent provider, and I'll look after everyone you want protected. In short,

I'm undoubtedly the best option you could hope for. Can you see that?"

"Within certain limits." She met his eyes. He was right. He was a very valuable asset, and clearly, he was not going to change his mind. "Whatever." She pulled on Domino's reins and whistled for Mack to follow her. "I was ready to go back anyway."

He suddenly smiled. "How lucky for me."

But she noticed he didn't move until she went ahead on Domino. "Yes, it is." She nudged Domino past the jeep. "I'll see you back at the manor."

He shrugged. "Perhaps not. I have quite a few arrangements to make before dawn tomorrow..."

And she suspected she would not have any input into those travel arrangements. But things would change once she reached Summer Island. She would be more in charge and able to run her own life.

And perhaps she'd also be able to do a little work on arrangements to show Harlan how very well she could perform when she was left to her own devices...

———•———

"What's the word?" Taylor asked the minute Donovan appeared on the deck of his cruiser. "Did you get the bitch?"

"No, Kira Drake got away and we didn't get either her or the niece." Donovan shrugged. "You knew attacking the castle was going to be a lost cause with all Harlan's men on watch there. Maybe next time."

Taylor cursed low and explicitly. "Don't tell me that. I told you I want her dead."

"And you'll get it. Don't I always come through for you? It wasn't me who left you in the lurch when we were on the cliffs. Mark Latham was the fool who did that." He added quickly, "And before you ask me if I took care of him, I did. The poor fellow didn't make it past the first raid on the castle. What a shame. And I managed to slip the note you gave me into Latham's pocket before I shot the bastard. Are you pleased with me?"

"I'm pleased. I'd be more pleased if you'd rid me of that bitch."

"But that would have been awkward. Though I did find out that she's being taken back to Summer Island by private jet tomorrow. I could set up a trap on the island and maybe bag both the woman and Harlan. Would you like that?"

"On Summer Island? You'd never make it. Harlan will have the damn place packed with his private army after the mess you made of that raid. You can scout around and see what you find. But your chances are practically nil."

"I might get lucky."

"Keep a sharp eye out. I want to see where the Drake woman goes next. That might be far more valuable..."

CHAPTER

7

"You know, I think I like your island," Harlan said as he started the descent to land his Gulfstream jet. "It's quite beautiful, and it reminds me a little of Scotland."

"Why would you think that? It's nothing like Scotland," Kira said as she gazed eagerly down at the ground. "Other than it's definitely wild country. It's all beautiful Caribbean views and lakes. And gorgeous flowers. But it's been my home base for a long time and I love it." She shot him a glance. "And it's not my island, as you probably know. It belongs to my friend Sarah. She just lets me use it for research and training. I'm surprised you haven't been here before. John Logan is your friend, isn't he? He comes here occasionally with Sarah when she visits me."

He nodded. "Friends and sometimes business partners. We have a lot of common interests taking down poachers and dealing with environmental issues. But we're both busy men, and I got the impression when he gave Sarah this island as a gift that he didn't want outsiders. So I politely backed away." He shrugged. "I could understand their need for privacy." He studied her expression. "And I imagine you can, too. You spend a good deal of your time by yourself trekking in the wilderness, don't you?"

She grinned. "I've always got Mack."

He chuckled. "Don't worry. I haven't forgotten what a competition he would prove to be."

She suddenly laughed out loud. "That reminds me of something Sarah said to me the last time I saw her."

"Amusing?"

"I thought so at the time. You might not appreciate it. It had to do with dogs and the desirability of the male animal in comparison. But then we live entirely different lives. I don't have a castle with a built-in dungeon to run back to when I need a schedule break."

"No, you just need to go treasure hunting to replenish your finances."

"It's an entirely different way to—" She suddenly broke off in alarm as she caught sight of movement on the ground below them. "What's that? Don't land! There shouldn't be anyone at the clinic at this time of day!"

"Easy," Harlan said as he covered her hand on the seat. He was gazing down at the large redwood building that occupied the hill overlooking the sea. "That's the clinic? I think it's okay." He took out his notebook and checked directions. "Yes, no problem. I sent

Charles Darue to the island last night. He's just setting up camps with his special guards to look out for your medical and training team. I told him to be on hand when we arrived today."

Kira drew a deep breath and then said dryly, "You could have told me. I thought we might be in for another invasion."

"Sorry." He lifted his shoulder in a half shrug. "I was just interested in watching your response to this island. It obviously means a lot to you. I believed you'd realize that I'd take care of you."

"Why should I? I never asked you to do that."

"No, but we agreed that the people you cared about were an entirely different matter. I believe I was supposed to regard them as my duty."

"Yes, you are. You're correct, it's completely different. But that's not me, Harlan."

"But I've found it's a hard habit to shake since that night on the cliffs. Who knows? Maybe you remind me of my niece. I'm used to taking care of her."

"Well, I'm not fifteen," she said caustically. "Do me a favor. Work on it."

"Certainly. I'll concentrate on doing that. But it's difficult when I find I'm so very curious about you. Every time I turn around, I find something new and different. It's been like that since you showed up in Colorado."

"Why?" She shook her head. "Or are you always like this with new people?"

"No, not always. As a scientist, when I'm working, I grow curious when I find a problem I need to solve. With people in social situations it's different. You might say that you're unique. I find the need to probe. I'm going to *know* you, Kira." He met her eyes. "Though I'll try not to make it uncomfortable for you."

She couldn't look away from those deep green eyes. So much power, so much depth, and he seemed to be searching...He'd used the word "probe," and she could see that, too. She forced herself to turn and stare back down at the ground. "You won't make me uncomfortable. I can take anything you throw at me." She finally managed to look back at him. "And you'll get to know only as much about me as I let you. Since we've agreed to be partners, that might be more than I usually permit." She lifted her chin and smiled recklessly. "Or it might not. I'll have to decide if I want to tell you to go to hell and get a new partner."

Harlan went still. Then he threw back his head and started to laugh. "Do you have any idea where you're going find anyone even half as accommodating as me?"

"But I don't know how accommodating you'll prove to be." She was trying to keep her lips from twitching, but she couldn't do it. "All I know is that that was a very arrogant statement, and I couldn't let it pass." She pretended to be considering. "As for your replacement...maybe that handsome French captain who was so polite to me at the dungeon?"

"Captain Darue?" He shook his head. "I have other uses for Charles than letting you play games with him."

"I don't play games. I'm very serious when I go after something."

"Or someone?" Harlan asked. "I'll remember that. It will be an essential part of my research." He was smiling again. "But I think you were playing games with me just now. You should know that you're going to have your hands full here."

"What does *that* mean?"

"Domino won't be the only horse joining us here tomorrow. Golden Boy will probably be arriving on the same plane, along with Fiona."

"What?"

"I feel better keeping Fiona close. And it wouldn't be fair to keep her from her training regimen."

Kira thought about this. "The fact that you waited to tell me this is definitely a half-assed power play. But I'm fine with it, as long as it's okay with Sarah."

"I think it is. I've already left the request on her voicemail. At least she hasn't said no."

"Unbelievable. You've already—"

Then Kira forgot everything else as she saw a familiar figure walking toward the airstrip from the direction of the pier. "Sarah!" She reached down and rubbed Mack's back. "There's Sarah!"

Kira and Mack jumped out of the plane as soon as it landed and ran toward the clinic at top speed.

Kira reached Sarah only a few moments after Mack and hugged her enthusiastically. "It's so good to see you," Sarah whispered. "I was so worried when Harlan called me the night he took you to the hospital. Are you okay now?"

Kira nodded toward Harlan, who had stopped at the plane to

talk to Charles Darue, the captain of the guards. "I wouldn't dare be anything else. Harlan has had me covered and guarded since that night on the cliffs. I'm not sure if it's because he wanted to earn another medal to add to his collection or just that he hates to lose. He told me you called about me?"

She chuckled as she rubbed Mack's head. "Several times. But you were in no shape to take the call, which only worried me more. Harlan was very soothing, though, or I would have been on my way to that damn castle of his. I told you that if you let Harlan help you, everything would turn out as it should."

"It didn't turn out quite that way." Kira paused. "And he's not the easiest person to get along with."

Sarah frowned. "But everything is going well?"

"It appears that it is," Kira said. "At least we came to an agreement." She hesitated. "But I might have to take a few weeks off soon, if you don't mind."

"Of course. You know you run your own clinic these days. You have better contacts than I do." She frowned again. "It's not because you're still ill?"

"No, I'm definitely on the way back. The doctor said I was very lucky."

"I believe it." She smiled. "You had Harlan on your side. John and I are very grateful to him."

"I wasn't exactly helpless." But that sounded a little churlish and she added quickly, "I'm very grateful for both my own and Mack's sake that Harlan was there. No, I just have to touch base with a few old friends. Then I'll be back here and working hard." She smiled teasingly. "Maybe on a few new concepts."

"Good," Sarah said absently. "'Old friends'..." she repeated. "That reminds me: I received a few calls from a friend of yours while you were in the hospital. Jabir Kalim. It rather surprised me because I hadn't heard from him in a long time. He would usually only speak to you."

"Kalim?" Kira repeated slowly, shocked. "What did you tell him?"

"What Harlan told me." She made a face. "And Kalim was not happy. He wouldn't talk to anyone but me. He called me twice more and was angry each time. I think you'd better call him back."

"I will." Kira had no choice. An angry Kalim was never good. "Thanks for relaying the message."

"Well, he was always your friend and good to you. You learned a lot from Kalim."

"Yes, I did." Her gaze went to Harlan, who was still talking to the captain of the guards beside the plane. He looked up and peered at her searchingly before he abruptly straightened as he caught something in her face. Then he started toward her with the same expression he'd worn before they'd landed the plane. Searching. Probing. She'd have to tell Harlan about Kalim as soon as possible. It was neither fair nor smart to keep anything from him. Particularly now that she realized Kalim might blame Harlan for putting her in the hospital. Until he learned the truth, there might be all kinds of violence in store.

No, she'd have to make certain Harlan knew about Kalim right away.

She turned quickly back to Sarah. "Can you stay for supper before you leave the island? Maybe even let me tell you about Harlan's niece and what I might be doing with her horses? She's bringing them here tomorrow, and I'm very excited about it. I believe you will be, too. There's one black stallion that you're going to love. Domino. We'll have to bring the dogs together when I get far enough along in training the horses…"

"I wouldn't miss it," Sarah said. "And I have to thank Harlan in person, so I might as well let him feed me supper tonight. I'd much prefer our island to that swank castle of his." She was walking toward Harlan as she spoke. "You took good care of her, Harlan," she said as she shook his hand. "I can't thank you enough."

"You're very welcome. But I heard what you said about my humble abode. Not kind, Sarah."

She laughed. "I'm like Kira. We have a problem with castles—and admit it, so do you and John. He told me about that rajah's palace in India, and how the two of you ended up in the jungle hunting poachers and ivory smugglers to get away from it. John knows after all these years that I have a simple soul."

"I doubt that," Harlan said. "But you're right, the castle isn't nearly as comfortable as your Summer Island here. It's safer when you need strong walls to ward off an enemy, however. I have quite a few of those wandering around."

She nodded. "So John told me. I'm sure he'd approve of you

taking additional care of my island. He insisted on furnishing me with a full security detail the day he turned the deed over to me. I usually leave all the security arrangements for the island and our townhome outside Miami to him. I'd rather deal with dogs and people than paperwork."

Harlan nodded. "Then you won't mind if I contact him and ask if I should add any special arrangements to my list?"

"No, I'm sure that, between the two of you, you'll have it covered."

"If you change your mind, just name it. Anything you want."

She chuckled. "That's hard to resist. Maybe staying in your castle might not be so bad. I'll have to ask Kira what she thinks."

He tilted his head, considering. "I can tell you that she likes the woods and her friend Sarah. Other than that, I'm still exploring what will keep her content."

"She likes a good many more things than that," Sarah said. "Maybe she's just bored with the palaces of the high and mighty. She's seen a lot in the short time she's lived. You'll have to ask her."

"I will. In the meantime, will you and Kira show me around your beautiful island and tell me how I can make my niece happy here?"

"Of course," Sarah said. She walked ahead of them up the hill. "It will be my pleasure. I'm eager to meet your niece. It will be like having a young Kira again. Did she tell you how we came together when she was a child I found climbing a mountain to get away from a volcano eruption in the South Seas?"

Kira tensed, and she realized Harlan had read her expression as he reached out and took her hand. Dammit, she didn't want Sarah to open any other intimate memories from her life to Harlan. He was aware of entirely too much about her already.

He sounded amused as he smiled slyly at Kira. "I don't believe she thinks me worthy of confidences yet."

"Nonsense," Sarah said. "You must have misunderstood. You saved her and Mack. Who could be more worthy of trust?"

"We'll get there," Harlan said. "I'm trying not to be too pushy. She's had a hard time lately. And she's such a delicate flower…"

Which immediately caused Kira to snort with disdain and Sarah to start laughing.

And at least it interrupted any wish Sarah might have to defend her or tell him any more about their early life together. Kira glanced at Harlan, who was nodding and smiling at Sarah. Every movement was probably creating exactly the effect he meant it to. Charming Sarah and yet letting her lead the way.

I'm going to know you, he had told her.

Well, he'd clearly begun as he intended to continue.

Yes, she'd better not waste any time telling him about Kalim or he'd try to take over her world…

"You're not a bad cook, Harlan," Sarah said critically that evening as they walked her back to the clinic where she'd decided to spend the night. "The biscuits were particularly good. Not that I didn't expect it. John is good with biscuits, too, when we go camping. I think it must be something in the male genes, or it might be a throwback to the Old West days when the cowboys sat around the campfire and did the cooking." She made a face. "Please don't tell me you had a French chef teach you the basics in that fancy castle."

"No, I learned while I was in the service. I was a SEAL. Not a chef in sight." He grinned. "But John liked my biscuits, too. I usually drew chow duty when we were hunting in the jungle."

"I can see why." Sarah stopped at the front door of the clinic. "You appear to be a man of many talents. But you and Kira really didn't have to escort me back here to the clinic. I'm used to taking care of myself."

Harlan glanced at Kira. "That sounds very familiar. Did she learn it from you?"

Sarah chuckled. "It's all blended together over the years. We learned from each other." She lowered her voice as she looked over her shoulder at the guards on duty on either side of the door. "I didn't really expect you to call in the marines to guard my island." She snapped her fingers. "Oh, that's right, it was the SEALs. Same difference."

"Not nearly," he said slyly. "SEALs are naval personnel. And you should have expected this reaction. You're a very precious commodity both to John and to your friend Kira. No one is going to touch you. I'll see to it."

"Listen to him, Sarah." Kira took a step toward her. "I told you earlier this evening about the trouble we're expecting with Taylor.

You still agreed to let me go forward with the new work I intend to do with the horses here. But I can't do it if there's even a chance it might affect you." She grabbed her friend by the shoulders and gave her a little shake. "Dammit, Sarah, let Harlan give you any protection available. I'll make sure it's done right."

Sarah was silent and then nodded with a smile. "Okay. But only if he teaches me to make those biscuits so that I can put John in the shade the next time we go camping."

"Done," Harlan said. "I'll give you a private cooking class. You won't regret it, Sarah."

"I know." She looked him directly in the eyes. "I haven't regretted a single thing connected with Kira since the day we met. I don't expect to begin now. You're the one who might be in trouble if you don't watch out." She gave Kira a brief, warm hug. "Take care and don't be too hard on him. I'll see you in the morning to get my first lesson, Harlan." She opened the door. "Now I've got to call John and then get to bed. I intend to have a different and exciting day tomorrow. Good night…" She closed the door behind her.

"Thank you for reassuring her, Harlan." Kira immediately turned away from the clinic and started back up the hill toward the tent area. "You made it much easier for me to get her to agree to bring the horses to the island."

"I think she would have done it anyway," Harlan said as he started after her. "She cares about you. Nothing could be more clear. How old were you when she rescued you from that volcano?"

"Ten. My mother and father had left me with a nanny at our

camp, but I tried to follow them up the mountain. I had a fall before I reached them. Sarah and her dog, Monty, were assisting in rescue efforts nearby, and she sent me to the local village hospital and then went after my parents herself." She paused. "It was too late. They were both killed by the volcano before she found them."

"And then she took you into her home?"

"It wasn't quite that easy. I was a wild child and full of guilt once I realized it might be my fault that my parents had been lost when that volcano erupted. The only way she could halfway tame me was to let me work with her own dog and some of the others at the clinic. One thing led to another, and she began to teach me everything she knew because it was the only way I'd heal. I eventually got a veterinary sciences degree. Sarah gave me everything she could during these last years, including a pup named Mack, and that's why I'm eternally grateful to her and always will be." She glanced over her shoulder at him. "End of story."

He shook his head. "Not nearly the end," he said. "You have a long way to go. I could see that the first time I saw you in Colorado. Or it might have been when Belson tossed that magazine with your photo on the desk in my study."

"The media again?" Kira asked. "I believe we've both had enough of that."

"Perhaps. But sometimes they can be helpful if you handle them right."

"You might have found that to be true. I haven't had your experiences. I tend to dodge and hide when I run into any of them."

"Then I'll make a bargain with you. Let me handle them for you. It will be part of our arrangement."

"I'm not sure I want to do that. It might give you a little too much power."

"You can't have it all ways, Kira," he said. "You're already trying to mold our agreement to suit yourself." He stopped her where she stood on the trail. "Did you think I didn't notice you trying to do that?"

"Of course you did," she said curtly. "I know who you are and all the things you can do. I could see when you first came toward me from the plane today that you probably wanted to take more from me than I'm prepared to give." She added quickly, "It's not that I was trying to cheat you. It was just that I knew it was going to be difficult and I had to allow a little time to prepare myself to tell you something. Sarah had just told me she'd received a call about me from an old friend. Then you decided that you'd do your best to charm Sarah, and I was relieved because that gave me even more time."

He smiled faintly as he slowly shook his head. "But I believe the grace period has run out, hasn't it?"

"Yes. I never meant not to tell you everything you needed to know."

"Good." He took her arm and nudged her the rest of the way up the hill. "Why don't I get us a cup of coffee, and then we'll sit at our campsite and you can confess all your sins."

"Don't be ridiculous."

"Nothing ridiculous about it."

They walked in silence the rest of the way, and Kira finally sat down in front of the fire and crossed her legs tailor-fashion. Mack lay beside her. "I'm sure you have more sins than I've ever managed to store up. I don't have that much imagination."

"I think you probably have a great deal of imagination. But you've already told me that you had a tendency to feel guilty as a child even when I'm sure you held no blame. Unfortunately, that puts me way ahead of you." He handed her a cup of coffee. "Now tell me why you were so edgy after talking to Sarah."

"She told me that she'd received a couple of phone calls from an old friend of mine, and it made me a little nervous."

"Nervous?" His lips tightened. "Taylor?"

She shook her head violently. "Under no circumstances would I ever consider him a friend."

"Well, you said Sarah was a little nervous And so were you, obviously." Then he asked softly, "Just who the hell is this friend, Kira?"

"His name is Jabir Kalim. He's an Egyptian national. You might have heard of him."

His eyes were narrowed. "Kalim? The horse breeder? Of course I've heard of him."

She nodded. "I'd be surprised if you hadn't, since his people have been known for centuries for raising some of the best-bred and best-trained horses in the world. He lives in desert country on an island not too far off the coast of northern Egypt."

Harlan nodded. "He's the one you made the bargain with about retrieving the treasure? I thought it might be him. Several years ago I tried to arrange a meeting with him to try to purchase a few of his horses for Fiona's stable, but he wasn't selling. What does he have to do with you?"

"I told you, he's my friend. I spent a college semester in Cairo, and one of my professors introduced me to him. I was working on a minor in archaeology, and I visited a dig in the Valley of the Kings, where you might remember a National Geographic expedition was exploring the possibility of Cleopatra's lost tomb being somewhere adjacent to a former desert well or shaft tunnel. I was very excited about it."

"You would be."

"Well, so was Kalim. He told me at the time that it was likely many treasures would be found near those dry wells in the desert—he'd run across a few on his own desert property, Hathor. He invited me to come there and explore before I went back to school."

"And you believed him?"

"Why shouldn't I? He was respected by my teachers and the Egyptian government. Even Sarah had heard about his work with horse breeding. Not only that, Mack and I discovered those Spanish medallions buried in Tortola a year earlier. To me it seemed the entire world was full of adventure and treasure just waiting to be found. Besides, I respected him." She paused. "And by that time he was beginning to respect me, too. My professor had told him about my life extension work with Mack and other animals, and he was very interested in letting me take a look at his herds to see if I could improve them. It seemed like a win-win invitation. How could I lose?"

"Any number of ways that I can name. Rape. Drugs. Human traffickers for three. Sarah should never have let you go alone."

"But she did and I'm glad. It was an experience to remember. Kalim and I both learned a lot from each other. I improved his herds and gave them training when I visited him every summer. In return, he showed me the location of those abandoned wells and caves that you'll be able to tap as a reward for helping me. So you have no right to complain."

"Then why did you look so nervous about telling me about him?"

"Kalim was upset that you gave me an assignment that put me in the hospital. He regards himself as head of the tribes and villagers who live on his property just as all his other ancestors in the family did before him. He didn't know you, therefore he doesn't trust you with a person he considers his responsibility. He's kind of adopted me as one of his villagers since we've worked so closely together. But he can be rather...intense at times."

"So can I," Harlan said grimly. "But I didn't realize I was going to have to prove it to one of your old pals."

"You won't," Kira said quickly. "Kalim will be very reasonable once he understands that you did everything you could to help me. And he's already guaranteed that any deals I make regarding the treasure will remain in place. Egyptian-made items will remain in the country. Only things with a foreign origin can be taken away. Most of the things I saw were left on an island by a trading partner. But you have to promise that you'll not do anything to tip the balance."

"And leave your old friend to furnish all the fireworks?" He finally shrugged. "We'll have to see what happens, won't we? I have no intention of taking down anyone but Joseph Taylor, but then I haven't run across your Kalim yet. Our situation is taking on new shades and textures even as we speak."

"Nothing is going to go wrong. I won't let it." She finished her coffee and set the cup down in front of the fire. "You saved Mack and you saved me. I couldn't let anyone hurt you. You'll just have to use a little restraint. And remember that Kalim has been a ruling force in his country for most of his life."

"You have no idea how much restraint I've already used up since you came into my life," Harlan said wryly.

She nodded. "Yes, I do. And there have been times when I haven't been kind or understanding when you got in my way. I have a tendency in that direction, but I'm trying to make up for it. Can you help me do that?"

He shook his head ruefully. "I don't know why, but I'll do my best. It seems to be my fate in life."

"That's good." She got to her feet. "Now I'm going to my tent to get some sleep."

"You're sleeping out here with the rest of us peons? You don't have your own place on the island?"

"Of course I do. But it's a fairly small apartment, and the visitor accommodations are full right now. It felt wrong for me to stay in my apartment while you and Fiona rough it in the tent village."

"It's hardly 'roughing it.' Fiona will consider it an adventure.

And I've always rather enjoyed the camping experience. Certainly more than I'll enjoy navigating the feelings of your old friend Kalim."

She stood up. "It really will be fine, Harlan. I wouldn't let anything happen to you."

"That's comforting to know." He took her arm and walked with her and Mack to her tent. "Because you'll have one more day to show off the horses and set up the training barriers and schedules with the dogs before we leave here tomorrow night. After that, I'll make final plans to move camp to go visit our new friend Kalim. You don't mind if I take Mack when I go check the sentries tonight? I'll be sure to bring him back to you when I've finished."

"No, of course not. Mack will enjoy it. He hasn't done any real work since the night on the cliffs." She shivered. "And I don't like to remember that night. Though I can't ever forget how Mack looked crawling toward me after he was shot."

"Neither can I. I promise to bring him back to you in great shape this time." He whistled for Mack as he turned to go down the hill. "And you don't have to worry. I've assigned an expert crew to monitor your tent area while you're here on Summer Island."

She watched his flashlight spear the darkness as he headed down toward the clinic where they'd left Sarah. "I'm not worried," she called as she heard Mack bark eagerly. It was true. There was no fear, but she felt oddly alone staying here when she felt she should be out there with Mack, doing her job.

Should she go after them? No, that wouldn't be either efficient or businesslike. Just keep an eye out in case of trouble...

———— • ————

"No problems," Captain Darue reported to Harlan as he bent to stroke the head of the retriever. "Mrs. Logan only opened the door about an hour ago to give me a cup of coffee and told me that she was retiring for the night. Nice woman."

"Yes, she is. Did you get any reports from anyone else making their rounds?"

"Gregot said he thought he heard sounds from the bridge area, but he hadn't gotten around to checking it out yet, so I may go up there myself and see if it's worth sending up another few men."

"I thought I heard something in that direction, too, before I reached the clinic." Harlan smiled. "But I thought I identified what I was hearing after a few minutes."

"You want me to check it out?"

"No, I want you to stay here and make sure Sarah Logan stays safe. I'll go up to the bridge myself and take care of any problem."

"Not your problem, sir," Darue said. "Let me call someone to assist."

Harlan shook his head. "I'm not expecting a full-scale assault. I don't believe Taylor would dare bring anything resembling a heavy force to this island after he saw how many of your men were occupying it." He took out his phone. "I'll call Belson instead. I told him when I talked to him before supper that he should scout

128

around the island and see if he found anything interesting going on. By now, I'll bet that he's as bored as I am and just as eager to be productive."

"And what do you believe is happening on that bridge?" Darue asked curiously.

"What I said. Nothing for you to worry about, but maybe enough to be interesting…"

CHAPTER

8

Ten minutes later, Harlan adjusted his earpiece as he walked through the trees. "I'm just clearing the tent city. Can everybody read me?"

"Go back to bed," a familiar voice said. It was Belson. "We've got this covered."

Harlan could hear chuckling from several others on their frequency. "But I'm not sleepy," Harlan said.

"Then go back to your tent and broker a few deals or whatever it is you billionaires do," Belson said. "I really don't have time to coach you right now. I'm here with most of your security detail, and the island's security team is out in full force. We got this."

Harlan chuckled. "I'm sure you do. But pardon me if I want to take a look for myself."

"Suit yourself. How about a roll call? Anybody see anything out here?"

A chorus of "negative" rang through the headset as everyone checked in.

"See?" Belson said. "All this for a nest of wild birds or something."

"Hold on!" one of the voices said. "Unidentified aircraft from the island's west side."

Harlan cocked his head. He couldn't hear it. "What does it sound like? A seaplane? A copter?"

After a moment, more of the security officers chimed in. "Drones!" several said at once.

Harlan heard the buzzing overhead. "They're heading for the east!"

"They just crossed over the river," Belson said. "We're heading toward the bridge now. Harlan, I really wish you'd hang back."

"Just when it's getting interesting? You know me better than that." Harlan quickened his pace. "I'll meet you on the other side of the river. Stay sharp, everybody."

Harlan jumped over the boulders that lined the main walking path and made his way toward the suspension bridge. It seemed there were now several drones in the sky, and they were all converging near the housing facilities on the other side of the river.

Boom! Boom!

Explosions in the distance.

Boom!

"What the hell is going on over there?" Harlan shouted.

"Possibly grenades," one of the security men replied. "And maybe some gunshots. We're seeing some flashes up ahead. We're halfway over the bridge right now."

"I'm right behind you. Keep going, I'll see you in a minute."

Harlan saw the flashes and smelled gunpowder in the air. What the hell was happening?

He pulled out his gun and charged onto the bridge. He could just make out the rest of the team thirty or forty yards ahead of him. If he put on an extra burst of speed, he might just be able to—

Boom-boom-boom-boom! A deafening string of explosions rocked the bridge from below. Harlan felt the vibrations beneath his feet, and he looked up just in time to see one of the bridge's two massive towers rocking from side to side.

Oh, shit.

The radio chatter told Harlan that the others on the bridge realized the same thing he did.

"It's going down!"

The bridge's superstructure groaned, and the steel cables snapped and whipped across the railing, slicing it in several places.

Harlan leaped for one of the cables and grabbed tight, hanging on as the bridge's roadway collapsed beneath him. The east tower tumbled into the river, turning the bridge into a one-way ramp into the churning water below.

Barking! Mack was crawling up the ramp trying to get to him. He reached out and grabbed the dog's leash, then pulled the retriever the rest of the way up as screams blasted through his earpiece. Mack fought the way to his side, trying to nudge him away from the abyss.

More screams!

At least half the team had been hurled from the bridge, and the others were still trying to grab hold of something, anything, as the remaining beams buckled.

Harlan felt his hands sliding down the steel cable. They were wet with blood, he realized.

Shit.

He gripped harder and swung his feet toward the railing.

Just short.

He tried again.

Another miss. He slid a few feet toward the yawning crevasse behind him.

He swung his legs out one more time and finally got a foothold on the now twisted railing. He pushed himself up.

He might be able to do this.

He moved his bloody hands across the cable and pulled himself up another few feet.

If he could manage that another couple hundred more times, he might be able to get the hell off this thing.

A voice crackled through his earphones. "Any survivors?"

It was Belson.

"Harlan here. Anyone else?"

Six of the other team members responded. More than he thought possible.

He looked up at what was left of the sloping bridge. Shards of metal and cable fragments rained down on him, some white-hot from the force of their twisting and breaking.

Boom! Boom!

More explosions rocked the bridge's foundations, and a team member lost his grip and plummeted toward the water. Harlan tried to catch him as he slid past, but the man tumbled away from his grasp in the last instant.

The bridge shook again.

Harlan dodged the falling debris and pulled himself higher, dragging Mack's leash with him.

Focus. Stay alive. Just fight the hell raining down on him and make it up to the other side.

He moved up five feet, then ten...

The water roared louder in his ears.

He was getting closer.

He could do this.

He crawled over one of the expansion joints, now pulled and twisted almost beyond recognition. Through the gap he could see burning brush along the riverbank below, blazing from the explosions.

He pulled himself higher. Another few feet, and he should be...

A strong hand grabbed his wrist. "Now will you start listening to me?"

Harlan looked up. It was Belson!

"You know, you didn't have to do all this just to get my attention," he said.

"Shut up and keep climbing."

With Belson's help, Harlan half crawled, half climbed the remaining few feet off the bridge. The five remaining team members were there, most nursing bleeding arms and torsos.

"Are we the only survivors?" Harlan asked as he dragged Mack off the bridge to safety.

"Two more checked in from the riverbank below," Belson said. "Hopefully there will be more."

Harlan turned toward the destroyed bridge. "They used the drones to lure us. The charges went off only after we were all on the bridge."

Belson nodded. "That's the way I see it."

Harlan pointed into the distance, where the night sky was lit with a vibrant orange glow. "It's the housing section. They'll be going after that now." He grabbed a rifle from one of the team members. "I'll get rid of a few of them to see if I can discourage their enthusiasm." He pitched Mack's leash to Belson. "Take Mack back to the tent area and turn him over to Kira. Make certain they stay safe. Then go and see what you can do about that housing section. Get going!" He was aiming at the nearest drone as he spoke. "And now let's see what I can do about you dirty sons of bitches."

————— • —————

Kira stood outside her tent with a pair of binoculars trained on the flashes of light coming from the other side of the island.

"Anything?" Sarah was suddenly standing beside her, holding her phone at her ear.

"Nothing since that series of explosions. Have you made contact with your security force?"

Sarah shook her head. "No. I think the cell service has been knocked out all over the island." She was frowning, troubled. "But I need to take these two guards and go to the labs. If we don't protect them from damage, we could lose years of research. Do you want to come with me?"

Kira looked back toward the orange sky. "You go ahead. I'll go toward the boarding section and make sure the dogs there are okay."

"Good idea. We have two staffers, Dane and Cathy, down there overnight, and I'm sure they can use any help you can give them. But take the ground path. It looks like the bridge may have taken a direct hit."

"Right." Kira sprinted toward the trees. "See you at the lab!" She followed the jungle path down to the riverbank and continued for a quarter mile. She rounded the bend and stopped short.

A direct hit indeed. There was little left of the once beautiful bridge, with the still-crumpling superstructure and pockets of flames marking the site.

She whispered a curse and moved through the wreckage. There were two corpses on the riverbank, still wearing their security uniforms and terrified facial expressions.

Keep moving. There was nothing she could do for them now.

She made her way down the riverbank until she reached a footbridge that would take her to the other side. She climbed the bank and moved through the trees until she finally spied the complex of buildings that made up the island's animal boarding facilities.

One of the buildings was on fire!

She ran toward it, even though she knew that the island's attackers could still be nearby.

"Dane! Cathy!" she shouted.

No answer.

Dogs barked inside the burning structure.

No!

She ran for the building's main entrance and yelled for Dane and Cathy again. She pulled on the door. Locked. The dogs' barking grew louder.

She had to get them out of there!

Kira ran around the building until she finally saw a large floor-to-ceiling picture window. She grabbed a beach chair and hurled it at the window.

It bounced away.

Shit.

She grabbed it and swung it at the window again. And again, over and over until a crack finally appeared.

Thank God.

The dogs were barking louder now.

She swung the chair again, and the window shattered. Over a

dozen dogs leaped through the opening, still barking and circling her. Kira ducked low and moved inside, checking to make sure there were no dogs in the private rooms. There were none.

Kira ran back and jumped through the window, where the dogs were still barking and whining. She clapped her hands. "This way. Come on!"

She led the dogs down the path toward the clinic, and before long, she realized *they* were leading *her* toward the clinic. The dogs' daily walks had obviously given them a working knowledge of the area. Kira turned back toward the burning building. Where were Dane and Cathy? Not in there, she was sure. Had they headed for—

"Thank the Lord!" It was Cathy, coming toward her from the direction of the clinic. And Dane was right behind her. "You got the dogs out. We ran down here to the clinic to get help from the soldiers, but they were already on their way to try to fight the fire. That's where everyone must have gone. The clinic was deserted."

Which meant that must be where Harlan had gone, too, Kira thought. "I'll go check." She was already turning around. "Look, can you and Dane take the dogs back and get them settled in the clinic for me? I'll send someone to help you as soon as possible."

"Sure," Cathy said. "That's our job. We'll take care of it."

"Thanks!" She was running back up the hill, heading toward the housing area. "I have to find Harlan and my dog, Mack..."

Kira found Mack almost immediately, but he wasn't at the fire. She found him tied securely to a pine tree right outside her tent and howling in desolation.

"Mack? What are you doing here? And where the hell is Harlan?" She untied him, and when she did, she saw the blood on his paws. Not Mack's blood. She stiffened. Mack appeared to be fine. Harlan's blood? What had happened to Harlan? She felt a chill run through her. It was absurd to feel this sense of panic. No one could take better care of himself than Harlan, with his military background and keen mind and sheer brilliance.

But none of those qualities could prevent a bullet from killing someone if the circumstances were just right.

And there had been bullets and explosives going off tonight.

Perhaps he'd gotten shot after he'd brought Mack back to the tent. It could be that he was lying somewhere in these hills bleeding. Helpless...

What the hell. Why stand here worrying when she had to *do* something. When she had to *find* him.

She ducked inside Harlan's tent and grabbed a khaki shirt she'd seen him wearing earlier in the day. She stepped out, untied Mack, and let him sniff the shirt. He lowered his head, turned, and started back through the woods, hot on Harlan's trail!

———— • ————

Damn Harlan! After miles of tracking, he was now just ahead of her, Kira realized. One more turn up ahead on the trail and she'd have him. And she just might kill the bastard. She was almost angry enough to do it. Just one more turn and she'd—

"Got you!"

Two strong hands grabbed her throat and threw her to the ground!

She couldn't breathe. She couldn't move. Who in the hell was this monster? Her throat was throbbing. Was it Taylor who—

"Kira? Son of a bitch. What are you doing here?"

It was *Harlan*! Indeed. Yes, she might kill him. She was coughing and still struggling for breath...

In the next instant, Mack had his sleeve in his teeth and shook it from side to side. Harlan finally released his grip on her throat.

Kira raised her palm. "Mack, down!"

Mack immediately released him.

Harlan backed away. "Why the hell are you—? Sorry, are you okay?"

She rolled away and clutched her throbbing neck. "Barely. No thanks to you."

"You shouldn't be here. This place could be crawling with Taylor's thugs. I thought someone was sneaking up on me. I could have broken your neck."

"You almost did, you idiot. And someone was sneaking up on you. It was *me*."

"Why on earth?"

"You didn't come back." She was trying to catch her breath as she pushed his arm away and struggled to a sitting position. "And then I heard the sounds coming from the bridge."

"So you came running straight for trouble," he growled as he pushed the hair away from her forehead and checked her for any wounds. "Not smart, Kira. Why didn't you stay put like I told you?"

"I tried. Because it seemed the most efficient thing to do. But then when you didn't come back right away, I decided to do what I thought best."

"It wasn't best." His fingers were moving over her face, and he stiffened as he felt the dampness. "That's not blood. Tears? You said you weren't hurt."

"I wasn't. But you were, and you bled all over Mack."

Harlan looked down as the dog gently licked his hand.

"Do you think I'd let you do that to me?" Kira said. "I told you that I did what I thought best. I had to free those dogs from a housing unit and take them down to the clinic where they'd be safe. You just got in my way."

"My apologies. But it definitely wasn't best in this case."

"Then you'd better start keeping your word so that I won't have to make decisions based on lies."

"They weren't lies. The situation just changed, and I had to change with it."

"You mean there was an opportunity and you decided to take advantage of it," she asked shakily. "Was it Taylor?"

"No, only a few of his men were using drones to attack us. I wanted to show them we're able to fight back."

"And enjoyed every minute, I'm sure." She got to her feet. "I could see how restless you were when you left."

He stood and grabbed her by the shoulders when she tried to

turn away. "Yes, as a matter of fact I did. But I was also tending to what needed to be done."

"I understand that." Her voice was suddenly fierce, her eyes glittering with anger as well as tears as she looked up at him. "But never again, Harlan. It was my fight, too, and I won't be left behind again. The next time you decide to 'tend' to business, you'll know I'm right behind you. I brought you into this and I won't let you do it alone. We're partners. I'm not going to have you risk your life if I'm not there to watch your back."

"Shh." His hands were suddenly gentle as they moved up from her shoulders to cup her cheekbones and brush a tear away. "We'll talk about it later. Heaven forbid I turn down a tough ally like you when I may need all the help I can get. I still have to meet your friend Kalim."

"No, we've already discussed that." She cleared her throat. "I just wanted you to know I accept my responsibilities where you're concerned. We're in this together."

"Whatever you say." He was pushing her gently toward the tents. "Now will you go to bed? I don't believe I'm going to need anyone to watch my back for the rest of the night."

"You can never tell." She was trying to smile. "I owe you. I'll be there for you if I think it's necessary."

He shook his head. "Kira, you might have heard I'm trained to take care of myself."

"So I understand. All that SEAL stuff that everyone raves about. I got to see it firsthand when Taylor closed in on me on those cliffs in Colorado. I pay my debts, Harlan." She looked down at Mack.

"You're lucky he didn't tear you apart. Mack is usually very protective. I think he realized it was you before I did, and he thinks of you as his buddy."

"I *am* his buddy."

Mack barked and wagged his tail.

Kira shook her head. "He probably thought we were playing a game. He's used to that here on the island."

"Not the kind of play I appreciate," he said. "Not with you, Kira."

"As you say, I'm tough." She didn't wait for him to reply. "I'll see you in the morning."

But she didn't move. She just stood there staring at him, somehow not wanting to leave him yet. She only wanted him to touch her once again.

And then he did touch her, reaching out to gently brush his hand against her neck. She flinched, and he jerked his hand away. "I *did* hurt you."

"No, you were the one bleeding. Maybe I should bandage it. Let me see it."

"It's nothing. I'll get a bandage when I get back to camp. It will give Belson something to do while I set up the work crews to help clear the bridge debris. You're the one who's going to have bruises." He touched her throat again.

Heat tingled through her this time. She inhaled sharply.

"I like that," he said softly. "Do you?"

She didn't answer directly. "I'm not sure. It was...unexpected." She went into her tent and whistled for Mack to come to her before she zipped it. "Good night, Harlan."

"Will you at least call me next time you decide you need to come to my rescue?" he asked gently. "If I promise to invite you along on all the fun and games?"

"That seems fair. But sometimes lately you've taken over all the action. Can I trust you?"

"You can trust me. I wouldn't dare do anything else. I need you to be where I can keep an eye on you at all times. Nothing could make this more clear than that moment tonight when I was on the verge of breaking your neck. I don't want to ever come that close again. Good night, Kira."

She heard his footsteps as he headed for his own tent and found herself smiling. She reached up and brushed her hand over her damp cheek and throat where he had touched her. It had been a wild, exciting, and upsetting evening, and she should want to forget it. But somehow she didn't. That moment had been special in a strange way, and she had wanted to keep it and Harlan with her for a little longer. It might change tomorrow, but right now she liked that feeling of closeness that had surrounded them and believed him when he'd said she could trust him...

Mack was nestling next to her because he had sensed her restlessness and wanted contact. She reached out and stroked him. "Did you have a good time tonight? I bet you did. I would have liked to have gone with you. Harlan is probably a good partner, but it wasn't fair to me. Next time, I get to go along..."

CHAPTER

9

"I *love* your island," Fiona shouted as she jumped out of the transport plane and ran toward Kira, who was coming down the hill to greet her. "I've already checked it out from the air, and Domino is going to love it, too." She grabbed Kira and turned her around in an exuberant circle. "He's a little nervous right now. I knew he would be, so I took the trip with him to soothe him. Though I don't really know why he should be. Those transport planes are luxurious as hell, and the horses are pampered like kings. I guess it's because he's not nearly as accustomed to being transported as Golden Boy. But he'll get over it. Golden Boy has had to be flown quite a bit since he became an Olympic superstar." She was motioning to one of the grooms to take Domino's lead. "The other transport plane landed an hour ago, and Harlan arranged to have Golden Boy taken to the stable and settled into a stall. He said to tell you to wait for him here until he gets back, that it was your responsibility to take care of me, and that Belson would be here in a few minutes." She made a face. "But I'd rather go up and get Domino settled. How about it?"

"Don't tempt her." Harlan was coming out of the clinic. "I've arranged breakfast for you, and she needs to introduce you to her good friend Sarah." He looked at Kira. "I thought you might like to be the one to do that, and I knew you'd want Fiona's first day to be as smooth as possible."

"No fun and games?" she asked with brows raised.

"Nary a one. I made a promise. Belson was told to bring you straight to the stables if you requested it. I thought that would be okay. But wouldn't you like to take her to meet Sarah?"

"You know I would." She turned and linked arms with Fiona. "Come on. She's an extraordinary woman and you'll see how lucky you are to have her in your corner. She taught me everything she knows about caring for animals and was right beside me whenever I wanted to experiment on something new and different." She looked over her shoulder at Harlan as she pulled Fiona toward the clinic. "I'll take care of Fiona. You and the groom can get Domino settled. If you're lucky, we might leave you a bite of breakfast."

He nodded and touched his hand meekly to his forehead. "Yes, ma'am. Whatever you say, ma'am." He was strolling toward the transport plane, gesturing to the groom to follow him. "I'll see you later, Fiona. It seems I have work to do."

Fiona gazed speculatively after him and then back at Kira. "Harlan is being very accommodating to you. Almost suspiciously so. It's usually my uncle who gives all the orders. Did I miss something?"

"Nothing that would be important to you. You'll still have all the security that you're accustomed to under his watch. Both you and your horses will be safe from any interference. We just clarified an agreement that we made about a few other details." She changed the subject. "He did tell you that we have to leave tonight for Egypt for a few weeks to take care of that business?"

Fiona nodded with a frown. "He called me last night. I told him I didn't like it. I'm not stupid. Usually whenever he goes anywhere and arranges protection for me, it has to do with Taylor. Coming here was going to be different, and I was relieved because I knew he wouldn't want to send you anywhere into danger after he'd just saved your life. Right?"

How could Kira explain that she was the one who had lured Harlan into risking his life by making this deal that gave him the chance to confront Taylor once more? Fiona had been a victim all her young life, and the only person she really cared about was Jack Harlan. Which meant the only thing Kira could do was to make the same promise she'd made Harlan. "I'll take good care of him. Nothing is going to happen to your uncle while we're in Egypt. He's just going to meet a friend of mine, and then we'll be coming back here and I'll start running diagnostics on your horses. Until then, you'll be in the hands of the trainers and vets who work here on Summer Island. They're experts hired by Sarah. You'll like all of them."

"I'm sure I will." Fiona shook her head ruefully. "And I promise I'll work very hard until you get back. If you'll promise to keep that promise you've just made me." She was nibbling nervously at her lower lip. "I can't lose Harlan, too, Kira. I can't tell you how good he's been to me. He's all I have."

"I know." Kira squeezed her arm. "You have nothing to worry about, I promise. Your uncle is very good at taking care of himself, and I'll take care of him, too. Now, can we forget everything but having a good time today here on this island I love? There are so many things I want to show you and tell you about how I trained Mack here." She saw Sarah coming out of the clinic and heading toward them and waved. "And how Sarah tried her very best to train me. Bless her heart. What a headache I was to her..."

———— • ————

SUMMER ISLAND
TWELVE HOURS LATER

The sun was going down in pink-and-violet splendor when Sarah walked Kira back to the jet that evening. "It was a good day. I like your Fiona. She's full of vim and vigor and maybe a little bit of the devil. She reminds me of you when you first came here. She has the same drive and stamina with those horses that you had with Mack and the other dogs." She chuckled as she glanced sideways at Kira. "I'll be glad to look in on her occasionally until you return, if you don't mind. That way, I won't miss you nearly as much."

"Are you kidding? I'll look forward to it, and she'll have someone to bond with that's not military or one of the horse brigade. She's going to miss Harlan."

"I can see how she might," Sarah said. "He's not only family, he's brilliant and charming and he's a good guy. By the way, where did she disappear to after dinner tonight?"

"She told me she was going to say good night to the horses at the stable and then meet us at the jet. I think she wanted a few moments with Harlan before he left. She's a little worried about him. She told me that he's always been good to her. She might even have a few plans that involve him and this trip. You can never tell what mischief Fiona will be up to."

"And how has he been to you?" Sarah asked. "You've appeared to be getting along well since I came here." She tilted her head, thinking. "What's not to like? Let's see...Besides all the things I mentioned...he's complicated, a scientific genius, a brilliant soldier and strategist. Many women would find him desirable enough to do some in-depth hunting in his direction. Why not?"

"You forgot that he can be very difficult."

"And...?"

Kira shrugged. "He's everything else you mentioned. What else can I say? I owe him. He saved my life and Mack's. But that's not why I'm going to get on his jet and fly off to Egypt with him. We both have a purpose and we have to do what's necessary."

"Taylor?"

"That's a big part. I want him out of our lives."

"Any other reason?"

Kira laughed. "You're matchmaking again, aren't you? Back off."

"I saw...something. I just thought it might be hope on the horizon."

"I owe Harlan," Kira said again. "And he wants Taylor dead if he can talk me into it. Not exactly the most romantic circumstances for you to work with, Sarah. Go home to John where you have the real thing."

"I do...constantly." She laughed. "And I can't wait, even after all these years together. That's how I know it *is* the real thing. I'm just trying to spread the good word to all and sundry."

"Kira!" Fiona was opening the jet cockpit door and then running toward them across the tarmac. "It's about time you got here, Kira. I've decided I need your help and support. I was just trying to talk Harlan into taking me along with you to Egypt. I've never been there, and you told me there are some magnificent horses raised by your friend Kalim that I might be able to persuade Harlan to buy for my stable."

"I doubt if Kira made any promises." Harlan was getting out of the plane and coming around to greet them. "I tried before, and her friend Kalim wouldn't even see me," he said dryly. "But I'll promise to try again while I'm there with Kira. She might have influence that I don't." He smiled at Kira. "I agree with Fiona that you're running a little late. I was about to come and look for you."

"I didn't think that you were in that much of a hurry. You said sunset." She gazed out at the red-streaked sky. "I'd say I'm right on time."

"You would be...if I hadn't decided we needed to leave a little earlier."

Kira glanced at him in surprise. "Then that was obviously your doing. That's hardly my fault, Harlan."

"True, that's why I was going to go find you. I didn't say I was right about it."

"And you admit it? Amazing."

"It does happen occasionally," he said solemnly. "I just try to keep it under control."

Kira tried to keep her lips from twitching with amusement. "Like you do everything else?"

He nodded. "It's so rare. I knew you'd understand."

Kira nodded as she looked back at Fiona. "Not really. But I do understand you'd probably want to talk to Fiona alone to say goodbye."

His eyes narrowed. "But since I've noticed the two of you have become very close indeed during the past few days, it may be you thought she'd have a better chance of getting whatever she wanted if she had more time to concentrate her attention on persuading me?" He gave Fiona a quick kiss on the cheek. "It's okay, Fiona. This is something I do understand."

"No, you don't," Kira said as she took a step closer to him. "Not everyone wants something from you, Harlan. Fiona doesn't. I'm sure she'd rather have your company than one of Kalim's horses."

"I was joking." Harlan was no longer smiling. "Sometimes I can only give what I can, when I can," he said quietly. "And I believe she knows me well enough to realize that. If she doesn't, then I've completely failed her."

Kira could tell he meant every word; she was probably the one at fault, she thought ruefully. As usual, she might have jumped too quickly to conclusions when it came to someone as complicated as

Harlan. "Then I apologize for poking my nose into your business when I had no right," she said. "It won't happen again."

He shrugged. "You were just protecting Fiona from me. It's no surprise. I've noticed you have a habit of trying to save the world and all the creatures in it. You didn't realize that Fiona and I don't need saving, not even from each other."

Then he walked across the tarmac toward where Sarah was standing and shook her hand. "It's been a pleasure getting to know you, Sarah. I'll tell John he's a lucky man. Thank you for letting my guards tear up your beautiful island. I'll make sure they repair any damage. You'll find it better than when you turned it over to me." He grimaced. "And the first thing on my list is a brand-new runway that will accommodate all the jets we'll need to bring in the rebuilding crews."

"That sounds great. I'm not worried," Sarah said. "You're an honest man, Harlan. Just take care of Kira, and we'll call it even."

"If I'm allowed." He held out his hand to help Kira into the plane. "Sometimes it's difficult."

Then he turned and took Fiona into his arms. "Take care of yourself. I'll work hard on getting you a horse from Kalim."

She held him close and said huskily, "I don't want his stinking horse. I'd find a way to get it myself if I did. Just come back soon, Harlan."

"I have every intention of doing that." He grinned. "And if you ever meet him, I wouldn't call any of Kalim's fantastic horses 'stinking' to his face. It's not only rude, it's inaccurate, and we might want to do business with him in the future."

"I'll remember." She was backing away from him across the tarmac. "And I'll take care of Domino for you, Kira. But come back soon or he might forget you. I can't be expected to do everything, you know."

"He is *your* horse, Fiona," Kira reminded her as she put Mack in his seat in the row behind her own. "But we'll both be back before you know it." Then she was buckling her own seat belt as Harlan started the engines and the jet taxied down the runway.

She didn't speak again until Harlan was in the air and setting their course. Then she turned to face him. "Why were you going to leave the island early? Is there a problem? I thought you said Captain Darue had everything under control." She stiffened. "More drones?" Then she relaxed. "No, you wouldn't have left if there had been any trouble."

"I'm glad you have that much faith in me at least." He nodded. "No current danger. I just thought there was a possibility we might need more aircraft once we've reached Kalim's Hathor. As it happens, I have a factory outside Morocco where it might be convenient to store my second Gulfstream if Taylor decides to make the situation difficult for us in the area. I sent Belson to fly the Gulfstream out earlier today with orders to get it ready...just in case."

"Why would you think Taylor might cause problems in the area? Is that a possibility?"

"Anything is a possibility where Taylor is concerned. There are hundreds of islands in the Mediterranean, some of them not even charted. Plus over a thousand Egyptian islands alone. It wouldn't surprise me if Taylor had found himself a cozy little paradise somewhere near where the media might have mentioned you'd been working lately."

She made a face. "That's not exactly reassuring. What are the odds?"

"Nothing for you to worry about yet. I have no idea. That's another thing Belson is going to try to determine on this trip. Besides collecting a few reports from my main executives in charge of engineering in the lab. Something about what you said regarding those wells off Kalim's island of Hathor made me wonder if one of my current projects might turn out to be useful to us."

"Why?" Kira frowned. "What kind of factory is it? What are you building in this lab?"

"That's what I'm wondering." He smiled mischievously. "I've found my work has a habit of changing and transforming as it goes along. I'm never sure until the final tests."

"Then heaven help us."

His grin deepened. "Oh, I do hope it does. But I think I can assure you it's not a super hydrogen bomb. No, it's actually a lab where I've been doing some preliminary research for the Pentagon. It's still in its early stages, but I plan to keep it out of the hands of the politicians until I decide whether I want to let them buy it. So I set up the factory in Morocco where I could have sole control."

"Your favorite state of being," Kira said mockingly.

"Yep," he agreed. "And I've noticed you have definite leanings in that same direction. You gave me hell in Colorado."

"You wouldn't let me do my job the way I wanted to." She paused.

"But we're still taking your jet to Hathor first? Kalim would regard it as an insult if we consider him an afterthought and not the main attraction."

"He's definitely the main attraction," Harlan said sourly. "I can hardly wait to meet him. I'll phone Belson on our way to see the great man and have him bring me the engineering reports after I'm sure Kalim's not going to behead me."

"Don't be absurd." She couldn't keep her lips from twitching. "I've heard Kalim hasn't beheaded anyone in decades. I'm certain he wouldn't make an exception in your case." She added thoughtfully, "Unless he thought it would gain him some kind of additional prestige among his people on Hathor. You are considered very important in some circles."

"Very amusing."

She was chuckling. "Relax. Fiona would never forgive me if I let anyone hurt you. You're quite safe."

"What a relief." Harlan shot her a glance. "But it's a long trip, and you've already had an exhausting day. I'd feel better if you'd take a nap on the plane, so that you'll be fresh when you have to confront Kalim and his merry band to save me."

"You might be right." She leaned over the seat and gave Mack a pat on his head. "When I'm sleeping, keep him company, Mack. I honestly believe he's trying to help us, and we can't let anything happen to him. Just like he took care of us... We have to regard it as our duty and privilege."

"Thank you for clarifying that for him," Harlan said wryly. "I'm truly touched."

———————•———————

Harlan gave a low whistle as his jet circled the private airport on Kalim's island of Hathor. "Very luxurious. Plus, I've seen air force training centers that didn't have as much ground equipment or personnel as what we're looking at down there. And I think he's got more military personnel than Captain Darue has in the escort coming out of that mini-castle down by that lake." Harlan was gazing at what appeared to be a gleaming, white marble palace with lattice carvings and curved windows that were pure Indo-Islamic in nature. "It looks a little like the Taj Mahal."

"Kalim will be pleased you're impressed," Kira said. "Everything about the island is meant to look like it was built for royalty. It's a family tradition passed from father to son for generations. I believe it may have started out as a question of pharaoh envy. After all, they lived like kings, ruling everyone on their property; the pharaohs came to them when they needed fine horses for battle or breeding. They probably didn't see why they shouldn't have everything surrounding them just as splendid as the royals possessed. Though actually, Kalim isn't nearly as ostentatious in his tastes as his parents and grandparents were. You should see the photos."

"I'll pass for the time being." He glanced at Kira. "Sarah said that neither of you is fond of palaces. Did she see where you were living when you were working with Kalim?"

"No, because I never lived here. I spent my first night in one of those palatial rooms and then I took my backpack and sleeping bag and moved up into the hills where I could be with the herds."

When Kalim wanted to see or talk to me, he'd come visit where I was working that day."

"And he let you get away with that?"

"Why shouldn't he? He respects hard work, and he wanted me to complete my research with his horses and the dogs. It was important to him. He works hard himself, and his family made sure that he grew up appreciating the beauty of the property and, most of all, the horses themselves. Everything that came onto the property had to be top quality. Even *Hathor*, the Egyptian name of the island, means 'everything beautiful in life.'" She gestured to the cliffs on the north side of the island. "In time, I even became accustomed to thinking of that north shore as beautiful, too. It's exciting and dangerous and definitely fascinating. The cliff is jagged and sheer, with a drop of over three hundred feet to where the Mediterranean crashes against the rocks below. During storms, that seascape has almost hurricane force, and the waves are very rough. Kalim told me that, during the time of the pharaohs, there were frequent shipwrecks right there on the north shore. Ships from Rome, Egypt, Greece, Macedonia, and the rest of the world came through here on their way to larger cities on the mainland. That was why I went down to explore the caves in that area. And those horses Kalim owns spend well over half a year in the upper pastures, and I had to decide what trees and border plants would be best to keep them calm and avoid any accidents that would send them tumbling off that cliff and yet give them soul-freedom."

"Soul-freedom?"

"You're well known as an environmentalist. I believe you're

aware that animals have souls, and freedom is important to them. It's particularly obvious when you run across a dog like Mack or a horse that's as highly developed as some of Kalim's."

He nodded. "Or perhaps also a few elephants that have wandered across my path. I'm not arguing with you about the concept—merely questioning the descriptive phrase. But perhaps I shouldn't have bothered. You were bound to come up with something unique to you. Well, how did you take care of Kalim's problem?"

"The best solution turned out to be super-intelligent dogs like Mack who could be trained to herd and yet still provide a familiar enough aura that the horses would accept them as belonging to the herd."

"*Your* solution?"

She nodded. "And one I'm proud to claim. They work beautifully together. It keeps them safe."

"Then Kalim owes you big time," Harlan said. "I hope he paid you well."

"It was more of a trade-off," Kira said. "Though I did insist that he show me those cave shafts and old wells that he'd promised, and I spent a good deal of time scuba diving and exploring the rocks and reefs. He even went with me a few times to show me where he and his friends had explored when they were boys. Some of the sea life around the island was very dangerous, and he wanted to make sure I'd be safe."

"I believe I'm beginning to approve of Kalim a little more than I did. Do you see him down there in that crowd?"

She nodded. "You won't have any trouble picking him out. He's the one with the gray-flecked beard and the air of authority. He's in his forties, but he's still one of the best horsemen I've ever met and tough as nails. He'd have to be able to run this island and keep his followers in line. He'll probably meet us at the airport as we land. I told you Sarah said he was very eager to meet you and check you out."

"Then let's get to it," Harlan said as he started to land. "This should be interesting. It's been a long time since I've had to struggle to get an approval from anyone." He shot her a glance. "Except you. But then you're an exception to any rule." They were on the ground now, and one of Kalim's followers was opening the cockpit doors. Harlan didn't wait for Kalim to step forward but got out of the plane and smiled at the fortyish, bearded man dressed in black-and-white clothing who was eagerly stepping toward Kira with outstretched hands. "You're Jabir Kalim, I trust? Jack Harlan. I'm delighted to meet you. As you can see, I've brought an old friend to visit you. I've been eager to see your beautiful island, and she thought you wouldn't mind if I tagged along."

Kalim's demeanor froze as he met Harlan's eyes. "I've heard of you," he said coolly. "But not from my friend Kira." He glanced at Kira. "Sarah Logan told me this man put your life in danger recently, and you were hospitalized. She approves of him. I'm not sure I do."

"Then you should," Kira said. "The doctors said I might have died if he hadn't saved me." She chuckled. "He even saved Mack,

Kalim. I'm sure you approve of that. I might not have been worthwhile in your eyes, but you know how your horses love Mack."

Kalim smiled faintly. "True. They would follow him anywhere. But I also found value in you on occasion, and you should not have permitted anyone I did not know to tend to your wounds. Why didn't you phone me so that I could send someone?"

"Perhaps because I kept falling unconscious? Yes, that must be it. Harlan was there to wake me and send me to that blasted hospital." Kira added, "And you were not, old friend. So stop being bad-tempered and thank him for taking care of me so I can torment you for the foreseeable future."

"Which you will probably do." Kalim turned back to Harlan. "I suppose she's right. In this instance she should have taken advantage of any safe harbor that was available." He frowned. "But she could have chosen someone more to suit me. As soon as I talked to Sarah, I did my own investigation into your background."

"And what horrible truth did you find out about me?" Harlan asked mockingly. "Even Kira couldn't find anything that was too terrible except one single flaw that she found too shocking to accept."

Kalim turned to Kira with interest. "Yes?"

She nodded. "Though you probably won't find it all that bad. He wants to kill the man who murdered his brother."

Kalim gazed at her thoughtfully. "You're right. I find that perfectly natural behavior. You've always been a bit squeamish."

Harlan threw back his head and laughed. "Forget everything that I've said about your old friend here. I'm beginning to like him."

"Be quiet, Harlan," Kira said. "Just because you have the same cultural beliefs in some areas doesn't mean you're blood brothers. Kalim realizes that I couldn't have fought harder to keep all his horses, his livestock, and the other people in his village alive and well. We just sometimes disagreed about the methods."

"As did we," Harlan said straight-faced. He turned back to Kalim. "Did you hear anything else that you found objectionable about me? If so, speak up and I'll get back in this plane and head out to Morocco. However, Kira might find me very useful if you allow me to stay. She offered me a deal and, if you agree to her terms, we might all come out of this with everything we want."

Kalim stared at him for a long moment. "Actually, I did find out something that displeased me, but not about the way you took her to that hospital. A number of years ago, you sent me an offer for three of my horses. I refused you. Your emissary was quite determined, and he kept nagging me."

Harlan nodded. "You refused me, and I wanted those horses for my niece. I told him to do his best."

Kalim nodded. "Oh, he did, and because of who you were I had newspaper and media people trying to get here to my island and interview me. You can imagine how that annoyed me."

"Absolutely," Harlan said. "But you were the best, and you had the finest horses in the world at that time. My niece, Fiona, deserved the best. She won two Olympic medals the next year, and she didn't even have one of your horses to do it. Think what she could have done if she'd had one of your magnificent beauties to help her."

"They're still the finest horses in the world," Kalim said. "And you're probably going to try to get me to sell one to you?"

"Yes, best to best is my policy. Isn't it yours? But I'm going to try to bring Fiona to your island so that you can see why you should do it."

"Best to best," Kalim repeated. "Yes, that's always been my policy as well." He glanced at Kira. "That's why I lured you here, isn't it?" He smiled. "And you haven't been sorry, have you?"

She shook her head. "But it was kind of a mutual arrangement. I hope neither one of us will be sorry that we came together."

He was silent a moment. "You want me to listen to him?"

"I wouldn't have brought him here if I didn't. I believe it will benefit all of us. You should at least try to understand him. That's what I'm trying to do. I owe him, Kalim."

"And I owe him nothing."

"But you might in the future. He's a man whom a good many people turn to in a jam."

"Did you?"

"No, I was too stubborn. But next time I might, as long as I can find a way to pay him back." She hesitated. "And I might recommend him to you if you get in trouble. Because you're my friend, and I can trust him to watch out for you."

"That's a fine recommendation. If I needed such a thing, which I do not." Kalim shrugged. "I will listen." He strode toward the palace bordered by the lake. "But I promise nothing."

"You never do," Kira said. "But I should tell you that I've been hosting his niece, Fiona, on Summer Island. I think you'd like her... she's magnificent with horses. Absolutely magic. I was very impressed. I know she'd like you. In a way you're like her uncle Harlan here..."

"I beg your pardon?" Kalim looked faintly enraged. "I thought I'd made it clear that I don't regard that comparison as a compliment."

"Ditto," Harlan said. "Except that Kalim was clever enough to talk you into coming here, Kira, when my agent evidently failed to do his job for me. I always appreciate success in any form. I think you might—" Harlan stopped as a servant opened the front door of the palace for Kalim with a low bow and then quickly scurried away when he saw his frowning expression. Harlan smiled with amusement and then dropped down on an elaborately carved bench beside the ornate arched palace entrance. "And now I believe I'll not intrude on you any longer. I'll sit out here in your lovely garden while Kira goes in and has her discussion with you regarding our arrangement and whether you still want me to leave after she finishes. Since she appears to still be in your good graces, I take it you'll want her to go up into the hills as you've done in the past and work with your horses?" He added, "However, you'll have to put up with me accompanying her wherever she goes while she's here on your property. I'm not fond of her situation at present. I've given my word to keep her safe."

"She's perfectly safe with any of my people on Hathor and absolutely secure with me," Kalim said coldly. "She will tell you that."

Harlan shook his head. "We made a deal. She won't break it. Will you, Kira?"

She slowly shook her head. "Not as long as you keep your word." She gazed at Kalim. "But some aspects of our deal depend on whether you will honor your promise to me regarding that treasure that I found for you, Kalim."

He stiffened. "I never break my word."

"I don't believe you would, but I agreed to give half my share of the treasure to Harlan for services rendered. Will you still agree?"

He scowled. "It's a foolish deal and not at all like you. I have no desire to give this Harlan anything."

"Yet I was the one who discovered the location of the treasure, and that was the deal we made. Fifty–fifty, and we dispose of it however we want. I've already needed Harlan to help me with a portion of it while I was on Summer Island. I may need to use him again, later." She stared him in the eye. "I repeat, is our deal still in place, Kalim?"

He hesitated. "I still don't like it." He made a face. "But of course it is. I'm an honorable man."

"Good." She gestured to Harlan. "Then I'll see you shortly, Harlan. Enjoy the sunshine here in the garden while I take Kalim into the library to fill him in. Because it's only fair I tell him all the details. It shouldn't take me very long if I don't have to keep the two of you from sparring with each other."

"Or if he doesn't change his mind." Harlan gazed steadily at Kalim. "Until then, just keep her safe when I'm not available to do it myself, which will be very rare." He added softly, "Do you hear me? I do hope so, or I'll be coming after you. I want to trust you because Kira does, but I'm having a few problems." He leaned back on the bench and took out his phone. "I have to make a few calls to get information from my employees in Morocco and tell them that I might require assistance if I find you less honorable than you claim. Run along, Kira. Do your duty by your old friend, but remember, I'll always be here when you need me . . ."

"I could hardly forget," Kira said. "And I don't need your permission, Harlan. Though neither of you has made it easy for me, I'll continue to do exactly what I please." She gestured to Kalim to follow her. "He's right, I'm going back to the hills after I tell you what you need to know, and I hope the next time we get together it will be a good deal more harmonious. I'm taking Harlan with me because he knows horses and he can help me with the herds. He might even know them better than you, Kalim. I've seen the stables at his home outside Paris, and I was very impressed. He also knows Joseph Taylor better—I'll tell you about him as soon as we reach the library. Who knows? He might even manage to keep me alive as an added bonus. I'll see you shortly, Harlan." She slammed the front door behind her as she and Kalim headed for the library.

CHAPTER

10

"How's it going?" Belson asked when Harlan's call reached him at the Moroccan factory a few minutes later. "Kalim has a rough reputation with the executives here. It appears he's a very important man in this area, and he doesn't hesitate to make his wishes known. Is he giving you a hard time?"

"About what I expected from the reports I've had on him," Harlan said. "But Kira is managing to keep us both under control."

"Is she?" Belson laughed. "It doesn't surprise me. She even handles Fiona fairly well, and you're the only other person who can do that with any degree of efficiency."

"I didn't call you to give you a report on my dealings with Kalim. What have you heard about Joseph Taylor?"

"He's not been apprehended by either the police or the governor's special forces." He hesitated. "But I asked the local gendarmes' informants here in Morocco and they said there had been a number of questions being asked here in the past few days by some of Taylor's local scumbags."

"Specify."

"Your name was prominent. Any news about treasure hunters. Activities of your nearby factories." He paused. "Activities of Kira Drake."

"Shit!"

"You knew it was coming."

Yes, he had, but it didn't make the confirmation any more palatable. "Taylor is moving fast as usual."

"Bribery is his middle name," Belson said. "You should hear the offers I've had. He knows I work for you. They've probably tried to bribe the other employees at the factory, too."

"Not Hannah Bryson."

"No, but she runs an entire engineering crew. Most of them are loyal to her, yet it only takes one Judas to blow top-secret material. Good news, though. She said to tell you that her work is done and ready for testing. Just let her know when and where you'd like your demonstration."

"I'll do that. In the meantime, keep Bryson and Yang, her chief engineer, safe. I don't want Taylor to get hold of either of them. Have you had any info about Taylor's having a possible location in this area?"

"No, but I've had a few solid leads about inquiries he's made lately."

"Follow up on them."

"I'm already doing it." Belson sighed. "When are you going to trust me?"

"But then you wouldn't be able to show off how clever you are and suitably impress me. Now put Yang on the line. I want details from my factory. If it turns out as well as I think it will, this could be extremely exciting..."

———— • ————

Harlan was still on the phone when Kira came out into the garden thirty minutes later, but he hung up immediately. A custom-made Bentley truck was pulling up in the driveway, piloted by a young man of nineteen whom Kira knew very well. He smiled broadly as he stopped in front of Kira and stuck his head out the window. "It's good you're back, Kira," he called out. "Kalim has been in a terrible mood. He hasn't let me go down to the shore once since you've been gone. I can't convince him that being a herdsman is really sissy work. I like the horses, but I'm a man who needs the ocean to complete me."

"So you've told me many times," Kira said. "Well, I'm sorry, but you're back with the herds for a while now. So get used to it."

"I already know." He sighed. "Kalim sent me down to the jet to pick up both sets of luggage to take up the hills to the summer camp. I'll deposit both in your tents the minute I drop you off. But it won't compare to going down to the sea. Can't you do something about it? Kalim listens to you."

The boy looked so disappointed, she found herself saying sooth-ingly, "Maybe we'll be able to do a little scuba later so you can exer-cise that manliness you're so proud of." She gestured to Harlan. "Aban, this is Jack Harlan. Aban is one of the best scuba divers on the island, Harlan. Kalim used to assign him to go with me when he thought I needed an escort."

Aban grinned. "She already had a good deal of experience. And after two weeks, she knew our waters well enough to lose me and go off by herself. She was so good that I didn't worry about her getting into trouble, even though we're not supposed to dive alone."

"And he never said a word to Kalim," Kira told Harlan. "Though I think Kalim must have found out on his own. He usually does."

Aban nodded. "He never said anything to me. But you know he has spies all over the island. And you were valuable to him."

Harlan was gazing at him thoughtfully. "I can see how Kalim might have been irritated with you if you lost Kira deliberately or otherwise."

"You might have trouble losing Harlan," Kira said to Aban. "He was a decorated SEAL. Be kind to him, Harlan."

"There are always ways to get where you want to go," Har-lan said. "It depends if he wants it badly enough. Evidently Aban wanted you to have as much freedom as he did down under the sea or he would have been more careful." He opened the passen-ger door for her. "Aban is going to show me some of the horses I've been hearing so much about. And he was willing to risk his boss's wrath to give it to you. I approve enormously." He glanced at Aban and smiled as he got into the car to sit beside Kira. "But not when it might be applied to me and my situations. Do we understand each other?"

Aban met his gaze for a long moment. Then he quickly nodded as he started the car. "Yes, we do. Very clearly. I'm totally at your disposal."

"You didn't have to be so stern with him," Kira murmured to Harlan. "He's just a kid."

"And I want him to live a long and enjoyable life. If he pays attention to the rules, he has every chance of getting there. How long do you think he'd last in Taylor's world? I'm surprised Kalim put up with it."

"He likes Aban. He wouldn't want to punish him. Aban was one of the boys he went scuba diving with in the past."

"Then Kalim's softer than I thought."

"Don't we all have our soft spots? You have Fiona."

"And you have Sarah Logan." He was leaning forward staring out the windshield at the scenery on the road ahead of them. "Is this another tent city like the one on Summer Island?"

"Not exactly," she said. "Though it is a tent city. You've seen all the beautiful flowers and waterfalls and landscapes at Summer Island. It's always been a place of serenity and healing. Sarah built Summer Island almost from scratch to be an animal hospital and sanctuary. She used to live and work in Arizona and commute to California, where John had his main offices. But one day, she visited Summer Island, and she fell in love. And since John was already in love with her and wanted to give her everything in the world, I guess he thought he'd start with Summer Island. Animals who'd been given up on by their vets were brought there from all over the world and were saved in surprising numbers, thanks to Sarah and her crew. The island became a mecca for researchers in the field."

"Like you?"

"Why not? It was beautiful, and it gave me everything I needed as far as research was concerned. Hathor, Kalim's property, looks wilder and more like a vagabond camp than anything else. Half beachy island and twisted trees and those stormy-looking mountains. The wild horses and Greco-Roman-influenced architecture add to the atmosphere, and so do the villagers, who are less dependent on technology than any of the workers at the modern clinics on Summer Island."

Harlan nodded. "It's also quite beautiful in an entirely different way." He was gazing at nothing but shining gold-white sand on the road ahead, which almost resembled a mirage. Yet the sand turned suddenly to shadowy darkness as they entered the foothills of the mountains and huge boulders and tall trees surrounded them.

And then he saw the horses fading in and out of the shadows as they ran through those trees! They reminded him of streaks of lightning. "Beautiful horses. All that power...magnificent."

Kira was watching his expression. "Yes. Now you know what you missed when Kalim wouldn't sell you those horses. They're totally fantastic. Wonderful. But you're not seeing everything. You're not seeing my work. I think I was kind of wonderful myself, don't you?"

Then he saw them. Dogs. Several dogs of all different colors and breeds running after those wonderful horses, weaving in and out, watching for all hazards. Guiding. Herding? He couldn't tell from this distance, but it must be what they were doing.

He turned to Kira. "That was what you were doing when you were working for Kalim?"

"I was working with the horses, too. But I'd just started with them. Because of the climate and ground differences, we needed super-intelligent dogs like Mack to guide the horses to safety if necessary. And I had to know if size or breed made a difference, so there were a number of experiments I had to conduct. We were getting along so well that Kalim was giving me hell about leaving here when I found it necessary to go after other jobs."

"So he offered you the treasure as a bribe to have you stay?"

She shrugged. "It was hard to resist when the animals were my first love anyway. I had no desire to hunt down the Taylors of the world. I only agreed to the assignment to please Sarah."

"And then you almost got yourself killed to do it."

"I'm here now. I can go back to work today if I wish."

"As long as Taylor doesn't show up to get in your way. I'd lay odds that he's making his plans now to do just that. I tried to tell you that was the way it would probably go down."

"Yes, you did." She wrinkled her nose. "But I didn't want to think about it. I still don't."

"Then leave it to me."

She shook her head. "His men almost killed those dogs in the boarding facility on Summer Island, but I managed to save them.

Yet he's already mentioned that treasure the media has been yammering about to me. What if he tries to track me down? What if he comes here?"

"I don't have the slightest doubt that he will. We'll take care of it."

"No, I'll take care of it." She drew a deep breath. "But right now I don't want to think about that asshole. I want to show you those horses and my wonderful dogs I've worked so hard to train. The hill country where we've built corrals to summer the horses is right around the next bend. Don't you want to see it all?"

He was gazing at her glowing face and eyes. "You bet I do," he said gently. "I can't wait." He reached down and stroked Mack. "Neither can he. He's practically trembling, he wants to join them so badly. Did you use him to train the dogs?"

"Of course. Otherwise the pups would have thought it was a game. They had to know it was serious business. Mack's a great example." The truck was coming to a stop, and she threw open the door. "Go say hello, Mack!"

Mack didn't wait for a second order. He was out of the truck and being surrounded by the other dogs in the clearing.

Kira jumped out and climbed the fence next to the huge corral. "Come and see, Harlan!"

Then he was sitting next to her on the top fence railing and Aban was leaning against the truck, laughing as he watched the dogs. "This isn't so bad," he called out to Kira. "You've taught them well. I think they have much better manners than that shark who chased me the last time we went down to the bay before you deserted us."

"I didn't desert you."

"Kalim thought you did. He was sulking and then he started worrying, which was even worse." Aban strolled toward the herders who were gathered on the other side of the corral preparing the horses' oats for bags. He started helping them. "But I forgive you because I have a good soul." He glanced at Harlan, his eyes dancing with mischief. "Can't you tell by the way I allowed you to intimidate me before? I wanted you to feel safe with me." Then he ducked through the bars of the corral and was instantly surrounded by the other herders.

Kira struggled not to smile. "Yes, couldn't you tell? He's a scamp of the first order."

"It's obvious that he's shown his true colors." Harlan shook his head. "Now you have to show me all the glories of your wonderful dogs and tell me about each one of these horses that Kalim will probably never let me buy. Then we'll have supper and sit by the fire and look up at the stars, and maybe have a glass of wine while you let me get to know all those herders you work with. We'll discuss how we're going to manage to keep everyone safe and still hold on to enough of the treasure you discovered to fund all your medical charities and save the animals that we've almost destroyed on the planet. How does that sound?"

She gazed at him uncertainly. "It sounds like you're going to be cheated out of your share of our partnership."

"Does it? But I almost always come out on top. It just may not be in the usual fashion. And as I told Aban, you have to want it bad enough." His voice lowered to velvet softness. "Because if you'll let me, I'm going to also ask you to take me to your tent and let me touch you in all the ways I've wanted to do since that night on Summer Island. Do you think you could let me do that?" He jumped down off the corral fence and stood in front of her, every muscle tense. "Because I'm beginning to think I've never wanted anything more. Show me your world up here, Kira." He held out his hand and took her own. "I promise you won't be sorry."

His hand felt strong, as strong as it had been that night on the cliffs when he had saved her from Taylor, and all the other nights when he had held her hand as he kept her from slipping away after he had brought her into his home and cared for her. "I don't think I will," she whispered. She shook her head. "But it could be a mistake for both of us."

"Take a chance. I've never seen you afraid to do that, Kira."

What was she thinking? she wondered with sudden impatience. He was right, she'd always reached out for every experience, and this was no different. Her hand tightened on his and she pulled him toward the dogs in the center of the corral. "Then by all means come on and I'll show you how terrific Mack can be at setting a prime example, and then as a teacher, with the pups. I don't believe I told you that he can also swim like a dolphin when I take him into the water with me."

"Obviously a dog of many talents. And then?"

"I believe it's a great idea that you let all the herders get to know you. I want them all to like you and realize why I brought you here. You seem to have quite a few good ideas."

"You haven't even addressed the best one yet." He was staring intently into her eyes. "What comes next, Kira?"

She couldn't look away from him. He was smiling quizzically at her and was everything that she desired at this moment. She could see how much he wanted her, and dear heavens she could feel the pulse pounding in her wrists and the way her breasts were taut and swelling with how much she wanted him. For tonight at least, she knew that she was going to do everything, take as much as she could from what he was offering her. She smiled brilliantly. "Then we'll see where we go from there, Harlan."

———— · ————

MAIN CAMPFIRE

FOUR HOURS LATER

"Have you noticed how good I've been?"

Kira looked up as Harlan smiled and knelt across the campfire from her. "Good?"

He nodded. "I've gotten to know most of your herder friends, and I believe they like me. I've let you ignore me most of the evening while they told me about their favorite horses and how much they admire your work. I've taken Mack for a walk around the camp to become very familiar with it." He held up a bottle of red wine. "And I bribed Aban to find someone in camp who would sell me a bottle of fine wine. I've gotten pretty close to the end of the list. Don't you think I should get a reward?"

She shook her head and smiled faintly. "Heavens, no. You would have done all that anyway. That's what it means to be Jack Harlan. Almost from the moment I met you, I could tell you had to be the best, know more than anyone else, take the most chances. Ask anyone."

He gave a mock sigh. "No reward?"

"I didn't say that." She got to her feet. "I've been watching you all evening and admiring the way you made yourself a star in Kalim's desert firmament. I was just wondering who should receive the reward. After all, I brought you here."

She turned on her heel and strode away from the fire. "And I was also thinking that I hoped when you took Mack for that walk, you found out where my tent is located."

He was laughing. "Oh, yes. That was definitely one of the first things I noticed."

But Kira was gone, streaking away from the main camp and toward her tent beside the lake.

She ducked into the tent a moment later and sat down near the door to wait for him. She was breathing hard. Her heart was pounding. He'd be here soon. In another few minutes. She lit her lamp, her gaze fixed on the tent opening. And then he was inside the door. She jumped to her feet and was in his arms.

She kissed him once. Twice.

"Well, hello," he muttered, "I'm glad to see you, too." He tried to pull her closer.

But she shook her head and pushed him away. "Not yet. I have something to say to you."

"Not now." He was pulling her down on the camp bed. "Unless it's no, but I don't think it is." He cupped her face in his two hands as he whispered, "Because I don't know if I can take it otherwise. I've discovered you're like a fever…"

"You're not listening to me, Harlan. I have to say this." She turned her head away from him. "It's not no," she said jerkily. "I don't know if it will ever be no when I'm with you. But you should realize you're not under any obligation to me. You don't owe me anything because I talked you into this partnership thinking I might need help."

"What a relief." He buried his lips in her throat. "I can't tell you how I was worrying about the way you tricked me by offering me a fortune in gold and jewels. It was keeping me awake nights."

"Shut up. I'm being serious. Ever since we came together, you've been helping me, saving me, stepping in when I most needed you. I'm the one who owes you. I just want you to know that I'm doing this because it's what I want. If all you want is a one-night stand, then I'll understand. I'm prepared for it."

He lifted his head and gazed down at her. "Truly?"

She stiffened but then nodded. "I'm trying to be honest with you." Then she stared into his eyes and said fiercely, "But to be honest, I have to tell you that I don't like the idea, and I might try to change your mind. Because you make me feel… Oh, hell, I don't know what you make me feel. But I had to warn you, because I don't remember feeling like this ever before." She pulled his head down and kissed him again. "Okay?"

"I'm duly warned." His hands were on the top buttons of her

shirt. "Now is it all right if I take your clothes off and get inside you? I want you so badly, you're driving me crazy."

"Oh, I'm so glad." She was tearing off the rest of her clothes and pulling him down on her bed. "That's exactly what I wanted." She gasped as his hands caressed her stomach and slid lower. "Though I...did mean what I said...but I can't think when you do...that." She arched upward and then spasmed helplessly and gave a low moan at what his fingers were doing to her.

"Do you like it?" Harlan asked hoarsely. "Tell me. Let me hear the words."

"You know I do, dammit..."

"Can you take more?" In an instant, he was on top of her and throbbing inside. He went deeper. "Oh, yes, you can take much more." And then the rhythm started as he twisted back and forth inside her. She was burning, flexing, the rhythm going faster, building. Then she gasped again as he plunged deep. He pulled her on top of him and she began to ride him. She screamed as he went beyond deep inside her, his hands clenching her buttocks to hold her still. "That's it! More..." he gasped with set teeth. "So damn good...Let me give you more." He was moving deeper, fuller, with every word... "I want every bit of you..."

She was giving him every bit and beyond, she thought dazedly. It was too much. No, it could never be too much. Not when she was so close...Not when she was also taking this almost unbearable pleasure with every passing instant...

"No fairy tale," Harlan muttered. "But definitely...magic. Don't...you dare...leave me..."

How could he think she would ever do that? This was where she had to stay. Magic... and he was causing her to arch once more as she gave another low, guttural cry and he took her down again and again into fiery darkness...

———— • ————

"I think I've had too much wine." Kira looked up at the stars and leaned back against Harlan near the entrance to her tent. "It was a good evening, wasn't it? Everything about it? You liked my dogs?"

"What's not to like? You and Mack taught them well." Harlan nibbled at the lobe of her ear. "And the horses are truly magnificent. You trained them, too?"

"Several of them. I did what I could with the time I had. The dogs were paramount because they had to learn how to protect the horses. But the horses were always Kalim's pride and joy. Fiona told me that there were rumors that Domino's forebearers were bred by the pharaohs of Egypt. Is it true?"

"Rumors that can't be proved." He shrugged. "I purchased Domino from a very high-end stable in Cairo, but there was no way to check ownership papers that far back. It's possible that one of Kalim's ancestors might have sold a few horses to neighboring tribes. If anyone could find a way to document that, it might be Kalim. But he wouldn't be willing to do it. At any rate, Domino was extremely expensive, and Fiona was delighted to have him. That was good enough for me."

"I can see that," Kira said. "Domino is fantastic. I enjoyed riding him."

"I enjoyed watching you. Are there any other of Kalim's horses that I could buy you that you'd like more?"

"Absolutely not."

"Just asking." He gently stroked her throat. "I wasn't trying to buy you. A gift can give more pleasure to the giver than the one who receives it."

"I realize that. It's still no. I haven't even paid you yet for your share of our partnership. We need to talk about that." She turned to look at him. "Which reminds me...did you find out anything from Belson when you called him earlier today?"

"A few things." He pressed his lips to the curve of her elbow. "Sorry. I became distracted. I like this particular spot..."

So did she, and she was getting breathless at just that light, caressing touch. But she was also beginning to want more. "I want to know. Tell me."

He sighed. "If you insist. But you're spoiling a wonderful evening. Where should I start?"

"Where nightmares start." She made a face. "I want to get it over with."

"Taylor?"

"Right the first time."

"No good news. He's still alive and kicking, and there's no sign that anyone is close to catching the son of a bitch." He paused. "A few of his scumbags have appeared in Morocco, asking questions."

"I don't have to ask about whom, do I?" she said bitterly.

"No. Actually, I was paramount but you came in a close second. Can we stop talking about him now? He's not going to be a threat for long. It's just always a good idea that I know where he is at any given time." His lips brushed her upper arm. "And that his location is never near you."

"And at a place where you can reach out and grab him if he doesn't get to you first." Her hands closed into fists. "I *hate* that, Harlan."

"Then it's time to change the subject," he said lightly. "And I'll give you the good news from Belson. My chief engineer has finished the project she was working on, and I thought I'd take you down to the shore tomorrow to watch the tests and let you see if my humble invention might be what we need to help retrieve your treasure."

"Tests? What is it?"

"Something that I hope will interest you."

"But you're not going to tell me exactly what? Maddening, Harlan." She had another thought. "'She'? Your chief engineer is a woman?"

"Why, yes. I thought you'd approve that I'm not biased where women are concerned. Hannah has worked with me on a number of projects. Her success rate is excellent, and I'm sure you'll like her."

"I don't have to like her. You're the one who needs competent people around you. I'm sure you know how to choose them."

"There's a rumor to that effect going around." He smiled teasingly. "But I could be wrong. It was Belson who chose you to go after Taylor. He had to convince me you'd be wonderful at whatever you did."

"And was he right?" He'd leaned around her, and his teeth were now pulling gently on her nipple. She could scarcely breathe. Her fingernails clenched on his shoulders.

"Without the slightest doubt." Then Harlan was over her, in her, pulling her thighs over his hips. "You haven't failed me yet..."

She lunged upward as the rhythm began again...She could barely speak as sensation after sensation tore through her. "You haven't...failed me either..."

"That's good to know." He was going deeper. "And for your information, I cannot imagine you as a one-night stand as long as you'll let me reach out and come into you like this...It's definitely a long-term commitment..."

CHAPTER

11

The next morning when she woke at a little before five he was no longer beside her. She sat upright in a moment of panic. *Get a grip. What did you expect? It was a fantastic night, but now it's over.* She had told him that she wouldn't expect anything else. It would be foolish of her to—

But there was a message to her from him on her phone propped beside the pillow on her bed. She snatched it up and accessed the message.

> I had a few things to do to prepare for the surprise I promised you with Hannah. I'll be back before daybreak. I'm only sending you this message because it just occurred to me that sometimes you have very peculiar ideas and I thought that I should guard against that at all costs. You were totally everything

I could ever hope to experience, and I refuse to let you think anything else. We'll straighten out every-thing else as we go along, but remember that and forget about obligations and deals and anything else you might decide to use as an excuse not to have what we just enjoyed many, many times again into perpetuity. Okay? Sleep well.

That was all. But it was enough. She put her phone down but didn't lie back down herself. Bastard. He shouldn't have worried her like that. And furthermore, she didn't have peculiar ideas, she thought indignantly. Everything she'd said had been sensible, and she'd only been careful to make certain he understood she wasn't trying to do anything that might make him feel caught or demand anything from him he wasn't prepared to give. Surely that was reasonable?

But she'd refuse to think about what he had said in that mes-sage. Except he'd said he'd be back soon and she'd rather think about every detail of what had happened last night and the way her body felt right now as it remembered every note of the way he'd made it sing...

But there was no chance of her going back to sleep now. She gathered clean clothes and her shampoo as she left the tent and headed to the lake for a swim.

Mack jumped to his feet from his blanket outside her tent and ran after her. She laughed as she started to run toward the lake. "By all means, come in for a swim. Yes, it was a good night, Mack.

Sorry we couldn't invite you in. But it was kind of a special time. And it might even be a better day. We'll have to see..."

———— · ————

Harlan did not get back to the camp before dawn. It was nearly nine before he arrived in the main camp, and when he did, Aban was in the passenger seat of the Range Rover he was driving. Aban jumped out of the car the minute he saw Kira. "I know I should have called and told you I was leaving camp, but Harlan said he might need me. How could I refuse?"

"You could say no." She turned to Harlan. "What have you been up to?"

"Didn't you get my message?" He got out of the driver's seat. "That said it all. But I thought that I should drive down to the pier and have Belson deliver this vehicle to me to use while I'm here. I didn't want to have to depend on Kalim for transport." He nodded toward Aban. "Accommodating as our young friend is making himself."

"Oh, shucks," Aban said with mock modesty. "That's what I'm here to do." He shot a sly glance at Kira. "Particularly since Harlan stopped by and talked Kalim into letting me go with you the next time you go down and scuba."

"Good." She turned and focused her attention on Harlan. "I could have gotten you any kind of transport you needed from Kalim." Kira was still frowning at him. "Why did you have to get that Range Rover from Belson?"

"Because it's got the kind of carrying and hauling power we're going to need." He was sniffing the air at the bacon cooking on the campfire. "I'm hungry. Kalim didn't offer me breakfast. Can you imagine that?"

"And what were you doing at Kalim's this morning?" Kira asked.

"I told you, Kira," Aban answered for him and then turned away eagerly. "I'll go get you bacon and eggs, Harlan." He was already walking toward the campfire. "Kira?"

"Not until I get answers," she said grimly.

"I think she'd appreciate a good meal, Aban," Harlan said. "She's going to need it today."

"Right away." Aban hurried toward the fire.

"Okay, let's start at the beginning," Kira said. "Why did you go wake up Aban and take him with you instead of me?"

"Because you looked so peaceful and beautiful, I couldn't bear to wake you. If I'd tried, we would have both ended up back in bed."

She wouldn't melt. Not until she got those answers. "Would that have been so bad?"

He grinned. "No, so good. But I had plans for today and I wanted you to share them. Aban was the practical solution. I had plans for him, too."

"What plans?"

"He wanted desperately to go back to his scuba diving, and Kalim wasn't going to let him, because he was afraid for him. But what if I insisted he go with us? I doubted Kalim would turn me down."

"He might. You're not on his favorites list."

"But I had a talk with Kalim this morning and guaranteed that I'd take care of Aban if he'd permit him to come with us on the hunt. I told him I knew that he'd want Aban to be known among his people as a great warrior, since Kalim was the one who taught him diving as a boy."

"And he agreed to it?"

"Not entirely in those words, but I also told him that I knew if anything happened to the boy, he'd feel justified to cut my throat." He added ruefully, "Then he was very happy to go along with it."

"Splendid," Kira said. "I don't believe I'd be equally overjoyed to let that happen."

"But you'd want Aban to thrive, and we can take care of the rest." He grinned. "Actually, he reminds me of myself as a kid. He's a boy who wants it all. To do it all. Let's try to give it to him."

In that moment, as she looked at him, she wanted nothing more. "I would have loved to have known you then."

"No, you wouldn't. I was a hell-raiser and always wanted to do things my own way. My brother, Colin, was the good guy in the family. He was always looking out to make sure I wouldn't get in trouble."

"You've certainly changed. Now you're the caretaker. Look at how you watch over Fiona."

He shrugged. "Sometimes you have to learn harsh lessons when you lose people. And Fiona was family."

"You didn't know anything about me, and you still watched over me."

"I knew quite a bit about you before you even showed up on my radar." He lifted her hand and kissed her palm. "And it was my pleasure...and will continue to be."

The melting had completely taken place. "Damn." She shook her head with frustration. "And I was all prepared to be angry about that snide message you wrote me. It's not fair."

"Snide? And I thought I was doing so well. Maybe just the thing Colin would have written."

She scowled at him. "You said I had peculiar thoughts. I believe I was being perfectly reasonable."

"Beautifully peculiar." He kissed her hand again. "Could I have breakfast now?"

She sighed. "Anything you want."

"Really? What a totally grand commitment. Will it be pirates' gold? Or perhaps a pharaoh's throne? Ah, let's go tell Aban you're not angry with me any longer." He winked and spoke in a mock English drawl. "I want to take you down to the sea, milady. Hannah will be waiting for us."

———— • ————

"It's about time you got here, Harlan. Just because you're my boss, it doesn't mean you can keep me waiting. I have obligations." The grinning woman who was coming down the pier toward them was in her thirties, with curly dark hair and deep-set brown eyes that twinkled with humor at the moment. "You're not the only billionaire who wants my services. They're standing in line."

"Sorry." Harlan was shaking her hand. "But I have a boss, too, and she's heading this operation." He drew Kira forward. "This is Kira Drake, and she'll be doing her best to keep me in line when we're trying out the diving sleds. Dr. Hannah Bryson, Kira."

"I'm impressed." Kira shook her hand. "Delighted to meet you, Dr. Bryson. Harlan didn't tell me you were the Hannah Bryson who did the work on the subs that were used when they found that lost city of Marinth. You're practically a legend."

Hannah shrugged. "That was a long time ago. I hope I've done even more interesting things lately."

"Evidently you have, if you're working with Harlan." Kira smiled. "Then may I compliment Harlan for having the sense to hire a woman to design his latest creation? It shows he's even more intelligent than I thought. I'm also delighted you're going to let me try to launch your new sled, Dr. Bryson."

"Hannah. And Belson has been telling me about you. He doesn't believe the word 'try' is in your vocabulary. I know it's not in Harlan's." She was looking out to sea at an incoming barge. "Here come my sleds. If you'll excuse me, I must go help my fellow engineers set them up for us." She gestured to a tent down the pier. "And if you want to change into one of the wet suits I brought, you can do it in that tent. Shall we get started, Kira?"

"You bet we should," Kira said. "I can hardly wait."

Hannah turned to Harlan. "I know you're going to want to examine your design creations before you let us toss them in the sea. You can change on the barge."

He nodded his head. "Whatever you say, Hannah. I don't expect any surprises." He glanced at Kira "But I hope you're going to have a great one a bit later, Kira."

She smiled. "You designed and built it, didn't you? I'm not expecting any surprises, either." She waved at him as she turned and ran toward the tent.

———————— · ————————

Less than an hour later, Kira and Harlan joined Hannah Bryson and her team at the water's edge, where four sleek devices were suspended on metal stands.

The devices' graceful curves and elegant lines almost suggested Italian race cars. They were much smaller than cars, however, measuring about five feet long and a little over three feet wide.

Kira stepped around them. "I didn't think they'd be so... beautiful."

"Thank you," a voice spoke behind her. Hannah stepped over a series of coiled cables and joined her, smiling. "When Harlan presented me with all the ideas he wanted incorporated in these sleds, I was blown away. I'm used to dealing with military clients, who often don't have the most revolutionary ideas. But Harlan is... brilliant. He deserves the reputation he's made for himself. Every time I presented my latest round of plans to him, he came up with another half a dozen amazing suggestions that took the project to another level."

Harlan grinned as he approached them. "Hannah is being too generous. When I came up with these ideas, I knew there was only one person on earth who could make them work, and that's Dr. Hannah Bryson. Though even I was surprised at how beautiful she made them."

Kira turned toward one of the dark blue sleds. "Me too. They're breathtaking. I have to reach out and touch them." She turned to Hannah. "May I?"

Hannah gestured to Harlan. "Ask the owner."

"Of course," he said. "From what I hear, every visitor to Hannah's shop at the factory has wanted to touch these things."

"That doesn't surprise me," Kira said. "They're stunning." She ran her hand over the sled's smooth curves.

"I'm flattered you think so," Hannah said. "I've always thought that my designs should be more than just utilitarian. They should invite people to engage with them."

Kira stepped back and admired the sled from a few feet away. "I'm definitely getting the invitation."

Harlan was also obviously thrilled. "Hannah, you've outdone yourself," he murmured.

She laughed. "You haven't seen them do anything yet."

"I have faith."

Hannah turned back to Kira. "See? If you design something that looks nice, you've won half the battle."

Harlan shook his head. "It's your reputation I have faith in. If these things can do half of what's in the design specs, we're all going to be blown away."

"No pressure or anything," Kira said.

"I think you're going to be very happy." Hannah motioned

toward a seating area in front of the sleds. "Shall we begin? I've brought a few divers as well as my engineering team here for the demonstration." She held up her hand as she saw Harlan start to protest. "Don't worry. All of them are sworn to secrecy regarding the details of the sleds. Naturally, the technical innovations won't be revealed. But they've worked hard, and they deserve to see what we've created." She grinned. "And I thought you'd enjoy having an audience to applaud your new toy, Harlan."

"By all means," Harlan said as he watched the stream of people pouring out of the barge. "And you deserve to have your co-workers appreciate what an amazing job you've done, Hannah."

She chuckled. "You're damn right. So hold on for the show!"

A couple of minutes later, Hannah stepped in front of two large video screens that had been wheeled behind the sleds. "Welcome, and thank you for the hospitality you've shown me and my team since we arrived here. When Mr. Harlan approached me to build a new generation of underwater sleds, he had some ideas that had never been implemented before. Which is exactly why I wanted to be a part of it. As most of you know, I usually design submarines, but I was inspired by Jack Harlan's desire to create a craft that puts us into the water in a way unlike anything else ever designed."

Hannah walked toward her devices. "Most of the underwater sleds with anything close to these capabilities require days or even weeks of training. Not these. Most divers can be up and running in less than an hour."

This elicited a round of surprised and skeptical comments from the crowd. Hannah smiled. "I'm serious. And I have confidence that each one of you will prove me right." She bent down and picked up what appeared to be a small scuba mask. "And it's mostly because of this."

"A mask?" Kira said.

"Yes, but it's also the nerve center of this entire project. It wirelessly interfaces with the sleds. The diver won't have to master a steering mechanism. All you do is look at your destination, and the sled will take you there, navigating itself over, under, or around any obstacle to get there. Once the sled locks on to the target, the diver just hangs on."

As she spoke, the two screens displayed an animation illustrating the concept. There were several "oohs" from the crowd, even from some who had expressed doubts only moments before.

"You can grip the sled on side handles, or—" Hannah slipped her hands into slender fissures in the sled's rear side. "—place your hands in these silicone-lined areas that wrap around your fingers like gloves." She leaned forward until she was in the device up to her elbows. "When I flex my fingers, you'll notice something happening in front."

The crowd reacted in surprise as a pair of mechanical arms suddenly protruded from the front of the sled. Each arm was outfitted with a mechanical hand that moved with the dexterity of a human appendage. Hannah smiled and turned to face the crowd as the device's steel fingers flexed and rolled as if playing an invisible piano.

"Cute," one of the divers said. "But if we're down there anyway, we can just use our own hands."

197

"You can," Hannah said. "But can your hands do this?" She leaned forward, and the mechanical fingers picked up a large rock on the ground in front of the sled. The hand squeezed the rock until it shattered into hundreds of pieces.

The diver stepped back. "Whoa."

Hannah turned back toward the crowd. "These appendages can be used to clear debris, move wreckage, or move heavy objects to the surface."

Kira turned to Harlan. "Nice. Is that one of your contributions?"

Harlan nodded. "You never know when you might need an extra pair of hands."

Hannah stepped away from the sleds as her small crew picked them up from their stands. "As you can see, their size and relatively light weight makes them easily transportable to wherever they might be needed. It's one thing for me to talk about what they can do, but another to actually demonstrate their capabilities in the water, which is what my dive team will do for you now."

Kira raised her eyebrows. "She's going to use that dive team she brought?"

"Plus one." Harlan unbuttoned his shirt and unfastened his pants to reveal a red-and-black wet suit under his clothes. He tossed his shirt and pants aside.

Kira chuckled. "You're kidding."

"You believe I'd let an opportunity like this go by? Watch and be amazed."

Harlan joined the three members of Hannah's dive team at

the water's edge. As each sled was placed into the water, a diver took his place at the rear; each undocked his swim mask and put it over his face. Harlan slung a scuba tank over his shoulder and adjusted his mouthpiece and regulator.

He and the other three operators inserted their arms into the sleds, which whirred to life and propelled them ten yards from shore before silently disappearing beneath the water.

Hannah pointed to the screens, which now showed a point-of-view shot from a sled in the rear. Kira could see Harlan leading the group, easily apparent because of not only his uniquely colored wet suit but also his broad shoulders. "Our divers are headed for an area we've set up with wireless video cameras so we can watch. These sleds are designed for exploring in all sorts of conditions. We've prepared some tests that will be a surprise even to our divers. Let's see how they do."

A moment later, dozens of tennis-ball-sized spheres appeared on the screen, fired from tubes on the ocean floor. Clear shields immediately shot up on the sleds' top surfaces, blocking the spheres. "As you can see," Hannah said, "the divers are protected from any debris they may encounter. These shields will stay up as long as foreign objects are detected in the water in front of them."

Then, as the spheres made contact with the sleds, they exploded in what appeared to be white clouds, covering the cameras' entire field of view in a milky mess. Hannah paced from one screen to another, showing a new image that almost looked like a video game. "When the visuals are compromised, these sleds emit sonar and lidar pulses that enable them to construct images, which are sent to the divers' masks. They can see in almost any conditions. We're now seeing what the divers are seeing."

Kira found herself gaping at the crystal-clear images in amazement. She looked around and saw that the others in the group were sharing her surprise.

Hannah pointed to the right screen, which was still clouded over. "You can't see them here, but we've released several plastic cones into the water. The shields will block them from the operators, but with a flick of the wrist, the sleds will now navigate around them with incredible speed and accuracy. It's technology developed by Mr. Harlan for the Department of Defense."

As the murkiness dissipated, Kira could see that the sleds were indeed dodging and weaving around the underwater cones. She turned toward Hannah. "They're doing that without any help from the divers?"

"Yes. The operator can resume manual control at any time, and from his logs in the software simulator, I've already seen that Mr. Harlan enjoys showboating a bit."

As if on cue, Harlan executed a breathtaking barrel roll as soon as his sled cleared the cones.

The viewers laughed and applauded.

"When the diver is finished, his sled will return to home base, even if that base is on a boat that has moved many miles from where it started. The sled will always find its way home."

"Incredible," Kira said. "I can't wait to try it myself."

"Harlan has already booked you for a training session," Hannah said. "But like I said, it won't take much time at all."

The four sleds and their operators returned to the surface and glided to a graceful stop at the water's edge. Harlan, smiling broadly, pulled off his mask and walked toward Hannah.

"Amazing!" he said. "I could have spent hours down there."

"You will," Hannah said. "The sled batteries are good for at least sixteen hours of continuous use."

"Excellent," Harlan said. "But I think there are a few adjustments we should still make. Do you have time for a quick conference?"

"Of course. I have a few tweaks of my own."

Harlan turned toward Kira. "What did you think?"

"I loved it. It's fantastic. What a cool toy!"

"It'll take us wherever we need to go. And there are a few things you haven't even seen yet." He cocked an eye toward Hannah. "If everything is operational."

"Don't worry." Hannah was scribbling in a pocket notebook. "Everything we talked about is in there."

"Good." He turned back to Kira. "Ready for your first lesson?"

Her eyes widened with excitement. "Now?"

"No time like the present."

"I couldn't agree more," Kira said. "Hannah told me you already booked some appointment time for me."

He took her hand and led her toward the sleds. "I did. For right now. I guarantee you're going to love it."

———— • ————

Harlan was already aboard the barge when Kira brought her sled close enough for Hannah's crew to anchor it firmly in its berth next to Harlan's more than an hour later. But it was Harlan's face she saw first as he bent over to help her out of her sled and lift her onto the deck of the barge. He was grinning from ear to ear as he swung her in an exuberant circle. "Have a nice trip?"

"Wonderful! You know I did." She gave him a hug. "Can't you tell how excited I am? What a fantastic new toy you've managed to develop this time, Harlan. You really know how to show a girl a good time."

"I actually thought it was you who was showing me the good time." He kissed the tip of her nose before releasing her. "I'm glad you thought my humble effort was worth your attention. You were the one in the lead; I was only trailing behind you for most of the run. I expected you to wave me back to the barge and go find that treasure by yourself."

"I wouldn't do that. This was something we agreed to do together. Besides, it was the wrong location. Good for a spin with your sleds, but I've already found the approximate area where I thought the treasure would be found. This side has the wrong structure and lack of caves on this side of the shore." She saw Hannah coming out of the control room and whirled toward her. "It was great, wasn't it? Aren't you proud of him?" She added quickly, "And yourself and the team, of course."

"Of course," Hannah said solemnly. "We all did well. Or so the progress reports told me today. But the genius in our midst might have had a good deal more to do with it than the rest of us. He tends to do that, I've noticed. That's why I came to work for him all those years ago. I knew I'd get all the glory and attention that rubbed off from him if I hung around long enough."

"Stop being modest," Harlan said. "It doesn't become you. You tell me often enough how many times you get asked to leave me in the lurch and go to work for competitors. Were the reports on the sleds really that good?"

Hannah nodded. "The preliminary was great. I'll be doing the final once I check out the onboard data recorders."

"Then let's do it," Kira said. "Harlan needs to know what a great job he did. May I help?" She frowned. "No, I might get in the way. But I'll learn more later. Oh, well, I guess I did my share earlier with the test dive."

"And an excellent job it was," Harlan said soberly. "So let me go along with Hannah while you get busy on making a report to show me what you meant about the wrong cavern structure and lack of caves. I don't want to be left in the shade again."

"I'll do that," Kira said. "I'll go change and then when you've finished, can we take Hannah up to the hills for lunch and let her see the dogs and horses? I want to hear more about her work, and you can introduce her to Aban. He's such a terrific scuba diver that I imagine he might be a big help to her."

"We'll give her the opportunity to find out," Harlan said. "No pressure, Hannah."

"Never," Hannah scoffed. "Not from you, Harlan. But I'm afraid

I'm more interested in submersible vehicles than dogs or horses. However, I'd like to hear about some of your experiences, Kira. Belson had a few fascinating tales to tell. Lunch it is."

Kira watched them as they headed for the control room.

Harlan glanced back at her before he followed Hannah. "Okay? If you want to try your hand at going through those reports, it's up to you. It's just that it can get pretty boring. I didn't want to inflict it on you since you've evidently had such a good day."

She shook her head. "You don't have to hold my hand." She smiled. "It has been a great day, Harlan. And I believe it will get better." She gestured for him to follow Hannah. "Go get your work done. After I change, I'm going to sit in the sunshine and look out at the sea and think about how good it was and what we might be able to find next time we decide to go down and have another look...It's good to realize that in a world that has ghastly ghouls like Taylor running around, there's still adventure and brilliant people like Hannah Bryson, and maybe new things to discover. Tomorrow could be very exciting..."

CHAPTER

12

"Kira Drake is definitely here," Donovan told Taylor when he answered the phone. "My reports from Morocco that I sent you earlier said that Harlan's personal assistant Carl Belson had arrived at the Harlan factory there. But it seems Harlan brought Drake directly here to Hathor Island. Because a barge arrived at a seaport on the far side of the island today, and she and Harlan were definitely using underwater equipment to explore the area."

Taylor cursed. "You're sure?"

"Would I steer you wrong?" Donovan chuckled as he adjusted his binoculars more closely on the two people on the deck of the barge. "I couldn't be more certain. I'm on the cruiser you hired, and I'm a good distance away from the barge that brought in the submersible equipment they're using. But I'd recognize Drake anywhere after my trip to get you off those cliffs in Colorado. She's looking very cozy with Harlan at the moment. Sort of like a contented cat basking in the sun."

"We know what she's probably looking for," Taylor said. "If she's brought Harlan into the picture, it's even better news. Two for the price of one."

"For a raid on Kalim's stronghold?" Donovan asked. "I'll have to bring in additional men if we're going that route. That's no small island Kalim controls, plus there's the sea all around it to deal with."

"Not right now. Have them ready, but I'm not sure where I'll need them yet." Taylor started to laugh. "Though I'm beginning to have an inkling where that might occur. Just keep an eye on what's going on with Drake. I want to know everything she does."

Donovan didn't answer for a moment. "No problem. But you're still going after the treasure, aren't you? You promised me a fat bonus."

"Do you really think I'd give up a fortune just for a quick kill? I'm no fool, Donovan. The aim is always to have it all. Remember that, and you might get that bonus. Don't worry. There will be work for you very soon…"

———— • ————

Hannah Bryson stayed for lunch and didn't leave the hills until almost dark. The good thing was that she seemed to be getting along very well with Aban, and the young man was frankly besotted with her and followed her around like an eager puppy. Before the day was over, she'd invited him to the barge the next day, and he had accepted ecstatically and asked permission from Kira to drive Hannah back to the barge so that he could see the sleds.

"All is going well in Emerald City," Harlan murmured as he watched Aban drive down the road. "Now can we go back to your tent and see the underwater maps you drew for me?"

"I don't see why not." She moved away from the fire and strolled toward the lake. She was very contented with how the day had gone. "Emerald City...that's from *The Wizard of Oz*, isn't it? *Wicked* is one of my favorite musicals."

"That doesn't surprise me. It's a fairy tale. You're partial to them, aren't you? That's how you came here to Hathor Island. I'll wager Kalim told you a few tall tales, didn't he?"

"No, he didn't. That's your story, and it's not really true. He told me what he believed was truth based on what his ancestors had told him all his life about both the geology and customs of this island." She stopped in front of her tent. "And it turned out that he was being as honest with me as he could."

"Cleopatra's burial tomb?" he asked skeptically.

She shook her head. "No, that wasn't exactly true as we know it. But it could have been. The archaeologists are still looking." She pulled him into the tent and lit the lamp. "And we both thought there was a possibility she could have been buried near one of the wells or caves in the Valley of the Kings. So I was just as guilty as Kalim when he asked me to come here to check out the desert wells and cave systems in his own country."

"But Cleopatra hasn't been found yet."

"No, but that doesn't mean it won't happen tomorrow or the next day. Miracles happen."

"And so do fairy tales," Harlan said. "If you're willing to believe them." He leaned forward and kissed her cheek. "And if that's what you want, then it's fine with me. But a few words of reason would not go amiss if you'd care to expound a bit."

"Allow me," she said mockingly as she pulled him down beside her on the bed and opened her notebook. "The reason why we're not going to explore that same area we were in today is that although the basic structure that supports the island is principally limestone, the entire network of sea caves is on the other side of the island from where we are now."

"Caves?" Harlan repeated as he gazed down at her sketch. "Is that the goal you're going for, Kira? Why?"

"Because caves have traditionally offered both secure hiding places and a way to intrigue and intimidate anyone else who might be a little too curious." She shivered. "Though caves can be very inhospitable. But they've always fascinated me. I grew up on Summer Island and learned how to herd and track in other wild countries as well. Lots of caves to explore."

"Why inhospitable?" He leaned back on his elbow. "Did you find Kalim's cave inhospitable?"

Suffocating darkness. Sounds in the swishing of the blackness of the water that should never have been there...

She shook her head to clear it. "I was speaking in general. But I was always a great reader, both in college and with my duties herding in the fields. Naturally I'd come across stories about caves and the people who now and then discover something new about them."

"Such as?"

"Cavers who wanted to explore them principally for adventure. Or scientists trying to learn about the world around them by studying prehistoric history carved on the walls."

"What else?"

Kira searched wildly for another example. "I guess I should mention the Mayan leaders who sometimes drowned their sacrifices in the cenotes outside their temple caves?"

"That's interesting. I didn't know you'd been to visit those Mayan temples."

"What difference does it make? I've been to a lot of places you don't know about."

"It was just a comment. We ought to compare notes sometime."

"Why on earth are you being so inquisitive?"

"It goes with the territory. I'm one of those curious scientists you mentioned." He tilted his head as he gazed at her. "And there was something in your expression when you were talking about those caves...I couldn't quite put my finger on it. But it bothered me. Tell me more."

"You're being totally ridiculous." She shrugged. "Let's see..." She searched her memory. "They say Zeus was born in a cave, and the Japanese sun goddess Amatarasu hid in a cave, plunging the world into darkness." She snapped her fingers. "And how could I forget? King Arthur and his Round Table and hounds are said to be sleeping peacefully in a Welsh cave waiting for a powerful, mystical visitor who will summon them once again to battle."

"Ah, now we're getting into the real drama."

"May I stop now? Why are you so concerned about those blasted caves?"

"It's not the caves, it's how you felt about them that bothered me."

She had a sudden thought. "I remember the day we arrived on Summer Island, you were telling me that you were going to get to know me, everything about me. Is that what this is all about? I don't appreciate that, Harlan. Everyone deserves to have a little mystery in their lives."

"I'd guess you have more than a little."

"Perhaps I do. It makes life more exciting and different, doesn't it? Though you probably lead a far more exciting life than I do. I don't see why it's bothering you."

"Neither do I. Perhaps because it's you." He lifted his shoulders. "I suppose that's a big part of it. I appear to have an obsession about you. And I'll try to keep it from annoying you. But you do realize I won't be able to stop if I notice something is bothering you? I'll have to step in and try to solve it. It's a function of my DNA."

"I've noticed you have a problem in that direction. And those blasted caves sent up a red flag for some reason. Why worry about that now? Kalim might not even let us do any scuba diving near those caves. He considered it too dangerous before. He never permitted any of his people to do any underwater exploring in that area after he lost a couple of his villagers when an overhead stalactite crashed down on them. Kalim was always very careful about taking care of the people of Hathor Island."

Harlan looked up from the sketch Kira was drawing, his expression grim. "But perhaps not as careful about taking care of you? You were an outsider, and you were probably very curious about those caves."

She shrugged. "I was told not to go near them. It wasn't Kalim's fault, and that only made them more attractive to me. I did make sure that I conveniently lost Aban when I decided I wanted to explore by myself."

His oath was low but profane. "I thought that was probably how it went when Aban was telling me about it. Dammit, it was Kalim's duty to keep an eye on you. He invited you here."

"And I wanted to come. He didn't know anything about my trips to the caves until I went to him and told him about them." She paused. "I figured it was only fair by then." Her eyes were suddenly twinkling. "Because I had to show him the box of trinkets I'd brought up from one of those caves. Since all those caves technically belonged to him."

"Trinkets?"

"An ebony-and-stone box I discovered jammed beneath the rocks in one of the caves that contained a generous collection of gold chains, diamonds, emeralds, and sapphires. I'm sure you've guessed that it's that particular cave I'm so eager to return to and explore. It would be foolish not to go back to the source and see what else we can find. Kalim was very impressed. Some of the stones were quite large." She thought about it. "And he was also a bit angry, but he got over it when he decided that I could have cheated him out of the entire collection and just walked away. That's when he offered to split the treasure with me if I'd arrange to do the hunting and gathering. I gave him the treasure box so that he could investigate the age and value of the contents."

"No wonder he was so worried when you disappeared," Harlan said wryly. "It wasn't only an expert herder and trainer he'd lost when I snatched you away that night in Colorado."

"That's not fair," Kira said. "He's been very generous to me. He didn't have to make that deal with me about the treasure."

"And you didn't have to tote that box of jewels to the surface and offer it to him along with anything else you might come up with. I believe it might be even steven if you look at it that way. You might even be a little ahead."

"I doubt it."

"Of course you do. But then you believe in fairy tales and even a glamorous Cleopatra who might just appear around the next bend."

She chuckled. "Or the next cave?"

"That, too."

"But I also believe in a man who followed me up in those mountains and saved my life even when I was more than a little rude to him. That's also kind of a fairy tale, isn't it?"

"Let me think about it." He paused, considering. "No, I'm not any kind of hero you might imagine. That was my brother, Colin. I just work hard and try to get along and do my best to keep you away from any nasty caves that might frighten you."

She stiffened. "Why do you think I'd be afraid of any cave? They just...interest me."

"Most of them. And I don't want to accuse you of not being brave as a tiger, but I believe you might have a few withdrawal symptoms when it comes to facing that particular deep, black cave nemesis."

He was joking, but Kira was still having a sudden vision of swirling water, a sleek, undulating body, and ultimate darkness as she struggled to carry that ebony box toward the surface.

"You're shivering." Harlan pulled her into his arms. "Not so funny?"

"Of course it is." She nestled closer. He was warm and strong and so different from the cold darkness of that moment she'd been suddenly remembering. "But you're right. I'd never had any trouble with claustrophobia or other cave-oriented problems. But that day when I brought that box up to the surface to give Kalim, it was different. It was too dark in the water...and I kept hearing things, and I thought I saw something moving back and forth in some of the streams. I couldn't tell what it was, but it made me uneasy. I couldn't wait to get away from the caverns and up to the surface." She ruefully shook her head. "It's never been like that for me before or afterward. I deliberately went down again the next day but I didn't feel anything..." She stopped and then corrected herself. "Yes, I did. I thought I saw something, felt something, a sort of...presence moving down there in the caves, but I couldn't tell what it was. Maybe I'll be able to decide once I can focus the lights of the sled on it."

"Possibly. Or maybe you won't want to know."

213

"Of course I will," she said curtly. "I won't let my imagination make me afraid of any natural element. I didn't tell you that there was another, smaller container I found that I left down there in the caves because I was in such a hurry to get out of there. I fully intend to go back for it. You wouldn't respect me if I didn't. I wouldn't respect myself."

"Okay." He held her closer. "You're completely wrong about that, but I'll let it go. Can we forget about caves and talk about what a wonderful time we had today? And may I tell you how I'm looking forward to tomorrow? Or maybe we'll just wait until afterward to talk." His lips were on her temple and his hands were caressing her throat. "Afterward can be pretty wonderful, too..."

———— • ————

Harlan was at the main camp making their biscuits when Kira came back from taking her bath in the lake the next morning. She smiled as she plopped down beside him. "My, that smells good. This is beginning to be a habit. I thoroughly approve."

"I saw you heading down to the lake when I woke. I would have joined you, but that lake looked a little too public for my taste. I like that you're friends with the herders, but I'm not into communal bathing. I prefer a more private arrangement with you. So I decided I'd cook you a decent meal and then go down later."

"How very snooty of you. How long before you finish cooking? I need to give Fiona a call before we take off for the barges.

I promised I'd stay in touch. I meant to call her yesterday, but I became distracted."

"I wonder how that happened?" He was grinning. "If you'd rather wait until later, it's not as if we've totally deserted her. I called her after lunch yesterday while you were talking to Hannah about her own career. She sounded fine, and all she wanted was for me to tell her about Kalim's horses. She said her own training with Golden Boy and Domino was going along splendidly."

"I'll still call her," Kira said. "I made a promise, and I want to tell her about how fantastic your sled is working out. She has a right to be proud of you. Not that she isn't already." She took out her phone and strolled over to sit beneath a tree while she placed the call. "Let me know when you're ready to serve breakfast and I'll come running."

"It will be another twenty or thirty minutes. Tell Fiona I said hello, and that Kalim is still not offering to sell me another horse, so she should make do with the prize horses I've already given her."

"Too bad. Much as she loves her own horses, Kalim's would have been special to her. She's not going to like it."

"Neither did I," Harlan said ruefully. "There's one stallion in that herd Adan showed me that first day that I would have paid a fortune to own. Maybe if I do something to make your old friend Kalim develop a special fondness for me..."

"Don't count on it." Kira shook her head. "I believe you're talking about Sinbad, and he's not going to sell him no matter what you offer. He's already refused an offer of more than a million dollars from some billionaire sheik; he didn't think twice. Besides the money obstacle, Sinbad is impossible to ride. All the herders have failed."

"Even you?"

She nodded. "I stayed on him longer than anyone else. But I didn't want to break his spirit. He's so wild that I was afraid it might even kill him. It happens sometimes with a horse that willful. I didn't want to take the chance with such a valuable horse. Kalim would kill me."

Harlan sat back and smiled at her. "But you wouldn't give a damn about Kalim's reaction, would you? Admit it, you love that horse. There wasn't a chance in hell that you'd risk him."

She nodded. "What can I say? He's glorious. I'd fight anyone who tried to harm him. You'd feel the same way. But then so does Kalim. So you can see why I told you to forget about owning him."

"I understand." He was still frowning thoughtfully. "You're an expert. What kind of rider would it take to tame Sinbad?"

She chuckled and shook her head. "You're impossible. Didn't you hear me? Forget it."

"But I have such a good memory, and you can never tell what will trigger it. We'll see..." Harlan went back to molding his biscuits.

Kira was still smiling when she finally reached Fiona at Summer Island. "Good morning, Fiona. I was just talking to Harlan about the conversation the two of you had yesterday. I believe you'd better give up on getting one of Kalim's horses for your stable. He's been trying, but it looks like Kalim is very stubborn. Still, Harlan said your own training is going splendidly."

"Of course it is," Fiona said. "I'm doing everything I can, and you have fantastic people here to help me. But after you told me how wonderful Kalim's stable is, it would be nice to see what they're like." She added, "And Harlan might be able to pull it off. He mentioned a certain stallion..."

"And he'll try, but don't get your hopes up. He's very busy with that underwater sled he's working on. It's quite wonderful."

"He's always wonderful," Fiona said. "And I'll be happy just having him come back here and see how good I'm becoming with my own horses. I don't want him to think I'm not grateful." She laughed. "And I think Domino misses you. There are definitely signs that he's in mourning."

"I don't believe you. He's your horse and I'm just a visitor at the gates. Though I will be glad to see him again."

"So when will you be back?"

"Soon. I do have some work to do here on Kalim's island before I leave."

"Then you should let me come to meet Kalim. We could ride together, and maybe I could persuade him to let me ride one of his own horses in the next Olympics. Think how he'd like all the fanfare over one of his herd."

"Probably not at all," Kira told her. "I'm not certain he recognizes even the Olympics as worthy of his precious horses."

"Then I'll educate him."

"We'll see. Are all of Harlan's men on the island taking good care of you?"

"Naturally, of course. All those soldiers and grooms trail around after me everywhere on Summer Island. But it's not like having you or Harlan here. Think about having me come to you, won't you? I have so much to show you."

"And you hope I have an equally vast amount to show you," Kira said teasingly, "right?"

"I admit it. But it does sound like you and Harlan are getting along just fine without me." She was laughing. "And you know how I like to be the center of attention. Can't you arrange that for me?" She went silent for an uneasy moment. "You two *are* getting along well, aren't you? I wasn't sure the day you left here. There were certain...vibes."

Vibes and fire and sheer sexual desire.

Kira had a sudden memory of the night she had just spent in Harlan's arms, but she wasn't about to mention that to Fiona. It was far too early in her relationship with Harlan, and it might upset the niece who clearly adored him. Instead, she said cautiously, "We appear to be. And we do have you in common. That's a very good thing."

"That's true," Fiona said. "So keep that in mind next time I talk to you about persuading Harlan to bring me to see both of you."

"You're impossible." Kira chuckled. "And it's time for me to go have my breakfast. Take care of yourself. I'll try to call you tomorrow." She cut the connection and jumped to her feet, then walked over to the fire to sit down beside Harlan. "You were right: Fiona is very determined about Kalim's horses. But she seems to be taking everything else in stride about her own horses on Summer Island.

And she takes wonderful care of them wherever they are. I suppose you know that about her?"

He nodded. "How could I not? Having them helped her survive— it helped her block all the pain and fear. She became almost another person."

Kira thought about it. "You know, that's kind of wonderful. I was thinking about her talent with horses when she was talking to me on the phone just now. You asked me who could ride an impossible horse like Sinbad. It might be Fiona."

"Because she's a horse whisperer?"

She nodded. "Of course you'd recognize all the signs. She grew up with you."

"Yes, I recognized them and I was grateful. I don't know what constitutes a horse whisperer—I just accept it and try to give her whatever help she needs."

"Like an impossible stallion?"

"Who knows if he's impossible unless we bring them together?"

"I applaud the effort. Every single one that you've made for Fiona. But this will be pretty tough, so don't get your hopes up." She couldn't leave it at that, though. This man didn't know the meaning of *impossible*. "She did try to talk me into bringing her here to look around a bit. That might include Sinbad."

"What did you say?" Harlan asked as he handed her a plate with biscuits, bacon, and eggs. "It's not really a bad idea. Much as I disapprove of Kalim's methods, you didn't turn out too badly working here in the hills with his herders. Fiona would probably enjoy it."

"How kind of you to admit that," she said bluntly. "I thought it was a very bad idea. I skirted the suggestion entirely."

"Am I allowed to ask why?"

"Isn't it obvious? Because we're sleeping together. She's your niece and she might not understand."

"Then it's time she learned. I don't ask her who I can sleep with. I realize you may be having trouble with the idea yourself, but you'll have to get used to it, too." He met her eyes. "Because we both know we're not going to give up what we've found, are we?"

"Aren't we?" Kira asked. "It's still so new, and I tried to tell you I'm not going to demand anything from you. Why bring her into it? You care about her. She's family. I'd be taking something precious from you. It's exactly what I said I wouldn't do."

"So sensible." He shook his head. "But I can't see it. Perhaps because I'm not feeling at all sensible at the moment." He sighed. "I believe we'll put this discussion on hold for the time being. Eat your breakfast. We have work to do down at the barge."

"Maybe not as much work as you think," Kira said as she picked up a biscuit from her plate and began to eat. "I've decided to recruit additional help."

He shook his head. "Hannah said Aban wasn't ready yet."

"No, but Mack is. You saw how well he swims down at the lake. It won't be the first time that I've taken him cave hunting. He did a lot of that when I was scuba diving at Summer Island, and he loved it. It was just another game to him. It should be pretty much the same here."

"Then I guess we'll be teaching him how to hitch a ride on one of my sleds. I have an idea how to make that work. But I'm not sure how to guide him or lead him through those caves. And you're the cave expert."

"You'll learn soon," Kira said. Her eyes were twinkling. "But you'd better give him a good breakfast, too. He'll need it. He can run me ragged sometimes when we're training on Summer Island!"

———— • ————

Hannah Bryson hadn't arrived yet when they appeared at the barge landing. But Kira was surprised to see Kalim getting out of his Bugatti Mistral sports car and strolling toward them. "I hear from Aban that you two have been doing quite a bit of diving in the past couple days. Anything interesting?"

"Not for Aban," Harlan said. "Hannah isn't ready to train him on the new sleds yet. I told you we'd take good care of him."

"What about you, Harlan?" Kalim asked. "Are you ready to take a chance on your new toys?"

"I never release a product unless I'm ready to take a chance on it," Harlan said. "And I guarantee you're going to want an entire stable of those 'toys' before this is over. That is, if I decide to sell them to you."

"Indeed?" Kalim shrugged. "Now, why would I want to bother with buying one of your new inventions when you know I much prefer to own the finest horses on the planet instead? Aban tells me he gave you an in-depth look at my herd the minute he got the opportunity. Were you properly stunned?"

Harlan took a step closer to Kalim's Bugatti and ran his fingers caressingly over the car's glittering black surface. "Absolutely. You didn't really need to bring this beauty to show off to me. The herd was more than enough. A car is just a car. Though I understand this mechanical miracle has all the bells and whistles. La Voiture Noire. Let's see, the last time I was thinking about buying one, it was priced at somewhere around nineteen million. Is it worth that much to you?"

"Anything I want badly enough is worth it to me," Kalim said, stiffening. "I support this island and educate my citizens exceptionally well. Why should I not buy anything for myself that I wish?"

"I didn't say that." Harlan shrugged. "I just didn't find it worthwhile for my purposes. Most of the time, I have simpler tastes."

"Oh, for goodness' sake." Kira had heard enough of this nonsense. "Will you stop?" She came forward and stood in front of Kalim. "Yes, Harlan was amazed and appreciative when he saw your horses—not to mention the dogs that I so carefully and laboriously trained for you. But you haven't had a chance to even test out his new sleds. They're a fantastic invention, and he's right, you'll want to own them. But you didn't come here so that you could taunt each other like this, did you?"

"Don't be rude, Kira," Kalim said. "No, I just wanted to make sure that everything was in order and Harlan was treating you and my property well. After all, I'm permitting him to watch over Aban, and I did allow those barges to enter my territorial waters when he requested it. I thought I should have a right to look the situation over." He turned back to Harlan. "I understand from Aban that Kira appears to believe you're not mistreating her. Though that term doesn't necessarily compute in either my opinion or my culture."

Kira stiffened. She had an idea what Aban had told him, and she needed to avoid any confrontation. "Don't go there, Kalim."

"I have no intention of doing so," Kalim said. "You're not one of my people, and you're a grown woman. I merely stated my opinion. I just thought I'd let Harlan know that you have a protector if you so desire."

"I don't desire it. You know that, Kalim. I take care of myself."

"I believe I've heard that mantra before," Harlan said suddenly. "But what if I desire it on her behalf? I'd appreciate your attention at any time, Kalim. I like the idea of having a man of your stature ready to help her if needed."

"Harlan!" Kira exclaimed in disbelief.

"It makes good sense, Kira," Harlan said. "I'm not so vain that I'd refuse anyone willing to be there for you in any bad situation. I'm beginning to like the way he thinks."

"I'm not," Kira said. "Back off."

Kalim was staring suspiciously at Harlan. "If that was supposed to influence me in any way, it's not going to work. I'm still not selling you any of my horses."

"I'm hurt, Kalim." Harlan sadly shook his head. "You misread me entirely. I believe you care enough about Kira not to focus on mere horses when her well-being is at stake. I meant every word I said."

Kalim was still gazing at him searchingly. "None of my horses can ever be referred to as 'mere.' They're all extraordinary."

"I understand the insult and offer my sincere apologies," Harlan said. "Particularly when we're talking about Sinbad."

"Ah, Sinbad." Kalim smiled. "I knew it would kill you not to get your hands on him. That's why I told Aban to be sure you saw him immediately."

"And it does," Harlan said. "But some things are more important than getting what I want. You've just given me a gift that towers way above it in scope. Now, is there anything I can do for you?"

Kalim didn't speak for a moment. "Are you conning me?"

"I most certainly am not," Harlan said. "We're on the same page. Sometimes I've found Kira to be less than appreciative of what we try to do for her, but I think we both believe she's worth it."

"Yes, I agree," Kalim said slowly. "I've always found that to be true. She's truly remarkable." He turned back to face Kira. "I believe that it's worthwhile keeping Harlan around. This does not mean I won't assist you if you need me. But considering my recent discussions with him and the way he has treated you and Aban, it appears he may prove useful."

"Really?" Kira said. "I always appreciate your opinion, and I'm sure Harlan will be grateful that the two of you seem to have reached a meeting of the minds." She added caustically, "Unfortunately, I seem to have been left out of the discussion."

"I'm not leaving either one of you out of anything," Kalim said. "I realize how valuable both of you are. I was going to call on the villagers and take care of this problem myself if my decision had been different. But that will not be necessary, and I won't have to involve them." He turned to Harlan. "Did you know that the two of you have been watched for the last two days? And if you did, why didn't you come to me and get permission to stop it, as you did when you brought those barges here? That was very clumsily done. I could have been very angry with you."

"What the hell?" Harlan said in bewilderment. "What are you talking about, Kalim?"

Kalim gestured to the north. "You actually didn't know about it? A cruiser. It's too far away to see from here, but they're using high-powered binoculars to watch what you're doing over here on the barges...and I assume in the sea itself. Abdullah, one of my villagers, thought I'd be interested in knowing about what these strangers were doing on my property. Five men are on the ship as far as he could tell. I told him not to approach them but to get close enough to try to get photographs of the cruiser and to send them to me." He handed Harlan his camera. "I thought you and Kira might want to see if you know them."

"I definitely do. Many thanks." Harlan was copying the photos and sending them to Belson. "You were right to keep your people away from that ship. The last thing we want is for you to have any trouble with your villagers." He handed the camera to Kira. "I'll send my assistant and a few other team members to check out what's going on with that cruiser."

Kira was studying the photos. "It's a good-size ship, but I don't recognize anyone aboard from those photos. Do you, Harlan?" She frowned. "Definitely no one from here on Hathor. But then the only one I might be able to identify would be Taylor. In Colorado, I was too busy fighting him off to pay any attention to any of his men. Though I did hear him talking to at least one of his helicopter pilots on the phone when I was stalking him at the ranch house—Donovan."

Harlan shook his head. "We'd already recognized Donovan from when he managed to help Taylor escape on the helicopter that night. And I was too busy trying to keep you and Mack alive during that period to pay any attention to anyone else. But I'll alert Belson."

Kira nodded. "But it won't stop us from going for another session in the sleds?"

"Not if Belson decides there's no risk from the cruiser. I take it we won't be operating in the same area?"

She shook her head. "I thought we'd take a chance on the west coast." She braced herself as she glanced at Kalim. "We need to see what's available in the caves, Kalim. It was where we managed the first strike. We may not go directly after treasure, but we should see what our options would be."

"I told you it could be dangerous." Kalim was frowning. "You know I refused to let my villagers go into the caves, Kira."

"Not as dangerous as it would be without the sleds," she told him. "It will be an entire new game."

"And we'll be careful," Harlan promised. "I'll keep an eye on her."

Kalim was still not pleased. "You'll not take Aban unless I

decide it's safe. He's young and reckless, and he takes far too many chances. The young fool believes he can live forever."

"Don't we all?" Harlan said. "I imagine that you took a great many chances yourself at the same age. I know I did. Now, if you'll excuse me..." He turned away and was dialing Belson. "I have arrangements to make."

Kalim hesitated for an instant, then turned and got into the driver's seat of his Bugatti and began backing out onto the road. "I hope you're not making a mistake, Kira. Harlan is clearly someone who likes his own way." He gave a half shrug. "But then so do you. I'll be in touch."

"I'm sure you will. That's how it's been since the day we met. And Harlan's shown me that I can trust him." She lifted her hand in farewell as she watched Kalim drive back down the road toward the castle area.

Harlan had finished his call and was coming back toward her. "Belson is on his way. We'll know something soon about that cruiser." He asked quietly, "Okay?"

"As much as I can be," Kira said. "It doesn't have to be Taylor or any of his men. It could be just some college kid or treasure hunter out to have a good time and make himself a fortune." Her lips twisted. "But neither of us believes that, do we?"

"Not bloody likely," Harlan said. "But we'll see when Belson and the team get here. Or I could take a couple of the barge hands as soon as they show and go over to take a look right away. That's what I'd prefer to do."

"No, wait," she said quickly. "We don't know what you'd find. You even told Kalim's people not to go exploring."

"Because I knew you'd insist on going, too."

"You're damn right."

He slipped his arm around her waist and brought her close. "Then we'll definitely wait for Belson. We can't have you leaving Mack out of his first treasure hunting trip, can we?"

CHAPTER

13

Harlan didn't get a return call from Belson until three hours later, and it was not good news. They'd delayed the dive so that they could first get the info about the cruiser. But they might just as well have stuck to their original schedule.

"No cruiser," Belson said when Harlan picked up the call. "Not a sign of any ship. I spoke to the villagers along the shore, and they said the cruiser took off from that area about the same time you called me. I followed up with that Abdullah who was giving Kalim his information, but I couldn't locate him. The villagers said he disappeared about the same time as the cruiser. Do you want me to continue to hunt?"

"Absolutely. And keep on doing a scan of the ocean and make sure they're not trying to find out what we're doing and where we're going on the dive."

"Will do. We'll monitor the entire area. They won't give you any trouble. Anything else?"

"Try to track down the name and registration of that cruiser and locate the lessor."

"I'm on it. Good luck today." He cut the connection.

Harlan turned to Kira. "You heard him. But we don't need luck, do we? You can take us anywhere we need to go."

"A little luck wouldn't hurt. But as long as we have Mack on board, he's bound to be a big help." She whistled for Mack to follow her as she headed for the tent to change. "You're going to be very impressed by him, Harlan. We'll just have to see how the rest of it goes."

———— · ————

It took less than an hour for them to board the launch barge and travel to the designated coordinates. The crew lowered three diving sleds into the water as Kira and Harlan watched.

"Are you sure Mack will be okay?" Kira asked. "These things weren't built for dogs."

"No, but they were designed to double as tow rigs, so that items could be placed on top of them and automatically follow other sleds they were paired with. We'll wirelessly pair that sled with yours. Wherever you go, Mack will be right behind you on the surface."

Kira looked at the diving sleds in the water. "You're sure? I'm very nervous about anything happening to Mack these days. It sounds good, but what if we hit rough seas?"

"There are incredible stabilizers built into each of these sleds. Anything short of a monsoon, Mack will sleep like a baby."

"If that's the case, I think I might want to curl up with him. Wake me when you see anything interesting."

"Tough luck. I'm counting on you to tell me."

"Aw, too bad. By the way, thanks for the wet suit. It's actually quite flattering."

He stepped back and looked her up and down. "And it's skin-tight. You flatter it."

She felt a rush of heat on her cheeks and instantly felt foolish. She wasn't some stupid schoolgirl, and here she was getting flustered over a few words from Harlan.

She tried dismissing the compliment with a wave of her hand. "As long as it keeps me dry."

"You won't need to worry about that. One of my companies made it. Let's get going."

———— • ————

Kira was surprised how quickly Mack jumped from the barge onto his sled. He didn't seem at all panicked, registering only mild interest as she and Harlan slid into the water and donned their electronic masks. They moved their arms into the sleds' control gloves and motored away from the barge with Mack floating just a few feet behind them. The dog wagged his tail excitedly.

"See?" Harlan spoke through the radio transmitter in his mask. "He likes it."

As Kira and Harlan submerged, she turned just in time to see Mack lie down on his belly. Kira laughed. "He's just treating it as another adventure. It's like he's been doing this his entire life. I *love* it!"

Harlan nodded. "I put a microphone module on his sled. We'll hear it through our earpieces if he starts barking."

"Or snoring."

"That too."

She gasped as they passed through a school of sunfish and beheld a valley of orange coral and a multicolored explosion of undersea life.

"It's stunning," she said.

"But you've seen it before, right?"

"Not like this. These sleds are wonderful. I almost feel like we're flying." She banked left to get a closer look at a crop of red flora. "I want to use these to explore every inch of this place."

"Next time. We're on a mission, remember?"

"If you insist." She focused her eyes on a spot ahead and tapped her forefingers to her thumbs inside the control glove. Her sled sped ahead, smoothly increasing velocity in a way that continued the sensation of flight. Harlan kept pace with her, and she looked up to see that Mack's sled was still overhead, perfectly tracking her.

"Are we getting close?" Harlan asked.

"Yes. See all that orange up ahead?"

"Hard to miss it. It looks like the entire ocean floor is lined with it."

"That's one of the largest coral reefs in this hemisphere. We're going to move through it in a way that a boat never could."

"That will take us to the cave system you've been talking about?"

"Yes. It's kind of a maze at first, but we'll surface in a cave system. Are you sure Mack's sled will keep up?"

"Positive. Where we go, he goes."

She put on an extra burst of speed. "Then let's hit it."

They moved through the orange coral, dodging and weaving amid the ridges with amazing precision. A far cry from the last time she'd visited the area, when it had taken hours to cautiously plot her journey past the sharp coral outcroppings.

She spotted something in the corner of her eye. "Wait, we just passed it."

"I didn't see anything."

"That's why I'm here." She turned around and moved back a few yards until she floated in front of a narrow crevice that was almost invisible from any other angle. "This way. It should be just wide enough for us to make it through."

"What about Mack's sled on the surface?"

"He can go part of the way up there, but after about fifty yards he'll hit a wall. I have an idea for what happens after that. Follow me."

She steered into the crevice and led Harlan—and up above, Mack—through a series of narrow passages until they found themselves in a large opening. They climbed to the surface until they reached a massive cavern. Kira and Harlan steered their sleds onto a stone beach, worn smooth by centuries of erosion.

Kira pulled off her oxygen face mask, stood up from her sled, and stepped over a pile of rocks. She turned around to get her bearings. "Mack! Mack!"

"You really think he can hear you?"

She pulled a whistle from a chain around her neck and shook the water from it. She blew three short blasts and waited for a few seconds.

Harlan shook his head. "If you want to point me in the right direction, you can just go back to him and wait. It probably wasn't a good idea to bring him out here if it was going to be such a—"

Suddenly the water churned, and then Mack leaped up onto the rocks beside them. He shook himself, spraying Harlan with water.

Kira laughed. "Serves you right for doubting him! I told you Mack has been in caves before. This one is just...different."

Harlan wiped the fresh spray of water from his face. "You're right. I should have known better. There was no way he'd let you go anywhere without him." He bent over to pet the dog's head. "Welcome, Mack."

Mack shook himself again.

Kira pulled a flashlight from her pocket and aimed the beam toward the back of the cavern. "We're almost there. This way."

They walked through what was quickly revealed to be a system of caves, some bone-dry, others centered by massive pools of water.

As they stepped around one such pool, Mack darted in front of them and growled.

He was making a sound Kira hadn't heard from him before. "What is it, boy?"

Mack turned toward her and slightly whimpered. Kira stroked his ears.

"Is he okay?" Harlan asked.

"I think so. He's just…unsettled." Kira shone her flashlight around the cavern. "But I don't like it. Mack is never skittish without a good reason."

Something moved in the water.

"See that?" Harlan spun around with his flashlight.

Something else appeared from the water and slithered into the shadows. Mack barked again.

Something hissed behind them. Then to the right. And the left. "What in the hell…" Harlan whispered.

Kira gasped. "Hell's bells! Prehistoric sea snakes?"

"You're joking."

"I wish I was. Get a better look, and you'll see. Though I've only seen them on TV and photographs in textbooks. But I swear that was a close cousin to *Titanoboa cerrejonensis*."

"No way. Those things were forty feet long. They could eat small whales. Besides, they've been extinct for tens of millions of years."

"Okay, so maybe these are younger and smaller cousins."

A huge snake leaped from the water of one of the dark pools near the rocks that led toward the sharp outcropping of orange coral. It missed Harlan by only a few inches! Then it slithered away and disappeared into another pool several yards away.

"Holy shit," Harlan said. "That was at least fifteen feet long. You could be right. At the Smithsonian, I saw the fossilized remains of one that had been discovered in a mine in Colombia. That was a pretty damn close resemblance."

"Did you take a look at its head?"

"I couldn't miss it. It almost swallowed my face."

She nodded. "I didn't see them the last time I was here. But the time before, when I brought up the treasure, I thought I was aware of something...strange in the water. They've probably been hiding in these caves for an eternity. If we could bring one back, that would be the true treasure."

He shook his head. "I'll settle for the gold and jewels, thanks. What do you say we scoop 'em up and get the hell out of here?"

She was already moving quickly. "Hurry. Those jewels should be in the very next cavern."

"If a prehistoric sea snake hasn't swallowed them yet."

"No promises. And that's not funny. I don't like the way Mack's tensing up. Watch where you step. And keep away from those dark, sluggish separate pools near the rocks. Those snakes seemed a little too fond of them. Maybe they think we're invading their territory."

"I only wish we'd brought cattle prods," Harlan said grimly.

"In all this water? We'd probably have ended up electrocuting ourselves."

Another snake slithered from the pool next to the path and came dangerously close to Mack. The dog yelped and quickly moved out of the way but stayed in front of Kira, protecting her. "Smart dog," Kira murmured. "Stay close, Mack." She started to run. "Come on!" Kira led Harlan and Mack to the next cavern, which was slightly elevated and completely dry. She stopped and glanced around. "We're looking for a small white boulder. It's lighter in color than the others, and it almost looks like a football." She pointed behind Harlan. "There!"

As she had said, there was a white boulder that roughly approximated the shape and size of an American-style football. Kira and Harlan knelt beside it and worked together to roll it away.

Kira looked down into the rock-lined hole that was left behind. "It's here!" She reached in and pulled out a white marble canister. She twisted off the cap, and Harlan aimed his flashlight inside to reveal that it was filled to the brim with a veritable rainbow of jewels, which reflected colored light all over the cavern.

"You weren't kidding," Harlan said. He reached inside and pulled out a string of diamonds. "These are incredible."

"And they're just the tip of the iceberg. But these will give you a hint of the quality we're talking about."

"I don't have to be a jeweler to see that. Just amazing."

Mack started barking again. He was looking back at the direction they had just come from.

"Oh, no," Harlan said. "More sea snakes?"

Kira cocked her head. "Do you hear that? It sounds like—"

"—water," he finished for her. He refastened the container's top and joined her back at the entranceway. The chamber behind them was now flooded and filling up fast.

"We were just in here," Kira said. "The tide isn't supposed to come in for hours."

"It isn't the tide," Harlan said. "It could be a thunderstorm miles from here. Underground streams could connect to this cave system and flood it in a matter of minutes. We need to get the hell out of here *now*."

A huge sea snake slithered past them.

"Shit!" Harlan stuffed the container into his waterproof knapsack. "We have to go back through here. No choice."

"Then let's do it!" Kira waded into the submerged chamber. She looked down and saw that Mack was beside her, apparently just as leery of the snakes as she was. They moved to the next chamber, which was now completely underwater.

Harlan shook his head. "How long can you hold your breath?"

"Hopefully, as long as it takes for us to get back to our sleds."

"Hopefully. Yeah, me too."

They took a deep breath and dove underwater, using their flashlights to guide the way back. Nothing looked the way it had just minutes before, and Kira knew that one wrong turn could be fatal. Her lungs were already starting to ache, and she knew she probably hadn't even made it halfway back yet.

Something moved up ahead. Could that be—?

A huge pair of jaws opened right in front of her face!

It was another sea snake, the biggest she'd seen.

Before she could even attempt to move away, the snake suddenly writhed back and forth and was hurled into the darkness.

Mack had grabbed this snake's neck in his teeth and flung it away!

"Good boy. But no more heroics. Just keep close to me. Move

fast." She grabbed Mack's leash and clipped it to his collar and then was pulling him through the water, using her own body as a barrier between him and any of those sluggish pools of water that might harbor danger, and hopefully keep him from trying to attack those blasted snakes. "Hurry, Mack. Don't pay any attention to those weird critters. Just move!"

And they *did* move at top speed through the series of caverns until they reached the small beachhead where they'd left the sleds.

They were gone. Floated away, obviously. Shit.

Harlan touched his diver's watch, and two headlights fired up on the far side of the cavern. The sleds, activated by a homing beacon, zoomed over to them. Harlan and Kira undocked their oxygen masks and put them on. Kira quickly positioned Mack on top of her sled, and they piloted their crafts out of the cave.

Less than a minute later, they broke the surface. Kira tore off her mask and hugged Mack close. "You're the best, Mack. You know that, right?"

Mack knew. His tail wagged furiously.

Harlan pulled off his mask and cruised alongside. "Is everybody okay?"

"Yes, thanks to Mack."

"Yes, I saw." Harlan reached out and rubbed the scruff of Mack's neck. "I suppose we'll need to take him on all of our expeditions."

"You know it. But next time he'll get his own version of a protective mask. Whether he likes it or not. I'm not going to risk him trying to save me and getting hurt himself. He almost gave me a heart attack."

"Yes, ma'am." Harlan nodded. "I'll go back to the drawing board and Mack will have his protective shield. I wouldn't have it any other way. We just weren't prepared for that kind of hazard this time. You have to admit prehistoric snakes and freak floods aren't what anyone would consider common threats."

"I know we can't prepare for every danger." She was still shaking as she held Mack even closer. "But both Mack and I have been trained to find bombs and disarm them. We don't think twice about it. It's our job. We accept it. And Mack made it through this more bizarre job with flying colors. But we have to do what we can to make any threat as safe as possible for him."

"That's what you did," Harlan said gently. "I watched you. You were ready to give your life to save Mack. You aren't the only one who almost had a heart attack. Do you think I'd let any of us go through that again?"

She shook her head. "Of course not. I was just so scared for him." She looked around. "Where's his sled?"

"It's heading toward you now. About twenty yards behind you. It's locked in on your location."

As it drew closer, Mack jumped off Kira's sled and paddled toward his own. He climbed onto its top surface and spread out with a sigh of contentment.

"He's tired," Kira said. She suddenly remembered something. "Tell me you still have those jewels."

Harlan patted his knapsack. "Yep."

"Good. Then let's get out of here!"

CHAPTER

14

"It was very interesting," Harlan said when he pulled Kira off her sled and onto the barge. "Those caves reminded me of the caverns I saw in Carlsbad, New Mexico. But the limestone surfaces were darker and more foggy while the waters flowing into them from the sea seemed brilliant and sparkling with life." He shrugged. "But no huge boxes of jewels yet to tempt Taylor from his life of crime. What a shame. I'm sure he'll be disappointed."

"Well, *I'm* not disappointed," Kira said as she took off her cap and shook out her hair. "I know it's there." She looked out at the sea. "And so does he, or he wouldn't have sent that cruiser to keep an eye on us. But I'm not eager to have him or his nasty thugs coming around and bothering us. I'd rather wait until we've located the majority of the treasure and we're ready to welcome them with the kind of response they deserve."

"I agree," Harlan said. "I just didn't expect you to be quite so enthusiastic about inviting them into our cozy circle."

"He's trying to *kill* you," Kira said coldly. "He wants to kill Fiona. You told me yourself that he'd already murdered your brother. It's not *right*. How long are we supposed to let him keep trying? We have to stop him. If the treasure will help us do that, then we have to find it right away and use it."

"I told you that Taylor would come to me. It's only a matter of time," he said. "You don't have to do anything, Kira."

"Just like you didn't have to help Mack and me when we were lying there dying on that mountain in Colorado. You don't make sense, Harlan."

He gave a low whistle. "You *are* upset. Since we don't even know if that was Taylor's cruiser yet, I don't think it's time to start planning to go after him. We'll talk about it when we get Belson's full report. In the meantime, let's get dressed and go over the data reports on today's journey to the caves with Hannah. Then we'll go up to the hills and have supper and maybe talk to Kalim and find out if he knows anything new. We'll have to turn the new stash of jewels over to him anyway and let him check out their history. Does that sound reasonable?"

"You mean that I'm not being reasonable?"

He took one glance at the tightness of her face and shook his head. "I wouldn't presume," Harlan said. "I'm just offering alternatives."

"Perhaps I'm not being as reasonable as I could be," she admitted.

"But neither are you. You're being entirely too calm about this. And we agreed we'd do this partnership together."

"I never said that I'd let you run up against Taylor again. Once was enough." His voice had turned abruptly harsh. "Too much." He turned to go back to the control room. "We'll talk later. Forty minutes back at the car. Okay?"

It wasn't okay with Kira, but neither was arguing with Harlan. Still, it evidently hadn't stopped her from doing it, she thought wryly. How could she explain that everything he did and said had an emotional backlash with her these days? She had begun to care too much for him. She had to either control it or find another way to handle her own feelings.

So that's what she'd do, blast it.

———— • ————

Forty minutes later they were driving away from the pier after she'd put Mack in the back seat of the car and climbed into the passenger seat herself. "You're right, I was upset," she said curtly to Harlan. "But I was also right about finding the quickest way to go after Taylor and you letting me help do it. So work that out, dammit."

"Yes, I will. There was no question about that," Harlan said impatiently. "I thought you'd realize that."

"Good, then I'll go along with any other suggestions you bring to the table. And tomorrow I'll do the best I can to find that treasure to lure Taylor into any trap we can manage to set up."

"As if you hadn't been doing that anyway." Harlan reached out and took her hand. "What sparked that little upset?"

"The fact that you didn't understand. I didn't see why you couldn't, when Fiona is always telling me how she can come to you with anything and trust you to fix it." She immediately released his hand and waved it dismissively as she went on. "But we'll forget it for now and just enjoy the evening. We had a great session in the caves with Mack, and I don't want it spoiled. Even though he was a little on edge toward the end." She smiled. "And it won't be spoiled as long as you're the one who cooks the supper! You have no trouble at all understanding the simple intricacies of cooking."

Harlan was staring at her speculatively. "I'm not at all sure that we should forget it. It may reach out and bite us if we don't get it out in the open."

"I'm sure," Kira told him. "Mack has had a rough day. I want to get him back with the other pups so he can relax. Drop it, Harlan."

He shrugged. "Heaven forbid we upset Mack. After all, he's the hero of the day." He stepped on the accelerator. "But later, Kira."

———— • ————

Kira made certain she became very busy when they arrived at the camp. She bathed and dried Mack, and then she had a talk with Aban about what they'd done in the diving sleds. By that time, supper was ready. She sat down with a group of the herders and got reports from them about their day and any problems with the dogs and horses.

"Finished?" Harlan asked as he sat down beside her in front of the fire.

"Not exactly. I still have to give Fiona a call and tell her how great Mack was today. She's a light sleeper, and anyway, I figure it's late enough on Summer Island that she should be awake. I know she'll be interested."

"So do I," Harlan said. "You've spread the good news throughout the camp, so why not include her?"

"That's what I thought," Kira said. "And by the way, that supper you cooked tonight was completely wonderful."

"Yes, it was. I thought so, too," Harlan said. "And before you ask, I also gave Kalim a call and he was delighted about the new treasure trove, but he hasn't received any more messages about the cruiser or his old friend Abdullah. He said he'd let me know when he did. No word from Belson, either. I'll call him again later."

"That's good," Kira said.

"*Now* are we finished?" Harlan asked. "I believe we still have some talking to do."

She nodded. "I'll meet you at the tent. I'll just make that quick call to Fiona." She took out her phone. "It's a promise. We both keep our promises, don't we?"

He flinched. "I have an idea that's going to haunt me until we're through with Taylor."

"It might." She smiled. "But I'll try not to make it hurt too much." She started to dial her phone. "And I promise to keep my word on everything else."

"Then all will continue to go well in Emerald City." Harlan tapped his forehead with his fingers and took off strolling quickly toward the tent area.

Kira found herself gazing after him a little uneasily for a moment before Fiona came on the line. "Fiona, it's good to hear your voice. It's Kira. How is everything going with you and your horses?"

"Well enough." But she immediately contradicted that. "No, that's not true. It's Golden Boy. I'm a little worried about him. The local vet here on the island says he's got a fever. Though he told me he'd probably be okay in a few days. It might be nothing, but I don't want to take any chances. And I know you trust this vet, but I've decided not to pay any attention to him. I've made a call to his regular vet at the castle to come and see him. He should be here anytime now."

"That's a good idea. But we use the local vet at the clinic all the time, and we do respect him enormously."

"I know, but Golden Boy is *mine*, and I have to take good care of him. How would you feel if it was Domino who came down with some nasty ailment?"

"You said it was just a fever," Kira said. "Don't borrow trouble."

"But fevers could turn into anything. It might be encephalitis."

"Then you'll take good care of him, the way you always do," Kira said soothingly.

"Well, I just wish you were back on the island to take a look at him. What's the good of you having all that fancy medical education if you can't use it? How close are you to coming back here?"

"I'm not sure. We'll come as soon as we can, but it might be a week or so. I'll be sure to keep you updated." She didn't want to leave Fiona in this depressed mood. "But the reason I called you was that I wanted to tell you how well Mack is doing with his underwater sled. You should have seen him today. He was magnificent."

"I bet he was," Fiona said. "I'm sure Domino would have been proud of him. All the more reason why you should come back and show off for us."

"I take it you're no longer nagging us to bring you here to see Kalim's horses?"

"Sure I am," Fiona said. "But that can wait. I need to get Golden Boy well from his fever. After all, he's my responsibility."

"That's very dutiful of you. I approve," Kira said. "But I have a few duties to take care of myself this evening. So I guess I'd better hang up and leave you to do yours. I'll call you again tomorrow to check to see how Golden Boy is doing with your vet. In the meantime, you take good care of him."

"I will," Fiona said quietly. "There's no question about that. I take care of all my horses. Like I said, it's my responsibility." She was away from the phone for a moment. "I'm getting a call. It's probably Sarah telling me my vet has arrived on the island. I've got to go, Kira. Bye." Fiona cut the connection.

Kira was smiling as she slowly pressed the OFF button and

slipped the phone back into her pocket. The call had been typical Fiona: a mixture of demands, affection, and responsibility that few fifteen-year-olds needed to develop. She was missing Fiona and found herself wondering if she could somehow arrange to give her that gift for which she'd been asking.

No, she told herself. *Don't even think about it now.* Fiona was hard to resist, and she'd let Harlan take care of that particular duty. Plus, as she'd told Fiona, she had made promises and had duties to other people than Fiona. One of those promises was to Jack Harlan, and she had to keep it. She jumped to her feet and strode away from the campfires toward the tents.

Harlan met her at the entrance to her tent with a glass of wine in his hand and a smile on his face. "Hooray," he said as he handed her the wine. "I was betting with myself if you'd show up on time. You fulfilled all my wishes."

"It was close. But as I said, I made a promise." She sipped her wine. "You should have bet on me to keep the faith."

"I was betting on you. It was Fiona where I had doubts. I thought she'd keep you on the phone a hell of a lot longer. She has a habit of clinging a little too hard if she cares about someone."

"I regard that as an endearing quality." Kira went into the tent and lit the lamp beside the bed. "And there's no such thing as clinging too hard if you care about someone."

"I agree, but there are times when you need a little personal time to come to terms with certain relationships. Particularly when it's with an individual as complicated as you." He sat down on the bed beside her and took a sip of his wine. "Now talk to me. Why were you so upset with me?"

"I've already told you. Fiona says you understand everyone and then set out to fix the problems. I didn't find that in my case. Not this time."

"Then how can I fix it?" he asked. "Because I am going to do that, Kira. It's very important to me."

"Of course it is. If it's something you might be able to fix, that's your nature," she said. "You said that you were going to get to know me, Harlan. I think you've succeeded. But have I gotten to know you? All I know is that you're the one who takes care of everyone. Fiona, Colin, all your employees, all the people on the estate, and your many, many, companies. I can't count how many people rely on you. And I appear to be just another person you took the trouble to save. But who took care of you, Harlan? Not Fiona, not your brother. Or anyone else that I've found. And you won't let me do it, either. I could see you pulling away from me today when I wanted to go after Taylor."

"It's what I do, Kira," he said. "It's one of the things I'm trained to do. How could I let you risk your life when it's a job I know how to do?"

"Because we had a deal and I don't cheat on deals," she said jerkily. "And I've found I'm particularly sensitive about this one. Imagine that."

"I'm very happy that you made me an exception. Would you like to elaborate?"

"I would." She reached out and turned off the lamp, plunging the tent into darkness. "If you don't mind." She came down into his arms and held him close. "I just want to hold you for a little while. Not for very long. I just want to take care of you and have you know that you don't have to do everything, be everything to everyone. Will you let me do that?"

He asked, "What? Great heavens, you haven't even mentioned sex? All I can say is that you're asking an awful lot, Kira."

She held him tighter. "Don't joke. This isn't funny to me. So you'll have to learn to live with it. I know you can do it. I wish I could have been there for you when your brother died. It hurts me that I wasn't. You were probably telling yourself that you could have somehow stopped it. Because that's what you'd do. Someone should have been there to tell you that none of it was your fault just because you once trusted that monster. You couldn't know what a demon he'd turn out to be. If I'd been there, I would have found out and told you."

"I imagine you would have." He was gently brushing her hair back from her face. "But I was responsible since Colin asked permission to have him stay at the castle. I could have refused."

She raised her head. "You see? I knew you'd be thinking some hogwash like that. If I'd said something like that, you'd have told me I was talking bullshit. I bet no one thought to ask what you were feeling. Everyone thought you were strong and mighty and king of the hill and could take anything that came along..." She tucked her head back down against his shoulder. "And you are. But you shouldn't have to do it all the time. So from now on, we do everything together and you let me have my moments of holding you. It will be a gift to me. Okay?"

"Are you finished?" he asked huskily. "May I tell you how touched I am now?"

"No, that would just embarrass both of us." She tucked herself closer to him. "Just keep holding me and remember that whatever we do, we're going to do it together..."

———————— • ————————

Harlan's phone was ringing, Kira realized as she got up on one elbow and saw that three hours had passed since she had turned out the lamp. Not only that, Harlan was already dressed and about to exit the tent.

"I don't believe you quite understood what I meant about doing things together," she said, covering a yawn. "Which part did you have problems with?"

"The part where Kalim sent me a text and told me that one of his men was going to pick me up and bring me to the village where Abdullah lives and he'd meet me there in the next half hour," he replied. "You weren't invited because Kalim thought my credentials were better than yours."

"That doesn't matter. And I'll tell him so." She started to get dressed. "I would have thought Kalim would know better."

"He does," Harlan said. "But the circumstances are a little difficult. Kalim asked you not to come this time."

She was still frowning. "Why not?"

"Because you're a woman and Abdullah was found murdered. Kalim didn't want the villagers to think he wasn't taking the death seriously. He had to call in the police from Morocco, and he also realizes I have contacts with them."

"Murdered?" she whispered. "How?"

"Stab wound in the throat," Harlan said. "Very nasty. Kalim said to tell you that it wasn't that he didn't respect you."

"No, I don't like it, but I understand," Kira said. "Abdullah was head of his village." She shook her head. "Give me a call as soon as you find out any details, and let me know what's happening. In the meantime, I'll try to get on the phone with Kalim."

"You'll probably know something as soon as I do," Harlan said as he kissed her cheek. "Kalim's man is outside waiting for me. I'll be back as soon as I can."

Then he was gone, and a few minutes later she heard the sound of a car as it left the encampment.

Murder.

Death.

Abdullah.

There was no way she was going to go back to sleep now.

She'd finish getting dressed and then go out to the campfire and talk to the herders about this horror. They would be even more devastated than she was because Abdullah was one of their own.

And it was Abdullah who had gone after the cruiser that might have been watching Harlan and her on the barge. Connection? Very likely. Which meant the threat was deadly and aimed in their direction. But how was he going to execute it? There was no question he would let them know soon—he enjoyed his vicious little games too much. Perhaps he'd already put them in play.

There was no question he wanted the treasure as much as he wanted the deaths he'd already planned. Harlan. Fiona. Not to forget her own. Taylor had probably struck at Abdullah because he was an easy target. So she had to go back to the other potential victims. How would he go after them? What was new or different in their lives that would make it easier for Taylor to pounce?

New or different...

She suddenly stiffened. There was nothing in that category about her life or Harlan's at present. Harlan had seen to it that they were both protected here on Hathor Island.

New or different.

But Fiona had something new and different in her life. Why had Kira not thought of that immediately?

Her hands were shaking as she dialed Fiona's number.

But Fiona did not pick up.

She dialed again. This time she got Fiona's voicemail.

Fiona's voice was cheerful and filled with energy when her message came on the line.

> Hi, I'll call you back when I get the chance. But things are happening and you'll have to stand in line. I promise to make it up to you. And who wouldn't want to wait for me?

For all of two minutes, Kira felt a little better about Fiona; her sickening feeling faded. But then she was dialing her phone again and leaving her own message.

Fiona. This is Kira. I need you to call me back right away. You're not the only one who's worrying about things happening. I got to thinking about Golden Boy and then about my own Mack. Taylor used Mack because he knew that I cared about him, and he was right. He's always going to use the people and animals we care about. What would be easier than making Golden Boy sick and then hijacking the vet you sent for to treat him? If your vet isn't on the island yet, I need you to be cautious when he gets there. I'm going to call Sarah and have her alert her guard detail right away. I hope to God it's not too late. Don't worry, we'll take care of this, Fiona. I'm not going to let anything happen to either you or Golden Boy. Please, please, call me back as soon as you get this.

She cut the connection and started to call Sarah.
But she was already receiving a call...
Unknown number.
Shit.
"Hello, Kira," Taylor said mockingly. "You persist in coming late to every party. Fairly soon you won't be receiving my invitations any longer. I know that would upset you."

"Yes, it would." She tried to keep her voice steady. "But I don't think I'll have to worry about that. You're not going to be around for much longer."

"Oh, I believe I will," he said. "Whatever would keep me from your charming presence? However, I have to compliment you on figuring out exactly how I could get my hands on Fiona. But you were late there also, weren't you? I think I'm coming closer and closer to having you exactly where I want you. I see that you've called Fiona twice recently but haven't made contact. I'm sure that your messages will give her hope for the future. She hasn't had much of that recently, poor child."

Don't show him how much he'd shocked and frightened her, Kira told herself. He wouldn't understand it. Listen to him and try to deal with him on his own terms. "Have you hurt her?"

"Not yet. I was saving that for when I can bring Fiona and her dear uncle together. What a reunion that will be. I can hardly wait."

Kira had been right. Deal with him on his own terms. "May I talk to Fiona?"

"Not right away. Unfortunately she became a little violent and I had to administer a strong sedative that would let her sleep. But you can see her." A photo flashed on the screen of her phone. "Just a little blood..."

Fiona was lying on a bed with wrists and ankles tied. The blood was on her wrists and upper lip. She was obviously unconscious. "You are a complete bastard." Kira tried to mask the bitterness she felt. "She's only fifteen."

"I'm aware of all her pertinent details," Taylor said. "I've been considering using her as a prize to give my men for special services. But she also has the misfortune to be related to Harlan. Too bad for her."

She tried to keep her tone as cold as his. "He'll kill you if you touch her, you know."

"Or it might be that this will bring us together in the way that I most desire. It would be a delightful punishment, and I've waited a long time for that. Most of the time, she's been penned up on those castle grounds and proving most elusive for my men."

Kira tried to think quickly. If she could find a way to turn his attention from Fiona, she might be able to strike some kind of balance...

Balance...bargain...strike a deal...think!

"It just shows that you can't have everything, Taylor. You shouldn't expect it." She paused. "And in this case, you're asking way too much. You made it clear what comes first for you. It's the treasure, and Harlan can't give you what he doesn't have."

"Nonsense. Harlan will give me whatever I want when I start hurting her," Taylor said bluntly. "In the past, the Harlan family has proved very generous and loving, and that gives me quite a decent weapon. Look at how long he's been hunting me since I killed his dear brother, Colin."

"But he can't give up what he doesn't have," Kira repeated. "That treasure you're so eager to take away from Harlan doesn't actually belong to him. It belongs jointly to Kalim and me. I was going to give Harlan a share for his trouble in protecting me from you. But in the end, the big bucks will be mine."

He paused. "I . . . don't believe you."

But he could be starting to, she realized. "Then do your research. Everyone knows that all the media stories about the treasure were about me, not Harlan. And what did Abdullah tell you about Harlan and the treasure before you killed him?"

"That you were probably sleeping with Harlan and that the underwater equipment you were using belonged to his Moroccan company."

"True. But also that Kalim was a special friend who liked me and supported me long before Harlan showed up on the scene. Didn't it ever occur to you that we'd also been lovers?"

"Of course it occurred to me," Taylor said slowly. "Just what are you offering, Kira?"

"What do you think? You're very good at trading, aren't you? I've heard you say yourself you always want it all. Isn't that right? Well, I want a chance to have it all, too. But I don't have the stomach for killing teenage girls that you do. I'll settle for a generous share of those jewels like the sample I brought up from the bottom of Kalim's caves. And if I can find a way to work it, I'll also try to get either Kalim or Harlan to share their wealth with me for the pleasure of my company in bed." Her lips twisted. "Though that might not happen with a bloodthirsty savage like you running the show."

"You'd have to be very clever to make that happen," Taylor said. "But yes, chances are still slim. It would interfere with all my prime motivations."

"Or it could make it easier to make the kills you were planning and also scoop up the treasure and get away with it in all the confusion. Are you smart enough to do that? I don't think so, Taylor."

"You don't know anything," he said harshly. "You're just a little whore out to score. You don't know what I've done in the past or what I'm capable of. But Harlan knows how difficult it is to fool me."

Kira said fiercely, "What I do know is that I'm really the only one who knows where the treasure is located and how to get my hands on it." She added, "And I know that you'll have to trade me Fiona to give to Harlan or he's not going to trust me or give me anything else I want. Since I'll have to have Harlan's sleds to bring up the treasure, I'll have to go through him to get them."

"And what do I get in exchange?"

"What do you think?" Kira asked. "What you *don't* get from me is Harlan or his niece to torture or kill to amuse yourself. That would cause too much trouble with law enforcement and they'd be all over us. You haven't been showing a low profile lately. So you'll have to work on getting that kind of kick on your own." She deliberately made her tone mocking. "However, in exchange I'll escort you down to the caverns to find and load that treasure onto a cruiser like the one you had spying on us from Abdullah's village. You provide the cruiser. I'll supply the treasure."

"That's not good enough. How do I know you won't betray me?"

"You don't. Set your own conditions. I'm sure you'll have a few ideas."

"Yes, I will," he said grimly. "One, you should realize that Fiona is no longer on your cozy little island. I had her smuggled out earlier this evening. I had that vet who was treating the horse she was so worried about tell everyone to keep away from the stable so he wouldn't spread germs to the other horses. So don't think you can just pick her up and snatch her away from me."

That's exactly what Kira had hoped, but it was clearly not going to happen. "Of course not. That would be foolish of you."

Suddenly he started to laugh. "Yes, it would. But I've just thought of an idea to guarantee that you won't betray me. Suppose I trade Fiona for you? Wouldn't that be amusing? Everyone knows that a whore like you would please Harlan more than a kid who is a constant expense and trouble for him. I return his niece and I get unrestrained use of you for the time you're with me. Twenty-four hours a day, which will also include the use of one of Harlan's miracle sleds and your services however I see fit." He was still chuckling. "And all his fancy friends will continue to think how noble he is and what a hard choice he had to make to get his niece back."

"Yes, very clever," she said. Diabolically clever, she thought, and she'd have to concentrate every effort to make a plan like that work for her. "As long as you go along with giving me what I want out of the exchange. I can probably talk Harlan into thinking later that I was only doing it for his benefit and get whatever I want from him, but you've got to handle it right. Do you understand?"

"Oh, I understand. But perhaps you don't. I'm going to enjoy this." He added, "Though I'm not certain that you will. You might change your mind, and that would make me unhappy. I like this idea. It's an entirely new way to sting Harlan."

"I won't change my mind."

"Women often do, and I'll think about it. Ah, but in the meantime I believe I'll let you have a little time to go over the possible ramifications of what could happen to Fiona while she stays on my cruiser at the mercy of my men. She's such an engaging little thing. How could they resist her?"

"Why should I care?" Kira asked coldly. "She's not my niece. Though your interference would just make my job more difficult because it would leave Harlan all the more angry." She added, "We'll have to do the exchange very quickly. Once Harlan finds out that she's missing, it will be much more difficult to come to terms with all the details. But I'm sure you'll see that we both believe it's the best way to handle the situation." She paused. "After all, it was your idea."

Taylor was chuckling again. "So it was. And that makes it doubly possible. I'll get back to you very soon when I get all the details straight in my mind. Probably in ten to fifteen minutes. Be ready. Goodbye, bitch." He pressed the disconnect.

Kira felt limp as she hung up her phone. She might have pulled it off, but she had grave doubts. The only person she really wanted to talk to now was Harlan. And that was the one person she couldn't talk to if she wanted to keep Fiona safe. Because Harlan would immediately go after Taylor to get her back, and that might start a chain reaction that would cause both their deaths. But if somehow she could get Fiona exchanged, she'd only have to worry about Harlan.

And of course herself, she thought wryly. Taylor would be trying to get rid of her at every turn; the only thing that might keep her alive would be the treasure that she'd dangled in front of him. How the devil was she going to keep that lifeline in place and still find a way to survive?

And why was she whining like a child when she had no other choice? she thought impatiently. She would do it because it had to be done and she was the only one in a position to do it.

Kira's phone was ringing again.

Unknown number. She knew who that had to be.

She answered the call. "You've made a decision, Taylor?"

"How could I resist?" Taylor said. "It was such a splendid idea. I've already told Fiona that I'd arranged for an exchange for her and she wasn't happy about it. You'll find she's not quite in the same condition as before. I had to punish her for being such a naughty girl. She actually threw a cup at me when I was describing how I'd killed her father. She's lucky she missed, or I'd have whipped her bloody. As it is, she survived with only a few more cuts and bruises."

"No!" Kira's hand clenched on her phone. "I told you, Harlan won't cooperate with me if you've put a hand on her. I need his new sled to retrieve that treasure." She tried to calm down and steady her breathing. "Look, I'll be at the pier in forty minutes. Don't let anyone touch her."

"Forty minutes," he repeated. "After that, our deal is off." He paused for a moment, then came back on the line. "Pier? Why did you mention a pier?" he said softly. "How did you know? Am I going to have to kill Fiona after all?"

"No! You mentioned Fiona was on a cruiser. The only place that could accommodate a cruiser anywhere nearby would be one of the two piers serving Kalim's island—at Abdullah's village and on the north shore. And your man killed Abdullah, chief of his village, so you would be very unwelcome there. So I'll guess the cruiser is anchored at the north pier."

"Very clever," Taylor said. "But if you try to turn our meeting into a trap, you'll find Fiona's decapitated head displayed prominently on the bridge of my cruiser."

"It won't be. Send Fiona down to the pier and I'll let you keep me within rifle range on the pier until she's away from that cruiser. After I consider her safe, I'll let you take me aboard. But if it's you who's staging a trap to keep both of us prisoner, I'll find a way to bring you down. And you can be sure that you won't get your hands on that treasure even if I have to drown myself in the sea to prevent it."

She hung up the phone.

The next instant, Kira was dialing Aban and grabbing her bag to run out of the tent. "Aban, I need your help. I'm going to need a lift. Pick me up at the edge of the forest."

"Isn't Harlan there? Can't he—"

"No, he can't. Not this time," she interrupted. "I don't want to ask you, either, but I need someone...Kalim probably won't like that it's you—" She drew a deep breath. "Meet me there at the road and bring your motorboat and I'll tell you everything. Okay, Aban?"

"I'm on my way. Of course. You are my good friend, Kira. It's not often I get a chance to rescue a damsel in distress. Anything you want."

"Thank you. I promise it will be all right." She hoped to heaven she was telling the truth. "I'm on my way."

CHAPTER

15

Ten minutes later, Kira was sitting beside Aban in the Bentley on her way to the north pier. She was driving.

He gazed at her curiously. "I still don't understand...Why did you have me bring my motorboat out here earlier?"

"Is it well hidden?"

"Of course. No one will find it in the reeds."

"Good. Because you're going to take a trip in it tonight and bring Harlan's niece to the encampment. You'll have to keep her safe there until Harlan can join you and do it himself. And I chose you because you know this island like the back of your hand, along with every inlet and tree and lake. No one will be able to catch you even if you need to hide out for a while."

"That is true," he said. "But you know Hathor Island almost as well as I do. Why do you not take her yourself?"

"Because almost is not enough in this case, my friend." She paused. No, she had promised to tell him everything. It was only fair she did so. "And I may not be available to make it safe enough for her. I'm dropping you off in the woods leading out to the pier and you'll take the boat down the path to the inlet while I bring Fiona to you. Once she's in the boat, you'll have to move very fast while I create as much distraction as I can manage."

"You're not coming with us?" he asked slowly. "I don't believe I like that plan. I know Harlan will not. Think of something else."

"There isn't anything else," Kira said. "Pull over to the side of the road." She opened the door when he did as instructed. "No one from the pier or the cruiser can see you going into the woods from here. Now take the motorboat to the inlet and get it ready to rescue a damsel in distress just as you promised. It's simply a different damsel. I'll be right back, Aban."

"I do not like this," Aban whispered again.

But Kira could see him moving toward the motorboat as she was heading down the pier.

There was one more thing she had to do, and it had to be done now. She dialed Harlan.

He answered immediately but sounded a little impatient. "I know I told you I'd call you as soon as possible, but Kalim and his villagers received info about where the cruiser might be berthed together with the people who were seen hunting down Abdullah. Kalim asked me to help him and his people track them down. I can't give you a full report right now."

"That's not why I'm calling you," Kira said. "You probably have all the wrong information anyway, because it came from Taylor. And I can see that cruiser you're talking about and it's only a stone's throw from where I'm standing right now."

"What the hell are you talking about?" he asked harshly.

"Listen, I don't have much time. Taylor is going to call you any moment and he'll be telling you a bunch of lies, but the one thing that's true is that Fiona will be safe and I made sure that Aban took her back to the encampment so you can keep her safe. The other thing that's true is that I had to make a deal with Taylor to find the treasure and give it to him to make certain he'd give me Fiona in return. That means he keeps me with him until I can do that. And I *will* do that, Harlan. Because I won't let him get his hands on Fiona again—and not those jewels at the bottom of the sea, either. I'll find a way of stopping him. Now quit muttering curses beneath your breath. I know that you're going to go after him and find me. It would be natural for you. And I'm glad you have Mack. Keep him close. He'll help you. Tell him it's a game. It's what I'd do for you if you'd done some crazy stunt. Except this isn't crazy. It's the only thing I could think of to keep Fiona alive. Taylor would have killed her. I *know* it, Harlan. Play his nasty game and we might be able to keep everyone alive."

"Will you be quiet?" Harlan asked hoarsely. "I'm trying to think of some way I can just manage to keep *you* alive. You know it's you he'll kill, don't you? You're number one on his list right now."

"No, that's definitely you. Though we might be able to use that in some way. But right now all I can think about is using the treasure." She heard Taylor coming down the ramp toward the pier.

"My time's up. I have to get back to him now so that he can start to torment you and tell you where to send my sled so that he can use it against you. He particularly liked that idea. And be sure that you act angry and a little heartbroken that he'd decided to use me against you, too. After all, I'm something of a precious jewel myself."

"Yes, you are. When you don't see fit to torture me into complete oblivion." He had to clear his throat. "Don't you dare let him hurt you. Angry? I'm going to kill the son of a bitch the minute I see him. But I'm begging you. Don't *do* this, Kira."

"Too late. It's already done. Taylor would kill me anyway for taking Fiona away from him if I didn't supply a replacement. We can do this, Harlan. Take care of yourself." She was walking toward the cruiser as she spoke and called out to Taylor, "I'm finished with talking to Harlan. You can talk to him now. I believe he'll go along with what I want. He'll let me use the sled as long as I turn over Fiona to him." She stopped and stood looking up at Taylor. "You need to hand her over now."

"You'll get her." He turned and grabbed Fiona's arm and shoved her down so hard, she fell to her knees on the pier. "Here."

"Come on!" Kira jerked Fiona to her feet and dragged her down the pier toward the woods. "You've caused enough trouble. Did you have to throw the damn cup at him? Are you trying to spoil everything?"

"You didn't hear what he said to me," Fiona said.

"And I don't care!" Kira shoved Fiona off the pier and onto the path leading through the woods. "Run!" she hissed. "As fast as you can! Now! I'll be right behind you."

Then Kira turned back toward the cruiser. "Did you have to hit her so hard, Taylor? Why make it so difficult? She can barely stand up."

Fiona looked at her in bewilderment and then started to run full-speed down the path into the woods.

Kira took another step toward the cruiser, blocking Taylor's view of Fiona. "And I see you have that rifle pointed at her. Don't you dare shoot her after I managed to talk Harlan into letting me use that sled. You're ruining everything!"

"Get out of my way, Kira." Then he heard the sound of the motorboat coming from the woods. "Damn you." He shouted, "Donovan, go after her. Don't let her get away."

Donovan was off the ramp and running down the pier. He brutally knocked Kira down as he passed her and then disappeared into the woods.

Taylor whirled back to face Kira as she got to her feet. "He'll bring her back," he said savagely. "And he'll be her first customer when he throws her back into that whore's room I gave her."

"No, he won't," Kira said. "I took care to keep her safe. Do you think I'd let you spoil all my plans? I told you that you couldn't have both of us. Now either shoot me or take me aboard and give me a room where I won't have to look at you or your men until I can arrange a delivery of that sled from Harlan." She was coming up the ramp toward him now, careful to still block his view of Fiona.

"Like I said, Taylor, you can't have everything. Be content you managed to get your hands on me. I'm a much better deal for you than his niece."

"I'm tempted." He was looking down at his rifle. "But maybe I'll let you live until I get that treasure."

Kira nodded. "And by that time maybe I'll be able to find something of equal value to keep you interested."

"Perhaps. It could be exciting watching you dangle, never sure when I'm going to pull the string and have you slowly suffocate."

She could see he was enjoying the thought. "Don't try to intimidate me. You'd rather have the treasure."

"I'm not that certain. You'll have to convince me. You'll never know which choice would please me most." He went back and leaned on the railing. "But you'll aways have that tiny worry gnawing at you, won't you? Ah, here comes Donovan. He's frowning. He never likes to fail me. It's made him very angry with you. Perhaps you might realize within a few minutes what your fate will be."

"I'm not worried. You're enjoying this too much." Kira gave a mock yawn. "And I still think you're going to go for the treasure."

Donovan was running up the ramp. "That bastard had a motorboat. I have to get a few of the guys and go after them. We'll hunt them down."

Taylor muttered an oath. "And how do we know it's not a trap? We've already been here too long. Up anchor. Lock her up in the bedroom, and let's get back to the safe house." He turned to Kira. "Well, there's your answer. It appears you have a little time to get all your ducks in a row. But you'd better be ready to move and give me what I want as soon as we're in position. Otherwise, you're not going to be happy."

They were obviously going to move the cruiser to a different location, Kira realized as Donovan roughly grabbed her by the arm and pushed her toward the cabin area. "I'll be ready." At least enough time had passed so that with any luck Aban should have Fiona almost back at the encampment by now; at least she wouldn't have that to fret about. Her only concern would be how to handle Taylor until she could get that sled in position and keep him greedy enough so that he'd have no choice but to go after the treasure. But what with his anger, greed, and lust, it might turn out to be a very long night for her...

Don't think about it.

Just concentrate on doing what had to be done to survive it.

———————— • ————————

ABDULLAH'S VILLAGE
TWENTY MINUTES LATER

"Where the hell are you going, Harlan?" Kalim was scowling as he stepped in front of Harlan's Range Rover. "I thought we'd agreed to take one of my trucks until we reached the shore."

"We did," Harlan said curtly. "But my plans suddenly changed. I have to make a side trip back to the encampment. There appears to be a problem we weren't counting on."

"And you can fix the problem if you go back to the encampment?"

"I hope to God I can," Harlan said harshly. "But I have my doubts. It might be too late. I can't get through to Aban."

Kalim stiffened. "Aban? What does Aban have to do with it? I gave him orders not to go with me on this hunt."

"Well, it seems Kira gave him different orders." He leaned over and opened the passenger seat door. "And yes, I told her that she wasn't wanted on this mission. But she doesn't pay any attention to me, either. Would you care to come with me? Perhaps Aban will answer your calls. You appear to have a good deal of influence with him. Though neither of us has as much influence as Kira."

Kalim stood there staring at him. "You're worried as hell," he said slowly. "And I don't believe it's about Aban. Is it Kira?"

"What a brilliant guess," Harlan said caustically. "Yes, it's Kira."

"What happened? Was she upset I wouldn't let her come on the hunt with us?"

"Yes, of course. But that didn't last long. Then she decided that she'd go on a hunt of her own." His lips tightened. "And that's what she did. Are you going to come with me or not? I've got to get to that encampment."

Kalim glanced at Mack, who was curled up on the back seat. "You're taking her dog back to the camp?"

"He won't be there for long. Kira told me he has to stay with me. I'm not about to do anything she doesn't agree with at the moment." He added grimly, "That may come later."

Kalim shook his head, troubled, as he got into the passenger seat. "I can't believe Kira would be that foolish. It wouldn't be at all like her."

"No, it wouldn't," Harlan said jerkily. "Unless she had a reason to think it was worth the risk." He started the Range Rover and headed down the road. "Sit back and I'll tell you all about it while we're on our way to give Aban the third degree. Kira found the perfect reason to go hunting down that son of a bitch," he said hoarsely. "Why not?" Because it was almost certain to get her killed...

Aban was waiting near the edge of the encampment when Harlan pulled up and stopped beside the campfire. He ran forward as Harlan put on the brakes. "I didn't like the idea," he said quickly. "I told her that you wouldn't, either. But she wouldn't listen. She just kept giving me orders."

"I believe you," Harlan said as he got out of the car. "But why the hell didn't you answer my calls?"

"She told me that no one must catch me while I had Fiona. I was afraid someone might trace the calls. I couldn't have that. No one was allowed to know where she was but you, Harlan."

"You still could have answered my call and let me come and pick you up. Where is Fiona?"

"I put her in Kira's tent. She wasn't feeling so good. Taylor knocked her around a little."

"And why did you ignore my calls?" Kalim demanded as he got out of the car. "I've called you twice since we got on the road. You do not ever do that to me, Aban. I thought that was understood."

"It is," Aban said quickly. "But Kira was very worried, and I thought you would not mind just this once. You always say I have to do what's best for everyone. Kira was very sad and worried.

273

She told me I had to rescue the damsel in distress even if it wasn't her."

"And I'm tempted to break your head open, young man," Kalim said grimly. "Next time I'll do it. Where is this damsel, Harlan?"

"Here she comes." Harlan gave a low whistle as he saw Fiona limping toward the blazing fire. "And not looking any too well," he said as he started toward her. "You're sure she's not badly hurt, Aban?"

"She said she was fine. Just a few bruises."

But Fiona was running toward Harlan now and then she was in his arms. "It was terrible, Harlan. I told him to take me to you, but he wouldn't do it." She was wiping the tears away from her cheeks. "It's all wrong. We have to go back to get her. I never would have left her if she hadn't lied to me."

He was looking at the cuts on her face. "These aren't too bad." He looked her in the eyes and asked gently, "Did Taylor hurt you in any other way?"

"Lots of threats and he made me drink that horrible stuff that put me out. And he socked me twice after I threw that cup at him. That made him really mad. I wanted to crush his face in."

"I imagine you did. I know just how you feel."

"But none of that matters." Fiona threw her arm out toward Aban. "He should have taken me back when I told him to. He wouldn't listen. Kira is with that asshole, and we have to go get her." Tears were flowing down her cheeks again. "He *hurts* people. He told me how he hurt my father. He laughed about it. I won't have him hurting Kira."

"You're right, we have to go back and get her," Harlan said. "But it's not your battle now. You'll have to leave it up to me."

"The hell I will," Fiona said. "It's always up to you. But this time I'm the one who brought Golden Boy's vet to Summer Island. I still don't know what Taylor did to him after he gave me that shot. He wouldn't tell me. All he said was that he hadn't hurt Golden Boy because he was too valuable. I've got to make sure I didn't cause any other harm."

"Don't worry about that," Harlan said. He didn't want to tell her that two of the guards he'd left to protect her on Summer Island were missing and now presumed dead, which was how so much time had elapsed without anyone realizing Fiona had been taken. "I don't know what role your vet played in this yet. But on the road here from Abdullah's, I called the captain of the guards at Summer Island, and I don't have the slightest doubt you were the target, Fiona."

"What difference does that make? Because Taylor still took Kira—" She whirled to face Aban. "—and it was *his* fault because he wouldn't pay any attention to me when I told him he had to take me back to get her. All he'd say was that he had his orders from her and you'd be angry if he didn't obey her orders."

"I did what I was supposed to do," Aban said sourly, "and everyone is already yelling at me. You're a pretty lousy damsel in distress, Fiona. I'll have to tell Kira that the next time I see her."

"If you see her again," Harlan said. "I'm not too pleased with the way you handled this either, Aban." He turned back to Fiona. "But it's probably not fair of you to blame him too harshly. We all know how difficult and determined Kira can be when she makes up her mind. You've seen it yourself. She wanted you back very much and was willing to do anything to make it happen. Now we've just got to concentrate on bringing her home. Aban will help us do that, and so will Kalim—to whom you haven't been introduced." He gestured to Kalim. "Kalim, my niece, Fiona, who appears to be just as upset as we are about the way Kira decided to go about getting our hands on Taylor."

"He's the one with the horses?" Fiona turned immediately to face Kalim. "Good. Tell him we don't care about his blasted horses if he'll help us find Kira. I'll even give him my Golden Boy. He could be as good as any one of his horses that Kira was telling me about. He'll probably win another Olympic medal this year."

"That's very generous of you," Kalim said. "But I'll have to refuse your offer. I regard your friend Kira as also my good friend, and that means I can't take anything in payment but your help in bringing her back to us. You may know a good deal about where Taylor and those terrible men were keeping her and can give us information. Is that possible?"

"It's possible," Fiona said. "And you're very smart to think about it. We can use him, Harlan."

"Thank you," Harlan said. "I'm sure he appreciates your approval. I was about to ask you the same thing, but I hadn't gotten around to it yet. Suppose we all go back to your tent and ask you all those questions right now. Unless you prefer to go to Kalim's palace?"

"Whichever is faster. I think Kalim will want that, too." She started back toward the tent area. "And Aban can come, too. He might remember something else Kira told him that he forgot to tell me. He said she's the one who talked to Taylor about you."

"Of course I will come," Aban said. "I do not need your permission. Kira is my friend. I am the one she called when you foolishly got yourself caught by that vermin."

Fiona looked stricken. "You're right. I've known that from the minute you jerked me down in that motorboat and took off with me. It was all my fault. I was the one who called the vet to come to Summer Island and take care of Golden Boy. I thought it was the right thing to do. But if I could change it now or have Harlan try to trade me for Kira, I'd do it. Taylor just might do it. He was very angry with me when I hit him with that cup." She glanced at Harlan. "How about it? It's either that or you take me with you when you go hunting for her. Otherwise, I'll go after Kira on my own. It's my fight now. It should have been mine all along."

"You were a little young," Harlan said. "And that would have been a special victory for Taylor that I'd never give him. As it is, I should have kept you safer while you were on Summer Island."

"Bullshit," Fiona said. "Make a choice, because it's going to be one or the other. You're probably right, I was only blaming Aban because I was feeling guilty myself. You can't expect me to stay here twiddling my thumbs—I'm not about to just sit this one out. Kira didn't do that when she knew I might be in danger."

"The young lady appears to be giving you a great deal of trouble, Harlan," Kalim murmured. "I could have her taken to my palace and put under heavy guard."

"No, you couldn't." Fiona turned back to face him. "I'd find a way to get away and then I promise you that I would be on my own." Her voice was suddenly fierce. "Because I'd never stop. Stay out of this, Kalim. That was a lousy idea. I respect you. I even like what I've heard about you from Kira. Since you're trying to be helpful, I'll be glad to work with you and do anything I can to please you. But don't think you can order me around. Look, maybe I wasn't as courteous as I should have been, and I know that all these people around here believe you're some kind of important royal demigod or something, but it doesn't mean anything to me. I grew up in the same house as Jack Harlan and I'm used to it. We can do this together. But don't get in my way."

Kalim gave a low whistle. He glanced at Harlan. "It's your call."

"It always is," Harlan said. "From the time she was seven years old. And I believe that we'd better take her along. She always means what she says, and she'll obey once she understands it's the right thing to do." He pushed her toward the tents. "But you'll obey without question, Fiona. And we're going to ignore that you're a bit banged up because that's what you want. But your first order is to keep an eye on Mack while we're on Taylor's trail. There may be more orders later."

"Mack is going along?"

"Kira may have a use for him. When I spoke to her, I think her intentions were a little blurry about whether it was me who was going to use him, or if she intended to do it herself. All she was sure about was that Mack could be a help. But then she believes Mack can walk on water anyway. However, we wouldn't want to disappoint her, would we?"

She shook her head. "Kira is really smart. She must have a good reason." She reached out and took Mack's leash from him. "And I'll probably be able to give you sketches of Taylor's men who were on the cruiser. I was careful to study everyone I saw after I regained consciousness. Would that help?"

"It might. Anything you saw or heard may help." They were at Kira's tent now. Harlan opened the flap and gestured inside. "I'll call Belson and we'll gather all the information we can from him about the location of that damn cruiser, then we'll start planning how this is going to go down. Let's all get to work, shall we?"

CHAPTER

16

The cruiser was no longer moving across the water.

Kira had been almost certain that the cruiser had stopped over an hour ago, and she thought she'd heard activity outside on deck.

They must have arrived at their destination near the coral reef. She had barely come to that conclusion when she heard the lock turn and then the door was thrown open.

"Welcome to my home away from home," Taylor said mockingly. He tore open the package he was carrying to reveal a navy blue wet suit. "I brought you a gift. You might need it paddling around in the Mediterranean tonight." He took her arm and pulled her out on the deck. "But first I wanted to show you my beautiful coral reef. And I would defy anyone to find either this cruiser or anything else that I choose to hide in this jungle." He threw out his hand to indicate the dense foliage surrounding them. "That's why I 'liberated' this reef from the families who lived here before I took it over. It took me only a week or so and two deaths of family members before the others ran like rabbits. Of course, one of the deaths was a grandfather that the others revered. I always pick and choose in these cases."

"I'm sure you do." She kept her face expressionless. "And I'm equally certain that they were so terrified, they decided never to return to their homes. So you've found a safe hiding place for your cruiser and for any guests you might decide to bring here." She met his eyes. "But since you've chosen to bring me, I'd bet that I can find my way around this reef of yours. For that matter, so would any experienced tracker. It would only take skill and determination. Jungles are difficult but not impossible. Though you appear to have tucked this cruiser neatly in all this jungle brush, and you probably have a good many men stationed and ready to intercept any interlopers."

"Yes, quite a few," Taylor said. "Eight to be exact. And they all realize what will happen to them if they don't do what they're supposed to do about uninvited visitors."

"What a shame," Kira said mockingly. "Just think about what a tragedy it would be if you lost such a talented bunch of hooligans. You might have to face a real threat all by yourself."

His lips curled. "You think you're so clever. You're *nothing*. Though I may decide to play with you for a little while to keep myself amused. Yes, I believe that might be the thing to do. But first, I think it's time for you to do your duty and give Harlan that call you promised to make." He reached in his pocket and pulled out his phone. "I want that sled as soon as possible. Tell him to arrange to air-drop the sled into the sea." He handed her the phone. "Call him and tell him that he's to send you the sled by midnight tonight. After you finish, hand me the phone and I'll give him exact directions where to drop it so it will be easy for me to retrieve. If he fails to do as I wish, he won't get a second chance. You'll not be of any use to me without the sled, so I might as well dispose of you." He smiled. "And that will at least give me the pleasure of knowing I cheated Harlan by making sure that he'll never have you as his mistress again. If he tries to go after the treasure on his own, I still might have a chance to steal the sled and go after him when he tackles those caves."

"Not much of one," Kira said. "You need me, Taylor." She started to dial the phone. "And you need the sled. I think I almost convinced him before to send it to me. Just give me a chance to persuade him."

"We'll see," Taylor said. "No tricks. I'll be listening." He turned up the volume. "Go ahead, Kira. Let's find out if he'll give up that sled to you. It's not only the treasure, it's the sled itself. Any invention Harlan brings out on the market is worth a substantial fortune. That's why I killed his brother. I couldn't resist the temptation to claim his latest invention as my own. If he does give it up to you, it will prove that he cares something for you. Which will mean that you'll have a certain value to me. It could save your life."

Kira shook her head. "You're lying. It didn't save Colin's. He thought you were friends, and you killed him."

"The situation was different. He caught me off guard. Though it didn't really matter. Make the call."

Harlan's phone was already ringing. Then he answered.

"Harlan? It's Kira," she said. "I told you that I'd call you back. We talked about the sled. Taylor is very eager to have it. He's listening now."

"That doesn't surprise me," Harlan said sarcastically. "He appears to lust after everything I own. Including you, it seems. Is he treating you well?"

"He's treating me as you'd think Taylor would treat me. He wants what he wants. I guess you've found out that the cruiser has been moved? He's sure that the cruiser and all his other possessions have been tucked away in a jungle where you'll never find them. I told him a good tracker would be able to surprise him. Just as I managed to do in Colorado. He's frowning at me now, so I'd better ask you to please send me the sled. It appears to be my only value in his eyes. He's not an individual who cares about anything else. Certainly not like family. I was just thinking about Abdullah and how much those villagers cared about him before he was killed. He was kind of like the grandfather of that entire village. His relatives must have felt as if they'd been deserted when Taylor murdered him. Taylor would never have been able to comprehend a relationship like that. He definitely couldn't understand how you felt about Fiona. That was why I had to get her away from him."

Harlan shook his head. "Oh, he understood. That's why he took her. He needed a weapon to use against me. You were foolish to go after her. It was bound to turn out badly."

"I couldn't do anything else. So why didn't you agree to give me the sled and let me try to save her? You do care about her. All I have to do is use the sled to retrieve the treasure and then turn it over to Taylor. You don't have to be involved at all. I'll return the sled to you and that will be the end of it. You get your invention back, and I have the jewels to give to Taylor. Everyone is happy."

"You might not be happy," Harlan said. "He could turn on you at any time."

"But he won't, if I can give him more coins for his cookie jar. I might have to offer him another treasure if he's not content with this one. But I'm willing to do that." She added coaxingly, "Give me the diving sled."

"Why would I want to do this when I've already given Taylor so much?"

"Do it for me. I've already given Fiona safely back to you." She paused. "I didn't mean to worry you, but Taylor keeps threatening me. I know you don't want him to hurt me, but you might have to give in on this one point to keep me safe. I don't believe you'd want to have anything happen to me."

"For God's sake, *no*," he said violently. "I'll take care of you, Kira."

"I thought you would. Now I'm going to turn the call over to Taylor, and he's going to give you directions. I hope to see you soon, Harlan." She handed the phone back to Taylor. "I told you Harlan would go along with it," she said softly. "He only needed to be nudged a little."

Taylor grabbed the phone. "And I'm very good at nudging.

Hello, Harlan," he said harshly. "Take these notes down. I want that diving sled by midnight, and no one can follow you if you want Kira to live." He rattled off the directions. "Understood?"

"You couldn't be more clear," Harlan said. "But if you touch Kira, I promise you won't live to see that treasure."

"The hell I won't," Taylor snarled. "I think I'm going to have to make her see how wrong she was about my little hideaway during the next few hours. She's very proud of herself that she managed to hunt me down in Colorado. Let's see if she can make her way through this jungle without getting her throat cut by one of my men. If she's lucky, she just might survive it." He cut the call short before turning back to Kira. "Harlan thought he could protect you just by threatening me? What a fool he is. Before this day is over, I'm going to be in a position to take him down." He pushed her toward the ramp. "Now it's time for you to take a little walk through my Garden of Eden and see if you come out of it alive. You're probably wanting to see if you can find your way around the reef in case you decide I might prove a danger to you. I'll give you a shot at it. I'll even give you a weapon to protect yourself. Do you believe that will be enough to keep you safe from those eight guards who will be very eager to slit your throat? Suppose I give you two hours to stroll around, and if you make it back to the cruiser alive, I'll let you rest for a while before we go pick up that sled."

"How very kind of you," Kira said. "But do I have to remind you that if you don't have me to drive that sled, you'll have a very rough time getting that treasure? Is it worth it sending those guards of yours after me just to frighten me?"

"But will they frighten you? You weren't frightened up in the mountains that night." He snapped his fingers. "That's right, you had Harlan to protect you. It made me very angry that you'd use him against me." He took the knife out of the holster at his belt. "Don't move, Kira. I'm very good with a knife, but I wouldn't want to damage you. You're right, I have to worry about you driving the sled." He threw the knife, and the blade pierced the wall next to her. "You see? Very good. Now take the knife and I'll see you in a few hours."

She drew a deep breath as she grabbed the handle of the dagger and ran down the ramp to the pier. "You're probably going to worry more about those guards than I will," she called back to him. "Every time you think of losing that treasure, you'll want to go after me and protect me yourself."

"You don't know that!"

"But I'm betting it's true. You're a greedy bastard." She was off the ramp now and running into the jungle as she slid the dagger into the waist of her pants. She had no idea if she was going to use it, but she might if it was a question of saving her own life. "I'll see you back here later, Taylor."

She heard him cursing as she ran down the trail. She stopped as she reached a bend to catch her breath. Taylor had been right about her planning to scope out the entire reef if she could, so that she'd be able to give exact directions to Harlan if it became necessary. She'd already tried to give him at least a hint about which area Taylor had chosen to move the cruiser. Eight guards, he had said...

Now she had to locate where those guards had set up their stations. But first she had to quickly familiarize herself with the reef itself.

Move swiftly but quietly.

Pay attention to all the trees and shrubs...

Particularly the upper branches of the trees. There could always be snipers.

Watch out for footprints of the enemy.

Seek out one of those guards, take him down, and search him for anything she could use to help her send a message to Harlan.

Finally, keep to the rule she and Mack lived by when they were on the hunt.

Keep alert every single minute...

———————— • ————————

Harlan started to dial Belson the minute he got off the phone with Taylor. "I just finished talking to Kira."

"How was she?"

"How do you expect her to be?" Harlan said harshly. "It was clear Taylor was pulling the strings. She even put him on the line to give me directions where to drop off the diving sled. But she also managed to give me a few hints about her location. It's an island or reef and has enough jungle foliage to hide the cruiser and probably another hideout or safe house. She kept talking about Abdullah and how Taylor had no feeling for family; there was something about how Abdullah was probably looked on by his villagers as a grandfather figure, but Taylor wouldn't have understood that."

"'Grandfather'?" Belson repeated. "What the hell?"

"Don't ask me. Kira was doing the best she could." He leaned wearily back in his chair. "It was clear she was walking a tightrope. Taylor was practically breathing down her neck. Just look for a reef or island with jungle, brush, and foliage that could hide that cruiser. It's probably not too far from Hathor, Kalim's island."

"And the grandfather?"

"That's up to you to make the connection. All I know is she was trying to tell me something. I've got to find out what it was before that bastard kills her." He pushed back the chair and got to his feet. "But right now I've got to arrange to move that sled onto a helicopter and get that drop to Taylor by midnight."

"Okay, I've got it," Belson said. "I'll find out where that blasted hideout is located. I promise I won't let you down."

"It's Kira you'd be letting down," Harlan said. "We can't do that, Belson, I don't think I could take it. We'll give Taylor that sled and then we'll find a way to take it away from him and keep her safe. She's given everything she could. Now it's our turn. I can't let him touch her."

"I don't believe that you'd allow that to happen. Particularly with me on your side," Belson said. For once, his voice had no hint of his usual dry humor. "I'll get back with you ASAP."

———— • ————

The guard was just behind Kira!

She ran faster!

She was almost back to the cruiser now. But she heard the crash of the guard's boots in the brush behind her. He'd been the last guard she'd run across as she'd been checking out the row of launches in the boatyard, which was only a few miles away from the cruiser. But he'd been more alert than the other guards—he'd definitely seen her, and she'd had to take off at a dead run. She'd managed to lead him on a race for the last couple of miles, but he was gaining on her. Instinctively, her hand closed on the handle of the dagger.

Though she might not need it. The ramp of the cruiser was right ahead...

But Taylor was standing there right in the middle of it and smiling mockingly at her as he blocked her access to the deck. "You almost made it."

"I *did* make it. Isn't this what you wanted? Me at your mercy? But now you'll have to make a decision. Let that guard have me or let me be there to run that sled for you."

"It's very close." He sighed and then waved off the guard, who was now starting up the ramp. "Leave her, Georgio. Maybe you can have her later. At the moment, she has a purpose." He reached out and took the dagger from her waistband and examined it. "No blood. I thought you'd come back with at least a sign of an encounter."

"It might have come to that. I was thinking about it. But I did hit the first guard I ran into with a very heavy branch that put him out of action." She reached into her pocket, pulled out a wallet, and threw it down on the deck in front of him. "Here's the ID I lifted off him. He never saw me coming. He was so inefficient I thought you might want to get rid of him anyway."

"It's entirely probable. I don't want anyone around who can be brought to his knees by a woman." Taylor was scowling as he bent and picked up the wallet. "I'm glad Georgio proved a little more of a challenge for you."

"Unfortunately, that guard behind me caught sight of me, and I had to run for it." She added impatiently, "Are you going to stand there blocking my way? I thought you said I could get a little rest before we went after the sled. Didn't I entertain you enough to deserve it?"

"Actually, you did." He moved to one side and permitted her on deck. "I can't tell you how much I enjoyed waiting for you to come back and imagining what those guards would do to you if they ran across you. I realized they'd eventually turn you over to me, but I was sure they'd have a bit of fun with you first."

"Instead, I was the one who ran across them," Kira said. "And no fun was had by any of us. I found your reef to be boring in the extreme, and those guards were hopelessly inadequate. May I go back to my cabin now?"

"By all means." He gestured toward the cabin area. "Go and rest. I'll even send you a supper tray to build your strength for the night to come. You're going to need it. I can't wait to see if Harlan will decide to actually do that sled drop to save your neck. Perhaps he doesn't care as much for you as you think."

"I guess we'll see, won't we?" She was heading for the door of her cabin. "But I think that sled—and the treasure—are as good as yours, Taylor." She went into the cabin and slammed the door.

She stood there, listening, waiting to see if he'd follow her into the cabin. Then she heard the key turn in the lock. Good. The sound of that lock would guarantee no one was going to surprise her while she was busy trying to prepare a message for Harlan.

She waited a moment until she heard Taylor walk away from the door, then moved across the cabin toward the desk in the corner. She reached into her jacket pocket and pulled out the phone she'd also taken from the first guard she'd encountered, slipping it into the desk drawer. She took out a piece of blank paper and a pen and closed her eyes for a moment, trying to remember all the details of the features she'd seen on the reef during the past few hours. It wasn't all that difficult. She'd done it many times before when she and Mack had been tracking in unfamiliar locales. Once she had things firmly fixed in her mind, she opened her eyes and began to transfer the reef to the paper, making certain she included the most important details. Placement of the guards . . . the boathouse . . . the cruiser, the tents overlooking the bay . . .

It took a little less than forty-five minutes until she was satisfied with the plan she'd drawn. She used the phone to snap photos of it. She tried to use it to send them to Harlan.

No signal. Damn. The boat had Wi-Fi but couldn't access the Internet satellite from its current hiding place. She'd probably have better luck later. She carefully folded the paper and slipped it into the waterproof ID section of the phone's container and put it in the very back of the desk drawer; she'd grab it again when the boat headed out into open waters. Since she'd be wearing that wet suit Taylor had provided, she'd be able to slip the waterproof container into the long, tight sleeves of the top before she was taken to the chosen site to pick up the sled. It would still be very risky, but it was the best she could do—and then everything she'd done today had been a risk, she thought wearily. She was lucky that Taylor had seemed so angry about her humiliating that first guard that he probably wouldn't look too closely to see what else she'd taken from him after she'd knocked him unconscious. She could only hope that Harlan would arrange somewhere for her to transfer the information when he dropped that sled into the sea. But Harlan was so damn smart. What good was being a genius if he couldn't do a little thing like read her mind? Heaven only knew if he'd been able to decipher what she'd been trying to tell him on that call. He'd told her that he was going to get to know her. Well, this would be a great test, wouldn't it?

Stop being absurd. Just relax.

Now all that was left was to rest and wait and hope that everything would go well and she'd be able to get that map of the reef to Harlan.

CHAPTER

17

Darkness. The sound of the water washing against the side of the launch. Taylor's harsh breathing and low curses from the seat next to her own.

There were six more of Taylor's men in this same launch, but the only one who was important to her now was Taylor, since he had spent the entire trip from the reef trying to intimidate her and forcing her to listen to his mockery.

"Are you ready?" Taylor asked as he turned to face Kira in the launch. "Harlan is cutting it kind of close, isn't he?" He turned on his flashlight so that he could see her expression. "I meant it when I told him that if he wasn't on time, you wouldn't live through the night."

She made sure to let him see that those words didn't bother her in the slightest. He would enjoy her discomfort too much. "That was only a threat. I don't believe you'd do it. You're far too selfish. You want that treasure too much, and I'm the key to getting it."

His lips curled. "We'll see if you're right. Maybe I'll be so pissed off that it will be worth it to me."

"I doubt it." She lifted her head as she heard the roar of an engine overhead. It had to be Harlan's chopper! "Because I'll bet that's Harlan bringing me the diving sled. I told you he'd do it. Now put on some lights so that Harlan won't drop that sled on top of this blasted launch."

"Not until we get moving so that they can't zero in on us." Taylor switched on the lights and started to speed in wide circles beneath the descending aircraft. Then the hatch of the helicopter was opening, and Kira could see movement as the sled was lifted and then pushed out of the copter.

It landed with a tremendous splash in the water, almost turning the launch over!

"Get in the water," Taylor ordered Kira. "I want you on that sled. You said you could run the damn thing. Now show me."

"I'm going." She turned around and surreptitiously checked the phone she'd taken from the guard. Still no signal. Damn. She had to do something else.

She slid off the launch into the water and then started to swim toward the diving sled. "Let me get settled on it and then I'll follow you back to the cruiser."

He hesitated.

"Move!" she said as she reached the sled. "I know you'd just as soon shoot me as look at me. Do you think I'd try to escape now? I'd pick a better place and time." She was crawling onto the sled now and found it completely covered in a waterproof tarp. Why? The diving sleds had never been covered in a tarp when she and Harlan had been using them before. She was sure the height from which the sled had been dropped would not have required the additional protection. Those sleds were lightweight but strong as cast iron. And if the tarp wasn't a safety measure, then it might be a way Harlan had chosen to communicate with her! She'd no sooner had that thought than she was running her fingers along the edge of the zippered closure of the tarp, exploring every inch of it. It appeared to be an ordinary seam...

No! It was doubled in the corner, and the underside was a zipper. She slipped the map of the island from beneath the sleeve of her wet suit and tucked it into the zippered pocket in the tarp.

But there was something else in that compartment! It was only a scrap of paper with a brief message scrawled on it.

I'll be there for you. Wait for me. H.

Thank God. She felt almost weak with relief. She wasn't alone any longer. Together. Incredible how those few words made such a difference.

"What are you doing?" Taylor was screaming at her from the launch. "Get that sled moving! We have to get out of here."

"I'm trying, dammit," she yelled back at him. "I have to get this blasted tarp off. It won't do more than crawl across the water if that tarp slows it down. It's all your fault. Harlan must have actually paid attention to those stupid threats of yours and wanted to avoid annoying you." She was silent a moment. "But I think I've got it off now." She tossed Harlan's note into the sea and watched it sink below the surface. Then she made a show of struggling to free the tarp, finally throwing it over the far side of the sled. "That does it." She was putting her arms into the sleeves of the sled itself. "You can take off now. I'll follow you."

"You'd better keep very close," Taylor said. "I'll be aiming this rifle at you all the way back to the reef." He lifted his head and looked up at the helicopter, still lingering near the place the sled had dropped from. "And if he makes any attempt to try to follow us, I'll blow him out of the sky."

"It's pitch dark tonight, not even a moon," Kira said. "He's not going to try anything. You've gotten what you wanted. He'll wait until he has a chance to do a lot more damage. Or else he might try to make a deal to keep me alive if he's feeling generous. I did give him Fiona back."

"It's whether or not I feel generous." Taylor chuckled. "And I never feel generous toward Harlan. There's been too much between us for too long."

She was adjusting the engine controls on the sled. It purred like a stalking panther. With the note from Harlan, all signs were good at this moment. "Then maybe your deal will be with me. I have my generous moments and I'm accustomed to taking care of myself."

"But I don't need your generosity," Taylor said. "I'll have everything I need once I take that treasure you keep waving in front of me."

"You haven't seen it yet. You might want more once you do. People like you never have enough." Kira squeezed the control trigger, and the sled sped around Taylor's boat.

Taylor gave her an impressed nod.

"You know that Harlan always satisfies his customers," Kira yelled.

He smiled maliciously. "And this time I'm the customer. After all these years, I think I like it."

"Of course you do. He said you like the idea of taking everything away from him." At this particular moment, she couldn't tolerate him any longer. She was just grateful that she could use his unfamiliarity with the sled to lie to him about its capabilities. "But it's not easy to run these sleds. I need to concentrate. I have to watch your launch every minute to be sure I won't run into you."

"Then be quiet and do your job," Taylor said with a frown. "I don't want you cracking up now that we're on our way to getting what I want. We're almost back to the reef anyway."

"Whatever you say," Kira said. She looked down at the controls. "You've made that more than clear to me."

I'll be there for you.

They were indeed almost back to the reef. But by the time Harlan got that tarp back out of the sea and checked it for messages, it would probably be almost morning. She doubted Harlan would choose Taylor's reef hideout to be the site of an attack at that time. He'd probably been talking about the caves, building his plans around them.

And she would build her own plans to coordinate with his.

Together...

————— • —————

ON BOARD THE HELICOPTER
ONE HOUR AND TWENTY MINUTES LATER

"Belson is on the phone," Fiona said as she left the cockpit and moved back to where Harlan was monitoring the hatch through which they'd dropped the sled over an hour ago. "He said it was important. Do you want me to take a message, or can I keep an eye on that blasted tarp you've been watching like a hawk? When are we going to go after it?"

"Very soon. I've just had to be sure that neither Taylor nor any of his men is anywhere near where we dropped that sled. I'm certain we're free and clear now. I've sent Aban over in a motorboat to pick up that tarp and bring it to the rendezvous point. It's made to float, and there's a GPS tracker in the lining. He should have no problem retrieving it."

"I could have done it for you," Fiona said. "You trusted me to help you drop the sled. Why couldn't I do that, too?"

"Because boating isn't your area of expertise and it's definitely one of Aban's," Harlan said dryly.

"What can I do to help you? Do you want me to take Belson's message for you while you wait to see if Aban gets that tarp?"

"That would be helpful," Harlan said. "And incredibly not at all like you, considering your desires about the matter." He moved toward the hatch as he saw the crew start Aban's final lift with the tarp into the helicopter. "Yes, take Belson's call," he said absently, "while I deal with Aban…"

———— · ————

PORT SAID AIRSTRIP, EGYPT

Fiona came out of the cockpit a little over forty-five minutes later. Aban was already drinking a glass of wine and looking very self-satisfied as he lifted his glass in a salute to Fiona. "Mission accomplished," he said with a grin. "Harlan was very pleased with me. Much more efficient than just tossing the sled into the water."

"Rub it in," Fiona said. "Did Kira send a message, Harlan?"

He nodded. "A very complete one. A map of the place where Taylor took the cruiser to hide it away."

Fiona gave a low whistle. "That's terrific. When do we leave?"

"You don't. That's not how we're going to handle it. This time Taylor isn't going to get away, and I'm not going to risk Kira's life or yours, Fiona. Not to mention, if you had your way you'd want to take any and every task involved with saving Kira. You're not the only one who feels that they need to help her."

"But I'm the only one who realizes it's her job," Fiona said fiercely. "Because every minute Kira is down there with Taylor, it's because I'm not and should have been." She gestured dismissively. "Yes, I know you feel it's your duty. You always feel like that." She paused. "And maybe it's more than that. I've been thinking that it could be."

"Maybe?" Harlan asked bitterly. "It could be a hell of a lot more than maybe, Fiona."

She nodded slowly. "But it still shouldn't keep me from being there and helping Kira."

"You've done what you could." Harlan was shaking his head. "No more, Fiona. You won't be involved in anything to do with freeing Kira. I have plenty of people we've brought into this area plus all of Kalim's villagers. We don't need you for this. Do you understand?"

"I understand what you're saying," she said slowly. "Though I believe you're wrong, Harlan. But I won't argue with you right now. I told you that."

"You're going after the treasure." Aban's face was filled with excitement. "The caves! You're going down to search the caves. May I go?"

Harlan shook his head. "Kalim wouldn't appreciate me taking you, and Taylor would almost certainly bring a boatload of his men after us. Perhaps we can find something else interesting for you to do."

"Yes, he can take phone messages," Fiona said caustically. "Just what we both wanted to do." She handed Harlan her notebook.

"Belson said that he thinks that Taylor's hideout we've been trying to find is a coral reef once inhabited by a desert people who were originally of Persian descent. But they were invaded within the last few years by a group of criminals who tried to take over their reef and finally succeeded recently. The head of their village was Babur Mateen, who was revered by all the other members of the group—kind of a grandfather to the younger members of the tribe."

"Grandfather," Harlan murmured. "Belson evidently struck gold."

"Not for very long. Babur Mateen was murdered by Taylor to set an example for his followers; so were two of his councilmen. Belson said he didn't know how many others were killed during that period, but it must have been enough that the other members of the village packed up their belongings and left for other islands and reefs in the chain. But word evidently did get around or Belson wouldn't have been able to track those villagers down this quickly."

"He did track them down?" Harlan asked.

She handed him her notebook. "Belson said those villagers wanted nothing to do with Taylor or his men. They were terrified that Taylor would hunt them down and kill them the way he'd already murdered so many of their friends and families. But they had no objection to someone else going after them. Like I said, they all liked Babur Mateen. They wanted revenge." Fiona nodded at the notebook. "And the location of their home reef appears to be fairly close to here."

"Yes, it does." Harlan was scanning the location and then checking it on the aerial map. "And with the information we've gotten from the interior map Kira sent us, we might be in a good position to move on them."

Fiona tensed. "When?"

"You haven't been listening," Harlan said.

"I've been listening," Fiona said. "I've just been hoping to talk you out of it."

"That's not going to happen," he said quietly. "I almost lost you, and Kira is still running a mega risk to keep you safe. Do you believe I'd let you put yourself in any other situation like that?"

Fiona's gaze searched his expression for even one sign of yielding. Finally, she shook her head. "No. But you're wrong. Kira would understand why I have to do it."

He nodded wearily. "I'm very much afraid that you're right. Because she'd probably do the same thing. Hell, I can almost see you following in her footsteps."

"They're terrific footsteps. I'd be proud to follow them."

"Oh, shit." He reached over and pulled her into his arms. "What am I supposed to say to that?"

"Yes."

"No." He pushed her back and looked down at her. "It's my job to say no to both of you. Kira didn't give me a chance to do it, so I'm taking the choice away from you."

She went back into his arms. "Not fair, Harlan." Her voice was husky with tears. "Change your mind."

"No way." He brushed his lips on her temple. "Accept it."

"It seems I may have to do that." She tried to clear her throat. "But not without you telling me what's going to happen and how you're going to find a way to get her away from that bastard." She glanced back at the notebook she'd handed to him. "Taylor wouldn't expect you to know anything about that coral reef. I thought this might be a way to get Kira away from him. Sort of a surprise attack? You might be able to use me as a decoy?" She saw he was shaking his head. "I thought it was a pretty good idea. What's wrong with it?"

"Not one thing if I thought the action was going to be focused on that reef," Harlan said. "And if I was willing to let you run the risk. But I'm not willing to let you do that, and we're not certain where the main action is going to take place. It could be on Babur's jungle hideout, or Taylor might send one of his units to attack Kalim's castle and the surrounding countryside to snatch all the treasure he can grab along with possibly a number of Kalim's prize horses. Hell, those horses might be worth more than the treasure. I'd certainly pay more for them."

She nodded. "I realize that. I've seen a few of those wonderful stallions since I arrived on Hathor Island, and I have to agree with you." Then she shook her head impatiently. "Now you've told me where the action might take place, but that's not why you let me help you throw that blasted sled out of the plane, is it?"

"No way," Harlan said. "Because my best bet is that Kira will find it easier to lure Taylor to use that diving sled to go after the treasure. A chest full of jewels would be easier to snatch and grab than transporting horses. I'm going to assume that's what she'll choose."

"And?"

"And I'll be down there in the caves with a team to give Taylor a surprise when he shows up with Kira in the sled."

"I should be there," Aban said suddenly. "I could help you. Let me go, Harlan."

"Don't you dare," Fiona said fiercely. "Just because Aban claims he's more fish than human doesn't mean that he'd help you more than I would. We could work around it."

"Neither of you is going with me," Harlan said flatly. "As I said, I'll have a strong, skilled team and I won't need you. I'll tell you what you're going to do instead. Actually, I'm tempted to send you back to Summer Island. You'd be safe there now. I contacted the guard units again and Taylor's thugs have all been routed and left the area, and the animals and medical teams are well and flourishing. By the way, Fiona, Captain Darue's men found Golden Boy's vet in the woods. He was bound and gagged but otherwise healthy enough. He had company because two of the guards I assigned to you had also been captured and tossed in a mine a few miles away. Evidently, Taylor wanted plenty of time to put any plans he had for you into place before we knew you were missing."

Fiona gave a profound sigh of relief. "It's good to know that I didn't cause anyone else to be hurt because I was foolish. Does that change the situation at all?"

Harlan shook his head. "I'm afraid not. Because I still don't like the idea of you being that far away from me. I'm going to tell the pilot that he's to take us to Hathor Island. I'm going to drop you both off in Kalim's care and leave it up to him if he wants to use you to help defend the villages and all his property on the island.

There's a good chance that you could see considerable action there. If he doesn't, then you may end up locked away under guard in that palace he calls home. You'll have to convince him that you'd be more valuable helping him than taking up his guards' time watching you."

Fiona frowned incredulously. "You're passing the buck."

"Maybe." Harlan smiled crookedly. "But you'll still be safer than if I let you go with me to the caves. Besides, it's about time Kalim had to handle a few more of the headaches that go with being king of all he surveys." He turned and headed for the cockpit. "Make peace with each other and then get together on a game plan to convince Kalim that he can't do without you." Before he opened the cockpit door, he looked over his shoulder at them. "One more thing. If you both want to do something to please Kira when you get to Hathor, I know she'd want you to go up to the hills and take care of the horses. They mean a lot to her. It's not a major rescue, but it's what she'd ask if she was here." He opened the cockpit door. "And we should be at Hathor in about thirty minutes."

CHAPTER

18

Kalim's primary airport was lit up with brilliant lights when Harlan landed at Hathor a little more than half an hour later.

"Did you lose something?" Kalim asked Harlan, strolling toward him after he left the craft. "You were gone far too long, and then you tell me you dropped Aban into the sea to retrieve that sled cover? I'm happy he was useful, but I expected nothing else. All my people are talented and superb. Did he do well?"

"Well enough," Harlan said. "But apparently he found the experience addictive, as I told you on the phone. He wanted to join the team that I'm gathering to go down to the caves."

Kalim nodded soberly. "Because you told him you thought Kira would be found there. None of us can fault him for wanting to bring her back. That's what we all want. Though I'm glad you discouraged him. We may need all the men we can muster here. I've been hearing that there have been a good many strangers sighted in and around the villages since Abdullah's death. Taylor may believe that this is the time to strike at them." His lips tightened grimly. "Strike at *me*. He'll get a few surprises if he tries. We know how to protect ourselves."

"I can bring in more men to help," Harlan offered. "Just call Belson, as I told you. He's on alert to send you whatever equipment or teams you request."

Kalim nodded. "I'll remember." He suddenly smiled as he saw Aban and Fiona exiting the plane. "Though by the look of those two, we may not need to bother with reinforcements." He tilted his head appraisingly. "Am I mistaken, or do they look as if they're ready to take on the whole damn world?"

"I gave them a few words of advice," Harlan said. "But I believe it's time I made my exit. I've already said my goodbyes. I'm taking a cargo copter to pick up my sleds and try to get them positioned before Kira shows up. Take care of Fiona." He was already heading for the helicopter. "Or as much as she'll let you. That's always the question. Good luck, Kalim."

"I don't believe luck will be required," Kalim murmured as he turned to face Aban and Fiona. "It's not as if I haven't had years of experience handling the population of this entire island. It's merely that one has to be firm..."

But Fiona was standing directly in front of him now, gazing at him accusingly. "He's gone?" Her eyes turned to the helicopter as it began to lift off the tarmac. "I was hoping to get to talk to Harlan again before he left. Why couldn't you have stopped him?"

"I realize you're disappointed," Kalim said. "But he told me that he'd had his discussion with you, and he asked me to watch out for you. I think you can trust me."

"That's not good enough." She was still gazing at the departing helicopter. "I wanted to help Kira. And I wanted to help Harlan, dammit. Instead, he sent me to you. Do you know how that makes me feel? I'm not a child, Kalim. He should have let me go with him." Her hands were clenched into fists. "I'm just as good as Aban if you give me a chance. You let Kira work with you here on the island, and look how much she improved your herds and even brought you a treasure trove. She wouldn't have been able to do that if she hadn't been much smarter than any other man you could have hired. I'm not saying I'm as smart as Kira. She's older and more experienced. But I could be, if you'd let me have the opportunity. I work hard, and all you have to do is let me try." She reached out and grabbed his arm. "Listen to me, you need help here? If you won't send me after Kira, let me stay here and help you catch Taylor so that he won't have a chance to hurt her. But don't lock me up somewhere I won't be able to do that. You need me, even if you don't know it yet."

"You very seldom appear to listen to me," Kalim said. "I'm hoping it's only a fault of the young and foolish." He shrugged. "But you seem to be very sincere, so I will take you at your word."

"You won't regret it," Fiona said. "Just tell me what to do and I'll do it."

"That sounds reasonable. Do you have any suggestions, Aban?"

"She does not swim nearly as well as I do," Aban said. "But Harlan has already said that I couldn't go and help him." He added reluctantly, "It seems she's been very good with the horses in the short time she's been here. She was even good with Sinbad. You might send her to help with the herds. That's what Harlan said Kira would want."

"Good. Then you take her and save me the trouble. Unless you have an objection?"

"Not if that's what you wish," Aban said resignedly. "You know I try to please you. But I've always told you herding isn't my favorite thing, sir."

"And he realizes I'm much better with the horses than he is." Fiona smiled slyly. "They like me and trust me. I promise not to hurt his pride too badly. Since he's one of your people, and I do respect you, Kalim."

Kalim shook his head. "I believe I've heard enough from the both of you to last me quite a while. All I ask is that you just keep your eyes sharp and take care of my property. Understood?" He didn't wait for an answer as he headed for his Bugatti. "Let Harlan and me worry about the rest..."

———— • ————

Kira looked at the four chunky black Jet Skis parked behind Taylor's cruiser. "You do know they're ugly as sin, right?"

"Looks aren't everything." Taylor scowled. "They're much more powerful than those ridiculous underwater sleds that Harlan and Dr. Bryson built."

"I doubt that." Kira wrinkled her nose in distaste. "I saw your men tooling around on them this morning. Your Jet Skis appear to be about as maneuverable as a supermarket shopping cart . . . with a busted front wheel."

Taylor's face flushed with anger. "They were custom-built for me by one of the world's finest marine manufacturers. I wanted to be ready if I needed to go after that treasure on my own."

"Really? For ordinary marine activities, they might be adequate. But what we're going to be doing is far from ordinary. You may have been cheated, that's all I'm saying." Kira turned away to keep him from seeing her smile. Now he was really pissed off. "But this is your party. I'm sure they'll get us to the treasure eventually."

"Are you quite finished?" he asked icily.

"I'll have more to say when you get on them. But your men sure didn't seem to be having too much fun. Maybe you should have consulted Harlan or Hannah Bryson before you put these things in the water. Possibly they could have helped you out."

"Enough!" Taylor growled. "I'm sick of your snide remarks. We leave now, bitch. And you'd better lead us right to that treasure."

"No problem. I realize what my purpose is at this party." She boarded the sled she'd brought from that midnight drop. But she couldn't resist one last needle. "Don't worry—if your sorry-ass Jet Skis break down, we can always swim!"

———— • ————

HATHOR ISLAND

FOUR HOURS LATER

"Come out, come out, wherever you are," Kalim called as he got off his horse and moved deeper into the woods. His voice became considerably more strident when Fiona didn't answer. "Now!" he snapped as he reached the edge of the forest. "Aban told me that you'd taken Sinbad out for a training session over an hour ago. He said he'd tried to stop you and told you that Sinbad was too wild for anyone to ride but Kira. But you ignored him. I don't believe you'll ignore me, will you? Because I don't have time for this nonsense at the moment, Fiona."

"No, of course I won't ignore you." Fiona nudged Sinbad forward out of the forest so that she faced Kalim. Her eyes were wide with fear as she searched his expression. "Have you heard anything from Harlan? What about Kira?"

"No word yet," Kalim said. "But Harlan will let me know as soon as there's any news." He added, "I didn't need to hear this trouble about Sinbad from Aban when I'm trying to get any information I can from the villagers, Fiona. What's it all about?"

"You told me to take care of your property, and that's what I've been doing," Fiona said. "From what Kira and Aban were saying, Sinbad appears to be one of the most valuable pieces of property that you have on your island. Anyone who wanted to damage you would choose Sinbad to do it. Just like Taylor chose Golden Boy to hurt me. I wasn't going to let him do the same thing to you." She stroked Sinbad's neck as she spoke. "I tried to explain to Aban that

I'd been working with Sinbad since I came here to the encampment. I thought he was ready to let me ride him. Usually all it takes is a few days for a horse to get to know me before we understand each other." She shrugged. "He wouldn't listen to me." She lifted her head and met Kalim's eyes. "And he was too afraid of you. So I thought I'd let you find out for yourself."

"How very kind of you," Kalim said acerbically. "Just what I needed when I'm so damn worried about keeping everything and everyone in my world safe and afloat." He was watching with amazement as she stroked Sinbad. "He's not displaying even a sign of wildness around you," he murmured. "Kira said you were magic with horses."

"Because I love them," Fiona said simply. "And how could I help but love Sinbad? Just look at him. He's absolutely beautiful. His coat shines like ebony. He's bigger and stronger than most horses that are considered to have Arabian blood, and his eyes are large and they positively glow with intelligence. He's already learned so much in this short time we've been training together. And the way he moves... Kira would understand all that because she loves him, too. Though she loves all animals. You know that because you've seen her work with them." She paused. "I want her back, Kalim. We have to make it happen."

"We will," Kalim said gently. "And she's one strong woman. She'll be out there somewhere helping us."

"But how can I help?" Fiona asked. "I thought if I hid Sinbad in the forest here, none of Taylor's men would be able to find him."

"Not a bad idea," Kalim said, "as long as Sinbad isn't going to buck you off his back and then trample you. I assume you're assuring me that's not going to happen?"

She smiled. "I'm safe with him. Give me another month, and he'll be safe for almost anyone to ride. He just didn't understand that his behavior wasn't acceptable. Can you blame him? He's been king of all he surveyed since the day he was born. It was obviously ingrained in his DNA." She was suddenly smiling. "Just as it was in yours." Then her smile faded and she frowned thoughtfully. "And you can tell just by looking at him. It would be no wonder if Taylor decided to go after him if he got the chance. He knows the value of an exceptional horse when he sees one. He saw it when he was using Golden Boy to try to kidnap me. He told me then that he was too valuable to destroy. I hated Taylor, but I was grateful at the time that Golden Boy was safe." She gazed at Kalim. "But what if he saw me riding Sinbad and decided he really wanted him? What could we do if—"

"No, Fiona," Kalim said firmly. "Don't give me any more what-ifs. Harlan would be justifiably furious with me if I exposed you to a risk like that. Besides, Harlan has enough on his plate down in those caves trying to survive. He doesn't need another challenge because you want to be involved in the rescue." He got back on his horse. "You stay here in the woods with Sinbad and do a little training just as you planned. I'll let you know any news about Kira as soon as I hear anything. Okay?"

She nodded. "No, it's not, but what can I say? As long as I can keep your blasted island safe and away from Taylor, I'll do anything I can." She paused. "Unless I find a way that sounds more foolproof. Then I don't promise anything." She pulled the horse's reins and turned back into the forest. "But you can give Aban a call and tell him that I'm not in any danger from Sinbad. The last thing I want is for him to come running after me because he thinks I'm still the lady in distress he rescued before."

"I can see how that would annoy you," Kalim said. "Aban meant well. His instincts are good. He's just not accustomed to ladies in distress being able to bring wild horses to attention with a single glance. Though he's known Kira long enough to be familiar with the concept. I'll give him your message, and I'll let you know as soon as I hear from Harlan."

"You're worried about him, aren't you?" Fiona asked.

He looked back over his shoulder at her. "I should lie and tell you I'm not," he said. "But you said you respect me, and I won't violate that trust. I'm beginning to respect you, too, Fiona. Yes, I'm very worried. I've been down there in those caves where they're playing their games with Taylor. It can be strange...and very intimidating. Kira and Harlan are exceptionally tough, and they have an excellent chance to survive. But you're right to be concerned. Just know that I'll be doing everything I can to keep the balance on our side."

Fiona tried to smile. "So will I. Thank you for being honest with me." She nudged Sinbad forward. "Come on, Sinbad, we're not quite on our own, but it's close...very close. Let's go find a way to show them that no one can push us around and get away with it..."

"Oh, shit," Kalim muttered.

Fiona could feel Kalim's gaze follow them as she and Sinbad vanished back into the forest.

———————•———————

Taylor and two of his helpers climbed onto the Jet Skis and motored behind Kira as she traveled toward the cave system. Although the craft were awkward and less responsive than the sleds, they performed better than Kira expected. But they were also noisier, scaring away marine life in a way that the sleds hadn't. As they approached the orange reef, the group dove underwater on their vehicles. She adjusted her mask and was relieved that it formed a tight yet comfortable seal over her face and ears. Like all the sled-connected masks, it came equipped with a radio that allowed her to communicate with the others in her group.

"Is everybody with me?" she asked.

"Right behind you," Taylor said sharply. "You're leading this parade."

Kira turned to avoid a cluster of vegetation. She was impressed by the Jet Skis' underwater capability, although they couldn't match the sleds' smooth feeling of flight.

Taylor's voice crackled over the radio. "Now what do you have to say about my Jet Skis?"

"Nice toy," she said. "But compared with Harlan's underwater sled, that's all it is. A toy. But it'll do the job, Taylor."

"You're damn right it will!"

They crossed over a ridge and beheld the valley of orange coral. Kira inhaled sharply as she recognized the shape of the rocks and the sluggish darkness of the flowing water. "Well, here we are. Didn't I tell you that you'd get what you wanted, Taylor?"

"This is it!" Taylor's voice vibrated with excitement. "You weren't lying to me. This is where you found the treasure, isn't it?"

"Yes. Get ready, everybody. We're going into that coral reef."

"Where, exactly?" Taylor asked. "Can you point it out?"

"No," Kira said. "Not yet. It's just past a group of white boulders. It's easy to miss, so we'll have to slow down to see it."

Kira slowed down herself. Suddenly it seemed there were white boulders everywhere. Where in the hell was it?

There!

She turned her sled hard left and followed the maze she'd traveled just a few days earlier. She was closely followed by Taylor and his men. Their Jet Skis were equipped with sonar sensors that made them relatively easy to navigate into the cave system.

Another voice spoke to her through the underwater helmet radio. "Hello, Kira."

She heard herself gasp. What in the hell...?

"Can you hear me?" It was Harlan's voice! "Don't worry, Taylor and his friends can't hear us. I just need to know you can hear me."

"Where are you?" she whispered. "How in the hell are you doing this?" She turned back to make sure Taylor wasn't privy to their conversation. He clearly wasn't.

"I have over a thousand patents and a couple of Nobel Prizes, Kira. You think I can't hack into a simple wireless communications system? I'm temporarily blocking them from hearing you."

"Foolish me." She moistened her lips. "Where are you?"

"Nearby, on the surface. How are you?"

"Better for hearing your voice. What's the plan?"

"Hey, turn toward Taylor and tap your helmet like you're having trouble hearing him. He's trying to talk to you right now."

"Shouldn't I answer him?"

"To hell with him. Let him think his equipment is faulty. It'll drive him nuts."

She chuckled. "You're right."

"I have a surprise planned for him and his men."

"And for me, apparently."

"I don't have time to explain. Just be ready to be very appreciative when you see the alternative transportation I've arranged for you."

"A navy submarine?"

"Better than that."

"Don't overpromise."

"Wouldn't dream of it. Okay, you're about to arrive at the first large cavern. You'll lead them in there, then back out immediately."

"They'll just follow me out."

"They won't be able to."

"How are you going to pull that off?"

"Did I mention that my sea sleds can be controlled remotely?"

"And...?"

"Don't worry about it. Just keep listening. Oh, and give Taylor a thumbs-up. He's getting a little frantic right now."

"I'd rather show him a different finger."

"Later. Right now, we want him to feel that everything is okay."

She turned back and raised her right thumb. Taylor nodded and raised his thumb in response.

"Just another few yards," she said. She eased off the throttle as they moved into the large cavern. She allowed Taylor and his men to drift past her, and she pointed vigorously at the far wall. They accelerated to take a look, and she spun around and roared back through the opening!

"I'm out!" she shouted to Harlan. "What now?"

"Keep going. Here's where the fun begins."

———— • ————

"She's getting away!" Giles shouted.

Taylor spun his watercraft around. "You idiot! Don't tell me about it. Go get her!"

The three men raced back toward the opening, but before they could reach it, one of Harlan's underwater sleds suddenly surfaced in front of them!

BLAM! Giles and Donovan struck the sled and were thrown from their Jet Skis. Donovan struck the cavern wall, and blood oozed from his forehead.

Giles struggled to get his bearings. "I can't feel my legs! Taylor, help...?"

The sled swung around and struck Giles, breaking his neck! It then raced toward Taylor, targeting him with deadly precision.

"Harlan," Taylor muttered. "It has to be Harlan…" He was controlling that damn sled from the surface, no doubt. Taylor gunned his Jet Ski and dodged behind a cluster of boulders. "Donovan! Where are you when I need you? Are you still here?"

"Yes," Donovan said weakly. "I'm bleeding. And I need to find my Jet Ski. I'm not sure if I can—" Donovan interrupted himself with a bloodcurdling scream.

Taylor turned just in time to see that a huge, thick sea snake had wrapped itself around Donovan's body and was literally eating his face.

Taylor stared in horror. Everything was going wrong. This shouldn't happen to him. It had to be Harlan who was causing it all. All he knew was that he had to get away from this place before he died like that fool Donovan. He had to get the hell out of here!

He rocketed out from behind the boulders, narrowly dodging the sled as it tried to ram him again. He sped past the snake and Donovan, who was now nothing more than a shredded bloody cloud.

The sled was after him again, he saw frantically. It was like some robotic monster Harlan had created to destroy him.

Taylor gunned his engine and raced back through the opening and past the orange coral formations that had seemed so beautiful and majestic on their way in, when he'd been certain they were leading him toward all those jewels Kira had promised. Now he was struggling to get away with just his life.

He finally cleared the coral and broke the surface. There, in the distance, was a yacht he assumed to be Harlan's, where Kira was undoubtedly headed. Bitch. Bitch. Bitch. She had done this to him. She and that demon from hell Jack Harlan. But none of it mattered. He would still win. All he had to do was bring in more of his men and attack from another direction.

This wasn't over yet.

CHAPTER

19

Death.

Screams.

Gurgling blood.

Kira's audio connection had been restored in time for her to hear the horrible end that the sea snake had visited on Taylor's henchman Donovan. But where was Taylor himself? And where was Harlan? She couldn't catch a glimpse of either one. As long as Taylor was alive and had weapons, he'd be a danger to Harlan. She had to locate him...

Then she caught sight of Taylor heading through the orange coral at top speed. Was he trying to chase down Harlan? She couldn't take a chance. She turned her sled around and headed toward Taylor.

She heard Harlan's voice again. "Kira, where are you? Are you okay? I've lost contact with you."

Kira adjusted her microphone. "Harlan, I'm heading through the coral after Taylor."

"No!" Harlan said. "Keep away from him. I sent one of the sleds after him, but I think he's probably reached the surface by now. I'll go after him myself."

"The hell you will," Kira said. "Don't you think you've done enough? Taylor has his own weapons and he might be expecting you. Your little gift of that remote sled was very welcome, thank you. But I'm not going to let you do this on your own. We'll do it together. I'm heading for the surface. I'll see you in a few minutes. Stop cursing and be there to watch my back." She hung up and adjusted the sled for surface travel.

———— • ————

"You don't have to be so cautious," Harlan said as Kira climbed over her sled and boarded his motorized launch. "Taylor is nowhere to be found. I thought at first he might have headed for the yacht I leased to try to set a trap for us. But I left Belson on board and he said that wasn't the case. He did, however, spot a Jet Skier making his way toward the east. He could have taken shelter in those huge boulders along the shore until he could arrange for pickup by one of his men." He paused. "Or he could have moved to what he thought were greener pastures."

Her gaze lifted to the massive cliff of the east ridge. She shivered. "Knowing Taylor, he's going to want to cut his losses any way he can. He'll go to Hathor Island. You should call Kalim and tell him what happened here. Warn him to be on the alert."

"I'll do that." He pulled her into his arms. "But not just yet," he said hoarsely. "I thought I'd lost you too many times during these last days. I want to hold you for a little while. Just hold you... Okay?"

She slid her arms around him and buried her face in his chest. "Why wouldn't it be okay? If I remember correctly, that's what I said to you the night this nightmare started." She suddenly stiffened. "Before I remembered that Fiona might be a target." She lifted her head and looked up at him. "And she might still be a target. She's at Hathor Island, isn't she? The nightmare isn't over."

"Don't start worrying yet. She might be fine."

"Might?" She turned to look at him. "And where is Mack? Is he still okay?" Her gaze flew to the yacht. "Is that where he is? Tell me he's safe."

"I sent him to be with Fiona. It appeared an ideal way to keep both of them safe. Do you agree?"

She drew a deep, relieved breath. "I think I do. I'm just used to taking care of all those kinds of details myself."

"If you let me, I'll be happy to take some of those responsibilities off your hands. I understand it's called sharing."

"I believe I've heard of the concept. I was glad to get a demonstration. But I'm still worried about Fiona. I don't like that word 'might.'"

But Harlan was already releasing her and turning toward the

launch's throttle. "She's under Kalim's personal care. We both trust him."

"But we both know what a wild card Fiona can be," Kira reminded him. "Make sure that Kalim knows what he might have to contend with if Taylor raises his ugly head anywhere near her."

"I'm already doing it." Harlan was punching the phone number as he spoke, and he turned up the volume when Kalim answered. "Harlan here, Kalim. I just wanted to tell you that Kira is safe and free and I'll be bringing her to your island as soon as possible."

"God be praised," Kalim said. "Fiona will be very happy. I'll call her right away."

"Call her?" Harlan repeated. "Isn't she with you?"

"Not at the moment. But she's quite safe and very busy. She's in the hills training Sinbad. It's not as if Mack isn't always with her. Tell Kira she was right about Fiona. She's doing an amazing job with Sinbad. I believe there's not a doubt about her being a horse whisperer."

"Of course I wasn't wrong," Kira said as she came on the line. "But bring her down from those hills and keep her close until we can reach the island. Do you hear me, Kalim? We're not sure that she's entirely safe there."

"So I take it the news isn't all good," Kalim said grimly. "Taylor?"

"Who else? The devil himself," Harlan said. "I eliminated the men he brought to the cave and prevented him from grabbing any treasure, but he appears to have wriggled out of the trap I set for him." Harlan paused. "He could be heading in your direction. Make sure all your border guards are on the alert."

"They will be," Kalim said. "And I'll call Fiona and tell her to bring Sinbad back to the stable so she can see you're alive and well, Kira. That should bring her running. She was very concerned about you when I talked to her earlier today. She was still determined to continue Sinbad's training, but she wanted to find a way to help you at the same time."

"That sounds like her," Kira said. "Always trying to control the situation."

"Which seems to be a very familiar trait," Harlan murmured.

"Hush," Kira told him. "Kalim, call us back after you've talked to her, will you? I'm going to go to Harlan's yacht to change into dry clothes, and then we'll be on our way to your island. Keep everyone safe."

"That goes without saying," Kalim said. "And may I mention that Harlan did extraordinarily well getting you away from that fiend from hell? I might have to compliment myself for allowing him to do it instead of going after you myself. I may even have to reward him in some manner. I'll have to think about it."

"Arrogance, thy name is Kalim," Harlan said dryly. "Naturally, it was all your doing."

"Well, it is my island," Kalim said. "And didn't I allow Kira to use the treasure to lure Taylor into the trap?"

"I don't remember you being consulted," Harlan said.

"Because you realized my consent was implied where Kira was concerned. I understood that." He paused. "However, I didn't find your handling of the encounter to be unacceptable. We'll discuss all this later. I need to call Fiona now and get her out of those woods and down here to the castle. Goodbye, Harlan. I'll see you shortly." Kalim hung up.

Harlan cursed softly. "Every time I think I might be able to actually like that bastard, he pulls the rug out from under me."

"Well, he did say that you weren't totally unacceptable." She was grinning. "And I think that you were absolutely splendid." Her smile faded. "But right now all I care about is getting to your yacht so that I can change and go check on Fiona."

He lifted a gym bag. "I have some clothes for you here. It'll be faster if we just take this launch over. I admit I'm a bit uneasy myself..."

———————— · ————————

"They're both safe, Kalim?" Fiona felt a swift rush of pure relief as her hand tightened on the phone. "That's wonderful. You're sure Harlan said he was able to get Kira away from that monster? It's almost too good to be true."

"I wouldn't steer you wrong, Fiona," Kalim said. "I spoke to Kira myself. I told her about your work with Sinbad, and she was very happy about it. But she was almost as worried about you as you were about her. She wants you to get out of those hills and come back to the stables at the castle. She said she'd meet you there."

"Why is she worried?" Fiona asked, puzzled. "Kira knows I wouldn't have any trouble with Sinbad." Then she stiffened. "But you haven't told me everything, have you? What did you leave out?" She inhaled sharply as it came to her. "Taylor!"

"I'm certain that Harlan must be very disappointed, but he didn't manage to kill that bastard down in the caves today." Kalim paused. "He also said there's a chance that Taylor might be heading in this direction."

"Probably more than a chance," Fiona said dully. "He'll be bitter and ugly and full of rage. I can remember his face when he had me prisoner on his cruiser, filled with hatred and wanting revenge so bad he could taste it. I threw a cup at him after he told me how he'd killed my father. Did you know he did that, Kalim?"

"I heard the story," Kalim said. "But don't be afraid. We'll all try to protect you. I'm going to take several guards to come meet you and escort you down here to the stables."

" 'Several guards'..." she repeated. "Here we go again. It seems as if I've been surrounded by guards all my life. Just to keep me safe from Taylor." Her lips twisted. "And this time he's going to get a real treat. He might even get another chance to take down Kira and Harlan. Because I'm the bait that can bring them running to the rescue." She found her hands clenching on Sinbad's reins. "And you're the master of this entire island, Kalim. How many of your villagers would suffer if anything happened to you?"

"No one is irreplaceable, Fiona."

"You come fairly close to that for those villagers. For instance, what would Aban do?"

He didn't answer for a moment. "Survive. I don't like the sound of this, Fiona. What are you trying to say?"

"I believe I'm saying it exceptionally well. I'm telling you that I'm tired of being bait, Kalim. Because it ends up hurting people I care about. Kira, Harlan, you. Maybe even some of your villagers. It's not going to happen this time. If Taylor wants me, let him come and get me. I won't hide behind anyone else any longer." She added recklessly, "Who knows? Perhaps I'll even go looking for him."

"Don't be a fool," Kalim said roughly. "You're little more than a child. Stay right where you are. I'm coming to get you."

"You won't find me. I don't believe Taylor will, either. Sinbad seems to know this mountain and all its many passes and crevasses very well indeed. It's like a maze, and he's been showing me all his secret places. What a truly intelligent horse he is."

"I'm glad you appreciate him. Then you wouldn't want Taylor to get hold of him. Let me take both of you down to my stables where you can be protected."

She chuckled. "Oh, dear, I think I must have scared you, Kalim. I have no intention of really going hunting for Taylor. I realize I'll need training and equipment before I'm able to do that. Unfortunately, someone neglected to give me a weapon, and that makes everything more difficult. So unless something else occurs to me, I'll just keep Sinbad, Mack, and myself safe—but none of us will be bait for anyone like Taylor ever again. Though perhaps Taylor searching for me will allow one of your people to zero in on him and get rid of him forever. Tell Harlan and Kira to take care of themselves and let me know when there's no more Taylor to torment any of us."

"That's not going to be enough. They're going to want to phone you and talk to you themselves. Will you take their call?"

"I wouldn't be rude and ignore it. Harlan's taught me better manners than that. Even though they're probably going to just repeat what you're saying. But perhaps only one call. I'm afraid that Taylor might be able to trace me through them. He managed all kinds of electronic and phone tricks when he snatched me away from Golden Boy and I ended up on his cruiser."

"They deserve the chance to at least try to persuade you," he said impatiently. "In the meantime, I'll be combing this entire area looking for you...and Taylor."

"I realize that, Kalim. Thank you. I'm sorry to cause you this trouble. Keep safe yourself. You've been a good friend to me..."

She cut the connection.

———————— · ————————

Harlan was helping Kira off the launch to the landing when he got the call from Kalim. "Shit," he muttered as he glanced at Kira's face. "Can't you do something about it, Kalim? You know it's not safe." Then he evidently gave up the battle. "Okay, we're on our way. Keep trying to locate her." He hung up. "Kalim wasn't able to talk Fiona into returning to the stables. She said she had no intention of being bait to lure Taylor toward either one of us again and took off on Sinbad farther up the mountain. Kalim hasn't been able to find her yet. He's still looking."

"Damn." Kira's gaze flew to the top of the stark cragginess of the mountain ahead. "And we don't know how much time we have before Taylor can bring more of his men to that area. He only brought two of his thugs with him to the caves; he left a lot more to guard his property, and they're still waiting for his orders to come and load up any treasure he finds. I don't believe there's any doubt that Taylor will order an attack on Kalim's island now that he believes I've cheated him out of that treasure."

Harlan nodded. "Kalim's been warned, and I'll call Belson and tell him to order reinforcements from among our guards in Morocco to head up there. While I'm doing that, why don't you call Fiona and see if you can persuade her to back down." He grimaced. "Though he said she was very determined and would only take one call."

"How kind of her," Kira said. "I want to shake her. But I know how she feels. She's been a chess piece since she was seven years old, and she loves you and wants it to end. I want it to end for her." She was dialing as she spoke. "But I'll see if I can persuade her to be reasonable. Don't hold your breath."

"You forget how well I know her," Harlan said. "I just want to keep her alive and away from that bastard. She might listen to you. You have a certain influence. And you're the one who got her away from Taylor the last time."

"Not likely." Fiona answered the phone, and Kira spoke into the receiver. "I just told Harlan that you're unlikely to listen to me, Fiona. Even though we both know you should follow Kalim's orders. That's true, isn't it?"

"That's true, Kira," Fiona said quietly. "It's time for it to end. I was so worried about you. And I always worry about Harlan. Don't worry, I'll be careful. After all, I have Mack with me. And I couldn't be anything else since I have Sinbad to take care of, too."

"You realize we're on our way up there to start searching for you? I know that mountain and the woods surrounding it very well. I might find you."

"You might," Fiona said cheerfully. "You have a better chance than almost anyone because Mack will want to help you." She chuckled. "Except he'll be torn because he's now been trained to also take care of Sinbad. I believe Sinbad knows the mountain even better than Mack, and I've got him on my side right now. He loves you but he knows I understand him. He's very complicated, and that's important to him."

"I imagine it is. Look, if you won't be reasonable enough to let Kalim take you down to the stables, will you and Sinbad hide out somewhere Taylor won't be able to find you?"

"That sounds like a plan." Fiona was laughing. "If I can make it work. I'll see you soon, Kira. Take care of yourself. Sinbad and I thank you for your concern."

"You're both welcome. Though I'm not sure that Sinbad deserves it. He obviously rejected me the minute he had a talented horse whisperer seducing him with soft words and compliments."

"He still loves you," Fiona said. "And I refuse to tell him that you were prepared to withdraw any aspect of your approval. It might hurt his feelings. And he's already a little edgy."

"Heaven forbid that I do that. I'm sure he's temperamental enough as it is." She was still smiling. "I hope you're wrong, and I'm able to dig you out of whatever rabbit hole you try to tuck Sinbad and yourself into very soon. Bye, Fiona!"

"No luck?" Harlan asked as she hung up.

She shrugged as she turned to him. "What I expected. Except that I saw a few more signs of maturity peeping out around the edges. These last few weeks have changed Fiona, or maybe they've merely defined her. I can't be sure. Perhaps we've all changed a bit." She shook her head. "Did you get what you wanted from Belson?"

He nodded. "He'll have a unit on their way to Kalim's island shortly."

"It can't be too soon." She gazed up at Kalim's craggy mountain seascape again. "I want Fiona out of there."

"Did she seem that upset?"

"No, on the contrary. As I said, she was...different." She shrugged. "It was Sinbad that she said was edgy. That bothered me a little."

"Why? Sinbad is a wild horse yet has magnificent breeding. He has to be very high-strung."

"I guess it was because Sinbad never showed me that side of himself. He was always so arrogant and sure of himself that he was never edgy. Very princely, even kingly." She looked back at the mountain. It seemed even more intimidating than it had a few minutes ago. The sun was dimmer and the sky was turning gray as it began to cloud over. "That was why it surprised me when she said Sinbad was edgy. It made me...wonder."

"Did it? You believe Sinbad might have been sensing something that made him restless?"

She shrugged. "I don't know. Probably not. Anything that's even a little offbeat tends to strike me as strange these days."

"Considering what you've gone through lately, that doesn't

surprise me." He reached out and took her hand. "But could I throw a little brightness into the picture? We're both alive and free, and so are the people and animals we care about. We just managed to foil the bad guy and send him on his way. Plus I'm trusting that we're going to bring the son of a bitch down very soon. Is that bright enough for you?"

Her hand squeezed his. "It's wonderful. You're wonderful. I'm feeling very lucky at this particular moment. I don't know how you could do any better."

He chuckled. "Is that a challenge? I believe I can meet it." He pointed at the mountain. "You know that edginess in Sinbad that you worried about? Those are storm clouds hovering over the mountain. I believe in a few minutes we're going to get a severe drenching. You might as well not have changed out of your wet suit. You're just lucky this launch had a few ponchos tucked away in the cabin." He tilted his head. "And we both know that horses can sense when storms are coming and become agitated. Particularly wild horses like Sinbad. True?"

"Quite true. But I refuse to give you a total victory. There could be other reasons. You've earned enough medals for one day." She was laughing even as the first claps of thunder roared in the distance.

CHAPTER

20

There was definitely a storm coming.

Fiona rode Sinbad up the narrow trail that she hadn't even known existed until a few minutes before. Sinbad had been restless for the better part of an hour, which often meant a thunderstorm was on the way. Now, with endless dark clouds rolling in, it was clear that the horse was right. The timing couldn't have been worse, with that monster Taylor on the loose.

She knew Kira and Harlan were doing everything they could to get to her, but a storm wouldn't make it easy. She looked down at Mack, who was running alongside.

"Just a little farther!" She was speaking to herself as much as the animals.

She heard a buzzing sound overhead. She looked up. It was a drone helicopter tracking her from above! She'd seen camera drones just like it during her time when she'd been a prisoner on

Taylor's cruiser. He'd found her! She felt a rush of panic. No way was she letting him get his hands on her again. She'd die first.

The hell she would!

She instantly rejected the defeatist thought. No, that would just be another victory for Taylor. She'd just find a way to hide and maybe set a trap...

She raised her middle finger into the air as the first drops of rain fell.

———— • ————

Taylor chuckled as he looked at the drone image on his tablet screen. Young Fiona kept her middle finger in the air for a long moment as she charged up the hillside on a magnificent horse. It must be the multimillion-dollar stallion that Taylor had heard about as belonging to Kalim, the owner of the island.

He showed the tablet to the two men whom he'd chosen to accompany him to climb to the island's upper reaches from the group he'd brought from his hideout on the reef. "She's flipping us off, gentlemen. I wonder if she'd be quite so bold if she knew how close we were to intercepting her."

Connor, who had impressed him on their recent lethal excursion to Latvia, scowled at the tablet. "Or if she knew we were probably going to make her watch that horse die in front of her eyes."

Phil Wendell laughed. "Yeah, she won't be such a smart-ass then, will she? Let's go get her." Wendell had come highly recommended by the late Zeke Donovan. He still hadn't broken a sweat from their climb. And his eagerness to please now was also a good sign, Taylor thought. He might be able to use him as a permanent replacement.

Taylor double-tapped Fiona's image on the screen, activating a tracking function on his camera drone. He might temporarily be missing out on that treasure trove, but Kalim's island, Hathor, itself had riches that he could take and build toward a new start for himself. Many of the villagers were very well off; Kalim had those horses and probably jewels of his own that he could be persuaded to turn over to Taylor.

And there was one more rich prize on that island that had nothing to do with treasure.

Fiona Harlan had been sent here for her protection by that bitch Kira Drake. What a wonderfully satisfying punishment it would be for both Kira and Harlan if Taylor was able to give Harlan's niece the final death blow. It would strike Harlan to his very soul. It was obviously meant to be.

"We need that girl," he said. "She holds the key to making me richer than Midas. Once we have her, there's no way we'll leave here empty-handed. Understand me?"

The two men nodded.

"Good. Then let's step it up."

———— • ————

Kira jumped nervously as lightning struck just a few hundred yards ahead. The storm had advanced from light sprinkles to pounding rain in less than a minute. She adjusted the hood on the poncho Harlan had given her. "What are you doing?"

Harlan stared into the sky with a pair of binoculars. He lowered them. "There's a small drone over the next ridge. It's almost come to a stop."

"You think it's Taylor's?"

"I'm sure it is." He raised his voice to be heard over the pounding rain. "And the fact that it has slowed tells me that it's found what he's looking for."

"Fiona!"

He nodded. "It's a good bet he has her in his sights."

"Then we need to get to her before he does."

Harlan raised the binoculars again. "In any case, that drone isn't going to last long in this storm. Let's go! I'll call Kalim on the way."

———— • ————

Fiona leaned over Sinbad's mane as they rode through the storm. For the past fifteen minutes, she'd been looking for a cave or even a cluster of trees to shield her from the sheets of cold rain that were hitting her full-force. She, Sinbad, and Mack were completely drenched, and her numb fingers could barely feel the reins. How much longer could she take this?

She'd lost sight of Mack, but it was difficult to see anything in this awful rain. He was probably okay, but what if...

Oh, God. If anything happened to Mack, she would never forgive—

Whiplash!

Something appeared in front of her and knocked her off Sinbad's saddle! She flew backward and hit the muddy earth with such force that the wind was knocked from her lungs. She lay on her back, facing upward as raindrops pelted her face. She couldn't breathe or move for a long moment, but when she raised her head, she saw what had knocked her down: a long piece of rope, pulled taut across the trail by two of Taylor's men.

The men walked toward her, both still holding the rope. One of them was laughing. Taylor walked up behind them, seemingly oblivious to the storm. He crouched beside her. "Hello, Fiona. Nice to see you again. Remember? Your friend Kira and I had a deal. I traded you for her, and she reneged. So I had to come for you. You understand that, don't you? It's all a matter of honor. None of it is my fault. You'll have to blame her. Of course, it's Harlan's fault, too."

Fiona sat up and let the cold raindrops roll down her face for a moment to help revive her. "You don't know anything about honor. But do you know who did? My father. He took you into our home and tried to help you and you killed him. Then you went after Harlan, who filled you with so much jealousy that you could hardly bear it. Everyone knows what a pitiful monster you are."

"And soon I'll be a very rich monster, which is the only thing that counts in this world," Taylor said. "And you will very soon be dead if you don't cooperate."

"No way. I'm not afraid of you, Taylor." By this time, Sinbad had trotted back to Fiona. She reached up and comfortingly ran her hand over his muzzle, then used the dangling leather saddle ropes to pull herself to her feet.

"That's right," Taylor said as he watched her. "You don't let much keep you down before you bounce back, do you? I remember how strong and defiant you were. I'll wait and give you a few minutes more to recover. Then you're coming with us."

"Like hell I am!"

Connor raised his gun and aimed it at Sinbad's head. "No. You'll do it, or we'll kill your horse."

Fiona tried to look as if she hadn't been punched in the gut. "You're bluffing. Taylor won't let you. It would be a stupid move. Sinbad is too valuable to him."

Taylor used his fingers to comb back his rain-soaked hair. "The metric has changed, dear girl. He's not very portable, is he? The only question that remains is if we leave him here alive... or dead? It makes no difference to us."

Fiona hoped the driving rain would keep them from seeing the frantic tears stinging in her eyes, but Sinbad could sense how upset she was. He suddenly started whirling, then bucking, his front hooves pounding the wet ground around them.

Connor raised his gun as Sinbad came too close to him. "That's enough. I'm putting him down!"

Fiona screamed and stumbled forward. "No! I won't let you. Don't do it!"

In that instant, she saw Mack tear from behind a tree across the path and leap for Connor's arm! The dog sank his teeth into his sleeve and thrashed ferociously back and forth until the gun went flying. Blood spurted from the wound! Connor screamed and fell to his knees holding his arm, trying to stop the bleeding.

Phil reached for his own gun, but before he could pull it from his holster, a shot rang out. A bloody wound appeared in the center of his forehead. His eyes turned glassy. Then he staggered and fell backward, dead.

Fiona and Taylor both whirled to see where the shot had come from. Harlan stepped into the clearing, holding his automatic in front of him. Kira was beside him. But she was already running forward toward where Connor was lying nursing his bloody arm. She grabbed his pistol to train on him. "Don't move!"

Harlan's shout at Taylor could barely be heard through the pounding rain. "You've lost, Taylor. Can't you see that? It's over!"

Taylor laughed. "Nothing's over! That's what you thought down in those caves. But I wasn't the one to die. I'm never the one to die. Do you believe I actually care about any of those men? Now I'm here and I'll get what I need and then I'll be gone again." He raised his gun and pointed it at them. "I may not be able to get all of you, but if you don't put that gun down, I guarantee at least one of you isn't getting off this island." He cocked his head toward Fiona. "Maybe it'll be her. Or perhaps Kira. Do you really want to take that chance, Harlan?"

Kira raised her hands to try to soothe him. "Just...relax. You don't want to do this. One way or another you'll die if you don't give up. We can work this out, Taylor."

"But maybe I don't want to work it out," Fiona said quietly.

Taylor's brow wrinkled as his gaze met Fiona's. "What are you talking about?"

She took a step forward. "Didn't anyone tell you that I've been training this wonderful animal you were going to kill? He obeys signals beautifully these days. And I guess you were too distracted just now by Harlan killing that asshole you brought to butcher him to pay attention to what I was doing." She gestured down to Taylor's boots.

His gaze followed Fiona's gesture and his eyes widened. "What the hell...?"

It took him only a few seconds to realize that Fiona had clipped the end of her saddle rope to the leather pull loop at the top of Taylor's left boot!

"Goodbye, Taylor." She clicked her tongue twice. "Go, Sinbad!"

And the horse took off!

Taylor screamed as Sinbad jerked him off his feet and started dragging him through the rocky terrain. His face and skull were bashed against dozens of boulders and clumps of vegetation as the horse galloped across the wet hillside. Taylor lost his gun during the first few seconds, yet he kept struggling and screaming for almost the entire distance. But when the screams stopped, there was no doubt that Taylor was dead. Sinbad eventually halted and looked over his shoulder, then slowly started to walk back toward Fiona as if puzzled that she hadn't signaled him to return.

She clicked her tongue again and held out her hand, and the horse trotted toward her. Somewhere along the way Taylor's body had come loose from the saddle ropes and rolled several yards until it landed face down in a gully of rushing water.

Mack was running toward Sinbad and was whimpering and rubbing against his forelegs as Harlan and Kira rushed toward Fiona, who seemed to be frozen in place as she watched.

"Are you okay?" Harlan asked her gently.

Fiona nodded. "I did what I had to do." She moistened her lips. "And I'm not sorry. You heard him. He would have killed at least one of us. I couldn't risk it. No more deaths, Harlan. It had to stop."

Harlan pulled her close. "I know, Fiona. I'm just very sad that you were the one to do it."

She shook her head. "I might be sad later, but I don't think so. He was a terrible, terrible man. And Sinbad had a right to protect himself."

"Well, I think Kalim would agree with you." Harlan glanced at Kira. "But do you, Kira?"

"Of course." Kira took Fiona into her arms and held her close for a moment. "A clear case of self-defense," she said. "No question."

Harlan nodded. "As soon as I tie up Mack's bloody prey that he left as a present under the tree, let's get out of this rain and call Kalim and have him help us round up the rest of Taylor's henchmen to deposit with the Moroccan police."

"Absolutely." Kira whistled for Mack as she put her arm around Fiona's waist and led her gently toward the path. "And for once, I'll be glad to see Kalim's castle!"

EPILOGUE

"You're sure Fiona's okay?" Kira asked Belson as she opened the door of the Gulfstream jet and jumped out onto the tarmac. "She wouldn't talk to me when I tried to call her yesterday. She said she had to speak to Harlan first. But then you called and said that Harlan might require my signature on some documents, and I had to come back and have them notarized or Kalim might get upset. Why didn't they tell me about this before I left to visit Sarah?"

"I have no idea," Belson said. "I just do what Harlan tells me to do."

"Sometimes," Kira said wryly. "When you want to do it. Is it a police or government document?"

"I don't believe it is. I honestly don't know the details. Harlan just told me to pick you up at Summer Island and bring you here."

"How frustrating. Maybe it has something to do with Fiona? Is she in trouble? What the devil is happening?"

349

He shook his head. "No trouble. Not unless it's the usual chaos that Fiona somehow manages to spread. Otherwise, she's fine. Harlan just told me to come here and take care of you until he could get here."

"Take care of me?" Kira repeated suspiciously. "I don't need anyone to take care of me. Particularly not Harlan, whom I've barely seen since Kalim took over his life when we went down to the castle the evening Taylor met his not-so-sad demise. You wouldn't think one super criminal would cause that much trouble. The entire island was filled with police and investigators of every description. We didn't get away from them until the next day." She shrugged. "But at least we didn't have to deal with the media."

"Due to my fantastic diplomatic influence," Belson said. "Harlan said he didn't want you to be troubled. Kalim was setting him up with interviews, and he said you didn't like them. Naturally, I obliged."

"What kind of interviews?" Kira was frowning. "Media?"

"No, only a few professors from Cairo and New York City." Belson shook his head. "Don't look so worried. Everything is going to be fine. We're taking care of all the details."

"How do I know that? What details? What if I don't like the way Harlan is taking care of the details? I haven't seen Harlan for more than a quick breakfast or lunch for the past few days and there hasn't been any time to talk. When he started to spend all his time with Kalim and law enforcement, I devoted all my time to Fiona up in the hills. She needed someone to talk to for the first few days after Taylor's death."

"Did it help?"

"She seemed much better. But then she started worrying about Golden Boy and wanted to make sure he'd fully recovered from those meds Taylor had given him. So Harlan arranged to send me back to Summer Island to check him out. He said it would be good for me to be with Sarah for a couple of days anyway."

"And was it?"

"Yes, isn't Harlan almost always right? At least everyone appears to think so. I took care of Golden Boy, and I always like to be with Sarah. Who knows? Maybe I also needed someone to talk to." She shrugged. "And maybe I was getting in Harlan's way."

"I don't believe that's a true reading of Harlan's intentions, considering his orders to me. He's been very busy."

"With appointments? I could have helped. What's he doing? *Talk* to me."

"Harlan said you might begin to fret," Belson said ruefully. "Oh, look, I believe I'm going to be saved." He gestured toward a larger Gulfstream plane landing on another runway as he opened the jet's door. "That's Harlan to the rescue."

"Yes, that's Harlan. And I don't fret," Kira said flatly. "I just have to know what's happening in my life."

Belson gave a sigh of relief as he saw Harlan coming across the tarmac. He tapped his hand to his head in a mock salute. "Over to you, Harlan. I've done what I could. Her last question involved why she didn't know what was happening in her life. It seems a fair question." He hurried away in the direction of Kalim's castle.

"An excellent question," Harlan said as he leaned forward and kissed Kira. "But you always have an answer, and most of the time you make them up yourself. The last time I spoke to you on the phone, you told me you were working with Fiona training Mack and Sinbad together, at least before she sent you to play nurse to Golden Boy. After you left, I sent Aban up there to keep her company, and Kalim dropped in every day to see how she was doing."

"Okay." She looked him in the eye. "So now I know exactly how she's doing. But I don't know nearly as much about you, Harlan. How are you? And why are you having interviews with professors? Do you have a new project?"

"I always have a new project in the works. It's how I live. But I have been busy. However, that's not why I called in the professors." He brushed his lips on her temple. "I was thinking of something you said to me when we were talking about caves, and it occurred to me that I wanted to give you a new project to amuse *you*."

She began to smile. "Are you joking? I believe I'll have enough to do. Working on my serums, dog and horse training, and we have to start bringing up the treasure that's being held for us beneath all those rocks down there in those caves."

"Very true, and I can never tell when you're going to decide to go hunting for another treasure. And if you do, then naturally I'll have to tag along after you."

"Naturally?"

He lifted her hand and kissed the palm. "Absolutely. Until you decide I don't amuse you any longer. But I'll work hard not to let that happen."

"I don't believe you'll have to work that hard." She met his eyes. "If you ever do get bored, I'll never try to—"

He put his fingers over her lips and said, "Suppose we discuss that in fifty or sixty years? We're going to be too busy before that. Look at how excited those professors are becoming about your new project."

"Harlan?" Her eyes narrowed as she tried to remember the clues he'd given her. "Caves? Excited professors? *Talk* to me. Is it Cleopatra's burial tomb?"

Harlan ruefully shook his head. "I'm not *that* good. Maybe next year."

"Now I'm truly getting pissed off. Stop teasing me. What did I say that intrigued you?"

He grinned. "We were talking about the prehistoric possibilities of the *Titanoboa cerrejonensis,* and you said bringing one to the surface would be the real treasure. I believe you were being sincere. Because that's who you are. If you weren't, then I've wasted a lot of scientists' time, because they're going to be here in a few weeks on an exploratory trip to examine those caves before we start disturbing any habitats."

She stared at him incredulously. "Of course I wasn't kidding." Then she hugged him exuberantly. "What a splendid opportunity to observe history at close quarters." She was suddenly giggling. "And what a wonderful gift, Harlan. I can't wait to tell Fiona. I don't believe she'll find it as thrilling as working with Sinbad, but you can never tell with her."

"I can come pretty close," Harlan said wryly. "And there's no way that she'd choose a monster snake over that fantastic horse. She'll politely look at it and then shrug and go back to work on developing Sinbad into the incredible animal she can see and touch and maybe even hug. She'll leave the scientific possibilities to you and me and history."

"And there's nothing wrong with that," Kira said soberly. "I love and appreciate all those other animals, too. I'm just curious to know what else is out there and what I might be missing."

"Do you think I don't know that?" he asked. "That curiosity is a precious gift, and I treasure it as much as I do everything else about you. Who else would put up with me?"

"I could name a few, though I'm not sure they'd want to embrace the idea of that *Titanoboa cerrejonensis*."

"See? You're stuck with me."

"And that document I was supposed to sign was nothing official, it only had to do with the professors?"

"Well, I didn't want Belson to spoil the surprise. The professors did want reports from you about what happened during the encounter." He started nudging her away. "I told Belson that he should take this plane and run interference with Kalim for the next few weeks." He was leading her toward his Gulfstream. "We'll need to take the larger Gulfstream so that we can get back to Summer Island with all possible comfort and speed. Who knows? We might even decide to take a few side trips."

"Why? I just came from there. Now you want me to go back?"

"Well, you're here because I didn't know if I could get everything done that I had to; I thought I might have to take you somewhere else to give you the surprise. But I should have had more faith in myself. It was close, but I came in under the wire. So now we can go back to that place you've always loved, and for the next few weeks, we'll sleep under the stars and talk and then make love and maybe even discuss those next fifty years. I don't want to be pushy, but I've always been one to advocate advance planning on any project. And this project is particularly important to me. If I do it wrong, it might even be a career breaker."

She laughed. "And we wouldn't want that to happen when you've had such a promising career so far. Too bad it's all in the past. But I'll be happy to cooperate with reviving it." Dear God, how she loved him! She held out her hand. "But first we have to go see Kalim and make arrangements for him to receive those professors in his fine castle if they arrive before we get back."

"That's all taken care of." He smiled. "I told you that I've been busy. I've also talked to Fiona and told her that she's to run this island, even and including Kalim, during the next few weeks while we're gone. Because you need a vacation before we start a new life after what you've gone through, and I'm going to see that you get one." He took her hand. She was delighted to cooperate. Why shouldn't she be?

She chuckled. "You think she can handle Kalim?"

"It wouldn't surprise me. I told her once that she was following in your footsteps. She liked the idea. Now stop questioning and let them work it out."

"Oh, I have every intention of doing that." Kira was grinning mischievously. "Because Fiona and I had a good many talks while we were working together in the hills during the time when you and Kalim were so busy ridding the world of Taylor's dirty crew."

"You did?" Harlan asked cautiously. "I'm almost afraid to ask the subject."

"You shouldn't be," Kira said. "Fiona and I both care enormously about you, and we're very fond of Kalim. We decided it would be fairly easy to persuade you to go along with whatever we need. But Kalim could be more difficult, and we might have to bring you into it occasionally."

"For instance?"

"Kalim isn't going fast enough to allow more freedom to the women on the island. We'll have to push him to speed it up."

He chuckled. "And that's my task?"

"*Our* task," Kira said softly. "And Fiona has a lot of ideas about combining her stable with Kalim's, which would allow them to be trained together. Can you imagine what a stunning and innovative group they'll be? What we could do with them?"

"I can see why the two of you would think so." He nodded. "It's a wonderful vision. Do you have anything else in store for us?"

"Yes, but I thought we could break it to you gently."

"I'm not sure that I shouldn't be making a list to prepare myself for what's to come," he said ruefully. "You appear to have a lot of surprises on the horizon."

"But a surprise is usually just a question mark, isn't it? And you like me to question. Isn't that what you told me?" She was already climbing the steps of the Gulfstream. "But this time, maybe I'll relax and let you answer a few of them. Remember? I kept telling you it was always better together! Every day and every way. I can't tell you how much I appreciate you giving me the opportunity to demonstrate that concept this week at Summer Island. Perhaps I'll even have Sarah and John stop by and give us a few lessons based on their years of experience." Her eyes were twinkling and she was smiling teasingly. "What do you think, Harlan?"

He chuckled. "That you'd better be kidding. I respect Sarah and John enormously but they're individuals living their own individual lives. We don't need lessons. It will be more exciting discovering everything on our own, including the surprises." He was starting the engines. "I believe we can create our own story and do a fantastic job of it." He reached over and fastened her seat belt as he smiled at her. "This is only the beginning!"

ABOUT THE AUTHOR

Iris Johansen is the #1 *New York Times* bestselling author of more than fifty consecutive bestsellers. Her series featuring forensic sculptor Eve Duncan has sold over twenty million copies and counting and was the subject of the acclaimed Lifetime movie *The Killing Game*. Along with her son, Roy, Iris has also coauthored the *New York Times* bestselling series featuring investigator Kendra Michaels. Johansen lives in Georgia and Florida.